HINTON

Mark Blacklock

GRANTA

In Memory of Ralph Ellis McRae Blacklock

And to Katie, Molly, Eve and Connie,
with multi-dimensional love

Granta Publications, 12 Addison Avenue, London W11 4QR

First published in Great Britain by Granta Books, 2020
This paperback edition published by Granta Books, 2021

A CIP catalogue record for this book
is available from the British Library.

1 3 5 7 9 10 8 6 4 2

ISBN 978 1 78378 521 6
eISBN 978 1 78378 522 3

Designed and typeset by M Rules

Printed and bound by CPI Group (UK) Ltd, Croydon, CR0 4YY

www.granta.com

Contents

Timeline   vi

Family tree   viii

Point   1

Line   5

Square   15

Cube   179

Tesseract   207

Cube   253

Square   261

Line   281

Point   291

Timeline

The life of Charles Howard Hinton

1853	Charles Howard Hinton – known as Howard – is born to James Hinton, surgeon and philosopher, and Margaret Haddon, at Bartholomew Square, London.
1855	The Hinton family move to the countryside near Dover while James works in London.
1859	The Hinton family live together at 84 Phillip Terrace, Edmonton, Tottenham.
1864	The Hinton family take a house near Regent's Park; Howard's older brother William is "showing some symptoms of delicacy".
1865	The family live between Barnet and Brighton.
1866	Howard starts at Rugby School in Moberly House (now named Cotton House).
1871	Howard is offered an exhibition to Balliol College at the University of Oxford. He leaves Rugby School and matriculates at Balliol as a non-collegiate student. The Hinton family live at 20 Golden Square, London.
1872	Howard spends a year abroad furthering his studies in Berlin where he attends lectures by Hermann von Helmholtz.
1873	Howard goes up to Balliol where he takes a 1st in his Mathematics Mods; James Hinton becomes unwell.
1874	Howard takes a 1st in Mathematics.
1875	Howard takes up a post as Assistant Master at Cheltenham College; James Hinton dies in Jamaica on December 16th suffering from "inflummata of the brain".
1876	Howard takes a 2nd in Natural Sciences and graduates from Oxford as Bachelor of the Arts; Howard's brother William dies.
1879	Howard leaves his post at Cheltenham College; he publishes an edited collection of his father's work, *Chapters on the Art of Thinking, and Other Essays.*
1880	Howard marries Mary Ellen Boole, daughter of the deceased mathematician George Boole and Mary Everest, in Marylebone on April 21st; his essay "What is the Fourth Dimension?" is first published in the University Magazine in Dublin; he takes up a post as science master at Uppingham College; the Hinton family have dinner with Henry Havelock Ellis in London.
1881	Howard and Mary live at 30 Stockerston Road, Uppingham. Mary's sister, Alicia Boole, is staying with the family at the time of the 1881 census.
1882	George, a son to Howard and Mary, is born on July 20th.
1883	Howard marries Maud Florence at a registry office on the Strand on January 19th under the assumed name of John Weldon; his essay

"What is the Fourth Dimension?" is re-published in the magazine of Cheltenham Ladies College.

1884   Edwin Abbott's novel *Flatland* is published to critical and commercial acclaim; Eric, a second son, is born to Howard and Mary on June 8th; Howard publishes his monograph, *Science Notebook*; *What is the Fourth Dimension?* is issued as a pamphlet by Swan Sonnenschein, publisher of the first English translations of Karl Marx and Sigmund Freud, as the first in a series of "Scientific Romances"; his affair with Maud Weldon is by now known to Havelock Ellis, Olive Schreiner and his aunt Margaret Haddon; Maud has twin boys by Howard.

1886   William, a third son by Mary, is born in January; Howard takes his MA from Oxford; in October he is convicted of bigamy at the Old Bailey and sentenced to three days imprisonment; having already spent a week on remand, he is released without further punishment.

1887   Having failed to find work as a tutor to support his family, Howard travels to Japan to join a mission; Mary and his children follow; Sebastian is born; Howard is appointed headmaster of the newly founded Victoria Public School in Yokohama.

1888   Howard's *A New Era of Thought* is published by Swan Sonnenschein in his absence, edited by his sister-in-law Alicia Boole and his Balliol friend Herman John Falk.

1891–93   Howard gives up his post at the Victoria Public School; the family travel in Japan.

1893   The Hinton family ship to the USA on SS *Tacoma* for Howard to take up a post as mathematics instructor at the College of New Jersey.

1896   *Scientific Romances II* is published by Swan Sonnenschein; Howard demonstrates his baseball cannon for the first time in the gymnasium at what is now Princeton College.

1897   Howard continues to demonstrate his baseball gun and it is widely reported across the USA; he leaves Princeton to take a post at the University of Minnesota.

1900   Howard leaves the University of Minnesota.

1901   Mary Boole Hinton publishes *Other Notes*, a collection of verse; Howard takes up a post as a computer working for the Nautical Almanac, part of the US Naval Observatory.

1902   Howard takes up a post at the US Patent Office as a patent examiner.

1904   A collection of Howard's essays, *The Fourth Dimension*, is published by Swan Sonnenschein.

1905   Howard makes a speech at the University of Minnesota Alumni Association dinner.

1907   *An Episode of Flatland* is published by Swan Sonnenschein; Howard dies on April 30th at the dinner of the Washington Philosophical Society.

1908   Mary takes her own life on May 28th.

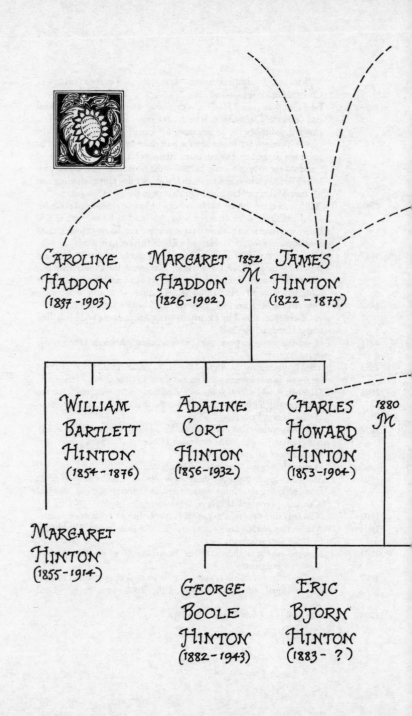

FAMILY RELATIONSHIPS

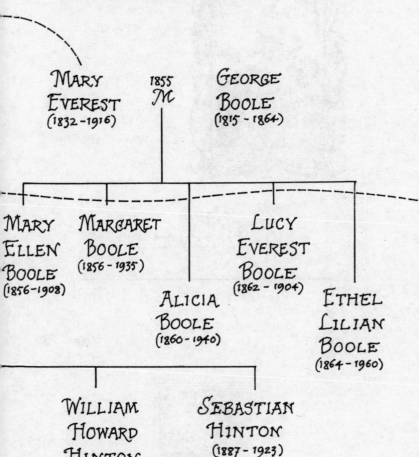

MARY
EVEREST
(1832-1916)

1855
M

GEORGE
BOOLE
(1815-1864)

MARY
ELLEN
BOOLE
(1856-1908)

MARGARET
BOOLE
(1856-1935)

ALICIA
BOOLE
(1860-1940)

LUCY
EVEREST
BOOLE
(1862-1904)

ETHEL
LILIAN
BOOLE
(1864-1960)

WILLIAM
HOWARD
HINTON
(1884-1909)

SEBASTIAN
HINTON
(1887-1923)

---- 1883
ⓜ MAUD
FLORENCE

?
(1884-?)

?
(1884-?)

Point

A

Others seek and achieve notoriety; Hinton has achieved almost total obscurity. He is no less mysterious than his work.

Hinton's *A New Era of Thought* (1888) includes a note from the editors which says: "The manuscript that is the basis for this book was sent to us by its author, shortly before his departure from England for an unknown and remote destination. He gave us complete liberty to amplify or modify the text, but we have used that privilege sparingly." This suggests a probable suicide or, more likely, that our fugitive friend had escaped to the fourth dimension which he had glimpsed, as he himself told us, thanks to a steadfast discipline.

Why not suppose Hinton's book to be perhaps an artifice to evade an unfortunate fate? Why not suppose the same of all creators?

Jorge Luis Borges, Prologue to *Scientific Romances* (1979)

Line

$$\overline{A \hspace{4cm} B}$$

A   B

1.

Never was a man so deep in thought. So limitless a field lay before him, so indistinct from the *terra incognita* beyond. He needed orientation. He needed to return to first principles. He needed simply to mark a point in the sand: let this be point *a*. By marking such points, so might a man draw fresh lines. By marking such points, so might a man construct foundations, axioms upon which to act anew. Let the commencement of this journey be point *a*.

Hinton stood so thinking upon the harbour's edge. Viewed from quayside, he cut a keen silhouette against the sheet-white sky, tailored Tweedside blocked against Yokohama cloud. A native artist would have drawn the rain that was falling as rods on the diagonal, with variations in angle; would have rendered the Western man's face as elongated, his nose as two sides of an obtuse triangle, his brows straight over narrowed eyes, paralleled by the brush moustache atop his upper lip. His hair would have been closely attended to, its swept wave and natural curl a particular interest for the artist accustomed to jet hair.

All would be flat behind him, and before, all on the surface of the plane, the colours soft but cleanly described in blocks of white, brown, blue and ochre. The schooner in the bay would be given equal weighting despite the foregrounding of the man, its three proud masts as significant to the scene as his hand thrust into his hip pocket. The more modern of the native artists, such as might sell his work to the newspapers or study at the Art School in Tokyo, would shift his perspective to bring into the background the steamer upon which the figure attended, making his picture emblematic of Tadayasu's *wakon-yōsai* – "Japanese spirit and Western techniques". Such an artist would – in a short passage of text adorning his image – record the man's noble work in education, his collaboration with Japanese mathematicians and philosophers, his journey of cultural exchange: the *idea* subtending the beautiful representation.

A European artist would give detail and perspective. In an already established tradition, the man would be framed against the immensity of the ocean, the terror inherent in its power dwarfing while elevating him, his status as heroic aesthete secured by his facing down the sublime force of nature from this stony crag. His forehead would be glimpsed in oblique profile, set against the elements, his shoulders set back in the broad tailoring of the great coat, his chin a jutting banner to the wind. In a newer tradition he would begin to merge with the haar, the confidence of his form deliquescing as sprays of light from an entropic sun fought through the haze, his very boundaries dissolved into his natural surroundings: a suggestion of a figure, dematerialised. In the very newest, he might appear as the Japanese version of himself, transposed and abstracted by a hemisphere.

This character carried documents in the inside pocket of his coat representing his entire family. His full name: Charles Howard Hinton. He was known to intimates by his middle name, Howard; had always been Howard to his parents, Margaret and James. James, even now, occupying his thoughts as he pondered distances travelled. He had been in Japan five years; his father dead some seventeen. How lives played out over their course. How might he redraw his own. He had suffered a fall, but rebirth was a possibility afforded him twice now, a possibility not afforded his progenitor.

His father, a philosopher highly regarded by society and

academy alike for his thoughts on issues as distinct as domestic life; the relations between science and religion; the physiological functioning of pleasure and pain; the need for self-sacrifice. Self-sacrifice above all. His father, James Hinton, a surgeon to educate and to feed his sons and daughters; a philosopher to nourish himself: great metaphysician, subject of biographers and obituarists. Howard was the inheritor of a once-illustrious name – how past that was – and the reputation attached to it.

In his youth Howard had burnished this reputation, conscious of its worth; had edited collections of his father's work and written prefaces for appreciations. He had published his own work on mathematics and its higher applications; had begun to enjoy a certain amount of success, to make a name for himself; had secured notices in *Mind* and other journals, winning praise from certain of his father's peers and appointment to a teaching post at Uppingham College. If he had not yet, by the time of his exile, piqued the interest of biographers, his life had been on that trajectory.

A jinrikisha came rattling along the harbour wall, pulled by a burly Japanese in straw rain coat in the custom of the rural workers in the surrounds of old Edo. In the trap, Howard's oldest son, George, was seated alongside a black, lacquered chest. George sat upright and alert, his fine blond hair slick to his scalp in the rain, his eye-glasses circles of opaque steam against his rosy face. Howard noted with pride the manner in which the boy had taken to responsibility. George was the least physically able of Howard's four sons but faced the world with a determined efficiency. Where he sensed disadvantage, he prepared methods for overcoming it. George had insisted upon travelling guard with the box, knowing its value to his father. He dismounted; Howard paid the shafu and together the three unloaded the box, placing it carefully on the harbourside.

The arc had been bisected: his career interrupted. He had been exiled. He had written to his publisher at the time of the shame that had befallen him since his trial, shame such as he would wish on no man, and had communicated his departure for work in distant lands: to a mission. He had not corresponded further with his publisher in the intervening years but had continued to write. While he now believed the direction of his earlier thought catastrophic, he was able to consider that he had found ways to think anew these difficulties by dramatizing them, making of them stories. Such stories had been the focus of his endeavours in Japan. Such stories might take flight in America.

He had inherited more than a reputation. For one thing, a gaze of considerable intensity. When he recalled his father, he recalled his father's eyes, beacons of a soulful mind, beaming, projecting the will for communion; active eyes, essaying a form of looking that wished to encompass all, to allow the object agency in the act of being seen. Despite the narrowness of his own gaze, such eyes glinted from within the creases. They had been noted, frequently, by the Japanese amongst whom he had been living these past five years and to whom their cobalt pigmentation was alien. His eyes had caused such comment that this sojourn had made him conscious of the organs as objects that were seen and contemplated by others, a dizzying inversion that produced a sensation of deep strangeness as he reflected upon it.

As Howard, George and the shafu worked, the second jinrikisha arrived, transporting Howard's wife Mary. Howard looked up and felt the sorrow and frequent frustration that had accompanied his relations with his wife since England. Mary, her hair tied back, a seriousness of expression squaring her jaw, was cradling their youngest son, Sebastian. Howard had much cause to rue the impossibility of knowing Mary's mind. He wished repeatedly to inquire after her thoughts. On occasions when he had acted upon such a wish, he had been disappointed. What was communicated was not thought, but something so attenuated that he became despondent of the hope of two minds ever achieving understanding. It was not that Mary did not have the words, simply that words themselves, however ordered, once external to her mind, were insufficient – woefully so – for the purpose he hoped they might achieve.

Sebastian had known nowhere but Japan and now would know nowhere but the new world to which they were set to chart course. Sebastian was English only on the documents Howard sheltered in his deep pocket: Sebastian Theodore Hinton. Howard conceded to the emergent narrative that Sebastian was cherubic, insisted upon by Mary. He brought God, she said, in keeping with his middle name, God and truth. He had more of his mother's features and frame and Mary allowed the boy's hair to grow, so that his soft face was cushioned in a blond mane. The boy was gentle of nature, thoughtful in his dealings with others far beyond what one would expect of a five-year-old. With no idea of their theory, Sebastian was the epitome of his grandfather's notions of self-sacrifice. That very morning, Sebastian had gifted to his mother the collection of pressed flowers he had lovingly assembled in Japan under the tutelage of his governess as a lasting memento of the Japanese nature Mary so loved. Howard noted how close to being overcome was his wife. A gift had not occurred to him.

A horse-drawn cart followed, bearing chests. These Howard directed towards the steamer, the *Tacoma*, moored further along the harbour. Already anticipating Mary's inquiry – where are William and Eric? – Howard contemplated retaining the second jinrikisha in order to commence a search. In the planning, all three traps had been due to leave the residence simultaneously and the two middle boys, despite their youth, seven and eight years apiece, were to travel together because the possibility of any interruption in the brief journey had seemed so remote. No longer.

Somewhere, somehow, between the home and the harbour, William and Eric had become delayed. Howard imagined the set of possible circumstances: an altercation of some description between the shafu and a passing pedestrian? It seemed impossible that the shafu should have become lost. The terrible thoughts to which the parent's mind is apt to fly in such moments loomed at the edge of his imagination, thrusting and parrying into consciousness: the mere forming of the word "accident" accompanied by a sickening sense of how vulnerable was childish flesh in the hardness of the world. No sooner had Howard begun to sound out the depth of his panic, felt as a falling away in the lower stomach, than the third jinrikisha rounded the houses at the harbourside and made its way along the quay, the two boys filling his lungs with relief by their grinning from the bench seat. That such extremes of emotion could be occasioned without external expression and within the span of a minute was the syrup torture of his quotidian experience.

"Papa, Papa, Eric nearly fell out!"

Eric, an almost perfect physical replica of his mother, robustly built, set jaw, closely cropped hair: always dressed in childish clothes against which his form chafed. Of spirit, something loose. In his more doubtful moments, Howard worried that the boy's senses had been altered forever by a head injury; that the boy was different since, that something in the matter of his mind had been shocked free of its moorings. There were questions of speech: his was more fluid, accruing recently heard words and phrases too readily and repeating them. There were matters of temperament. There was a troubling disregard for others in the child's actions, an antithesis to Sebastian's temper, against which

Howard wondered if it mightn't be some form of reaction. In times of more ascendant thinking Howard could glimpse in the boy a speed of mind, an impatience with the mismatch between his capacity for curiosity and its satisfaction. Frequently that void was bridged by self-styled entertainments involving the provocation of his brother William, as near as not his twin in appearance – slightly heavier, if the two were to continue to grow into adulthood on parallel paths – and in temperament direct and stubborn to the point of insolence. Willy appeared stuffed into his clothes; was, indeed, stuffed into those worn by Eric but twelve months previously. William had been named for Howard's beloved younger brother, a promising student and gentle soul, overcome by pulmonary paroxysm in his fifteenth year.

Six Hintons, gathered on the quayside, their chests and bags piled beside them. The Hinton family, detailed in documentary form on the papers inside Howard's pocket: a bill of passage and letters of introduction. Soon to be transferred in name and number, age and status, into the ship's log of the SS *Tacoma* by the man walking towards them.

Square

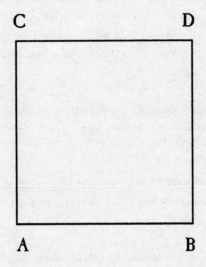

SS Tacoma
From Yokohama, Japan to Tacoma, Washington
August 16, 1893

I, J. R. Hill, Master of the above-named S.S. *Tacoma*, from
the Port of Yokohama, do solemnly, sincerely, and truly swear
that the above List contains the names and descriptions of
all the Passengers who were on board the said S.S. *Tacoma*
at the time of or since her departure from the said Port of
Yokohama, or that have been taken on board the said vessel
at any foreign port or place and that none have died on the
voyage.

COLLECTOR'S OFFICE, Port of Tacoma, August 16th 1893.
Subscribed and sworn to before – signed – James Osborne,
Collector.

LIST OR MANIFEST of all the Passengers taken on board
the S.S. *Tacoma* whereof J. R. Hill is Master, from Yokohama;
burden, 2550 tons.

Columns represent: Names, Sex, Occupation, The country
to which they sovereignly belong, The country in which they
intend to become inhabitants.

Cabin

1. Rev. W. M. Hayes	M	Missionary	USA	USA
2. Mrs. Hayes	F	Family	USA	USA
3. Child	M	Family	USA	USA
4. Infant	F	Family	USA	USA

5. Captain Keane	M	Ship Captain	Gr. Britain	USA
6. Mr. C. H. Hinton	M	University Professor	Gr. Britain	USA
7. Mrs. Hinton	F	Family	Gr. Britain	USA
8. Child	M	Family	Gr. Britain	USA
9. Child	M	Family	Gr. Britain	USA
10. Child	M	Family	Gr. Britain	USA
11. Child	M	Family	Gr. Britain	USA
12. Mr. H. A. Thomson	M	Engineer	Gr. Britain	USA

2.

"Seppuku," Howard preaches to the assembled diners. "Or hara-kiri. The word is the same, it is merely the positions of the characters that are exchanged. As in algebra. Kiri, I believe, means cutting. So se. And hara, and hara for belly. Hara or fuku. The samurai cuts across the belly, like so, from left to right." He becomes expansive, miming the actions.

Mrs Hayes straightens in her seat, William leans in. The table is set for the twelve cabin passengers, absent George, who is seasick in his bed, and the engineer Thompson, who attends to his duties. The Reverend Hayes is a missionary of a kind Howard is familiar with: determined in his faith, narrowing the entire world to fit its scheme. He senses in Hayes's wife the zeal for expansion: she must have brought them on the mission.

"A short sword called a tanto is used. The blades of Japanese swords are extremely keen but a sword for this purpose must also possess a point." Hinton plunges the imaginary point into his own guts and gazes beyond Keane, forming images somewhere behind him, on some screen of the mind.

"Professor Hinton, I am unsure . . ."

The Reverend Hayes is pale but the Captain wants to hear more. "Did you witness this personally, Hinton?"

"No, Captain. The practice is increasingly scarce. Though I am told that there were many such suicides during the final weeks of the war."

Willy, sat beside his father, toys with his knife, running his finger along the serrated blade. "I wonder how it must feel."

Howard observes his son, contemplating the boy's morbid curiosity. Typical of his age? Or something more deep-seated?

"Your grandfather made a study of physiological pain, William. The sensation is most profound in the instant of penetration. Thereafter certain mechanisms of the mind, or the body, we know not which . . . I assume something like release. Opening. The French word *vent*, for wind, shares a stem with the Latin word for stomach. I wonder if you mightn't feel the external breeze within you. It must be visually appalling. One's own viscera, there, before one's own eyes. The mind must flounder. The colours are extremely lurid. Also, steam, I shouldn't guess. Depending upon the external temperature, because the internal temperature of the body . . . But there is something in that ventilation, I think, that is like an inversion. The interior exposed. A freedom of sorts. An expression. A ventriloquism."

"It is a sin." Mrs Hayes cannot contain the words, nor their tone. She is appalled. Her eyes, sharper than the point of a tanto, aim to pierce Howard but he is distractedly unaware.

"Perhaps it should not be so, Reverend." Mary pats his hair as she fusses at Sebastian. "It is a matter of choice and the Japanese elevate it to an act of nobility."

Hayes has sensed doctrinal wavering. "Are you a Romanist, ma'am?" Words dragged through pews.

"I am, Reverend, though some years lapsed in attendance to my faith. I must confess that I lack the zeal possessed by missionaries such as my husband."

Howard is incapable of blushing, his skin inscrutably weathered to the last. "We were not at the mission for so long, Mary . . ."

"Rome is clear on this matter. The bible is clear." Mrs Hayes speaks over the husband. The wife does not fluster. Mary is not easily disturbed.

19

"I am sure there are verses."

Keane, seated across the table at the captain's chair, revels in Mary's accent, softened almost to nothing but tickling his ear. His own mother's accent was pronounced, her journey from Cork much later in life, but he recognises the lilt immediately, wants to have the Hinton woman speak again if only to hear that wisp, no more than a raised eyebrow of intonation.

"You have strong feelings on this matter, Mrs Hinton?"

She turns to him. It is as if she reads him.

"I do, Captain, and I apologise to the Reverend but with the greatest respect I do not hold to doctrines that do not offer something for life as it is lived. A life is nothing if not one's own. This sin of self-murder, I do not know how it can be a sin. Against whom is it a sin? Life is sacred, I am sorry Reverend, I feel that I have interrupted you there, I realise that this is the counter-claim, that all life is created by the almighty and that it is his and only his to take away but that is not, I think, quite so sound a doctrine as it might once have been. I exceed myself. I apologise."

She withdraws, pets Sebastian, leaves Hayes to attend to his shocked wife and Howard to entertain William. Keane marvels at the voice, giggles submerged within it but sunk so soundly they no longer bubble as they should. The Hinton boy acts out the ritual disembowelment of his father who tells the Captain of yet more outlandish Nipponese customs.

"Milk is drunk as if it were medicine?"

--

Having settled Sebastian on a bunk, Mary sets course to explore below decks. She thinks she wishes to find a lonely spot, perhaps to clear her mind, perhaps busy it, but as she wanders the corridors, feeling as much as hearing the muffled rhythms of propulsion, she crosses paths with Thompson, the engineer. He smiles from beneath grey smears. "Mrs. Hinton. Are you lost?"

Mary tilts her head. "Not as such. I'm becoming lost, I suppose. Is there a difference between the two?"

Thompson laughs. "I'm sure I'm not the man to ask. If there's anything I can do to help. I could show you the engine room. If you'd like that. I marvel at it."

Mary nods her assent with a gleeful skip of the chin. Thompson leads on, opens bulkhead doors with heavy clanks of handles, Mary glancing this way and that in an effort to memorise the route, and they emerge into a long chamber defined by regular, fluid motion. Four pistons, thirty feet apiece, gleaming steel rods sliding in and out of brass sheaths, perfectly regular but asynchronous with each other. Sighing, swooning metalwork copulates before her.

"I've just been in the stoking room, you don't want to see that, ma'am, filthy like Sodom."

"I don't doubt it, Mr Thompson."

"Piston rods drive the paddles."

Mechanism is alien in its precision, thinks Mary. All moves to perfect plan with neither pause nor interruption. It is the time of it. Time does not so flow. Time stammers and hiccoughs, falls faint and suffers fevers. This relentless power exceeds the human. There is something monstrous at its heart. No sooner has she seen what drives them forwards, to another new future, than she recoils from it.

"I wonder if you might direct me back, Mr Thompson. My weariness has surprised me."

"Of course, ma'am," says the engineer. He appears ever so slightly hurt. Just like a child.

George leans over the rail, the effluent from the steamer's funnel framing his head against the ocean sky. His nausea has retreated with calmer seas. Mere feet above his head, almost close enough to touch, gulls float, tracking the ship, tilting and correcting to maintain the sky, the current of the air allowing stasis within it. Howard and George observe the Chinese passengers on the lower deck. The Chinese are chasing the gold rush. One hundred and fifty gaunt faces, men, women and children, jostle for space within steerage. When the Hinton family boarded the passengers from Hong Kong were already established. They run lines from the deck hoping to supplement their rations: sporadically an angler hauls a catch on board, examines it, and pitches it, squirming, into a pail or whence it came.

There is scrabbling within the mass and it shifts to the starboard. To George, the mass is undifferentiated; the Chinese steerage passengers wear linen in various hues but it tends towards the same grey. As fever spreads like wildfire through steerage and may leap with ease the artificial boundaries imposed between decks they are checked for disease daily. The ship's doctor is recognisable even to the poorly sighted George by his blue smock, temporarily worn over his mate's uniform: each of the men doubles in roles and the doctor is a student in medicine though an experienced sailor. He examines tongues for spots, tests brows with the back of his hand, inquires after water supplies; they show him roots, herbs, unguents.

Howard observes from over his son's shoulder. "The system has become momentarily agitated by the introduction of the good doctor. His entry onto the deck has introduced a considerable amount of kinetic energy." George takes in the lesson, familiar with his father's mode of discourse. "The work of the doctor is important, essential. He is a form of moderation within the system. It would tend towards dissipation much more rapidly were he not to perform his checks. Any infection would spread at a great rate and with it the energy death of the steerage passengers."

"What are we, Papa?"

"We are observers of the system from a higher plane, George. We have little power to intervene, though we may bear witness to all that occurs."

George mulls on this. He has received instruction in forms of energy: potential and kinetic; in heat and the Brownian motion. He is unsure why this applies to Chinese folk as well as gases. He finds it difficult to imagine human beings as molecules. There is an insurmountable problem of scale.

--

A Chinaman stands as far to the aft of the steerage deck as it is possible to go. He leans perilously over the railing, swinging a weighted and baited line in his right arm in a wide arc, releasing it to fly upwards, towards the hovering gulls. One gull darts at it and takes the bait in its beak; in the same instant the Chinaman yanks downwards, pulling the gull from its flight. There is no need to reel it until the seabird finds its wings some feet from the deck. The fisherman pulls against its flapping until his companion can take hold of the bird and calm it. They remove the hook from its mouth, perform some indecipherable operation, and release it once more to the sky. The gull takes flight and resumes its position hovering above the higher deck. Some minutes later, a sound like the striking of a pillow with a fist, a fine crimson spray, and the gull falls from the sky, its viscera spilling from the popped bag of its stomach as the Chinamen collapse to the deck in screeching laughter.

Eric is thrilled. Never had he imagined such things possible. How did they do it? How did they *think* to do it? If these men can do such things for amusement, what else might they know? He determines to learn the trick for himself.

Eric has been in hiding from his own family since Yokohama, playing dice with himself. Father had given each of the boys a set of cubes before the journey: one-inch kindergarten blocks, coloured in fawn, gold, crimson, blues; scribbled over with a litany of Latin words; Fons, Plectrum, Vulnus, Arena, Mensa, Terminus, Testa. For Eric, every word is as hateful as the transparent attempt to have him study geometry while also studying Latin under the guise of play. Father had demonstrated the method: moving the cubes through sequences, imagining the points, lines and faces of each in motion. The instructions were frequently nonsensical to Eric. One had to remove self-elements. One had to think as a plane-being. The black square traces a cube, the colour of which is invisible, and ends in a white square. Eric had taken his cubes and made of them gaming dice, chiselling indentations into each of the faces. Bones. He throws them for himself and recites his own poems forged from his dreams and the echoes of the lessons that have lodged themselves within his mind: two vermillion dots, Ilex is hot. Five brown eyes, Mala subsides. He has indulged his knack for covert observation of strangers, learnt in Edo, where he would sneak up on washer-women and steal items of curious clothing. He has been rewarded now with this secret trick of exploding birds. He will learn it. He will know how.

--

Howard contemplates the ocean surface, George having indicated the spectacle of silvered, winged fish, emerging from waves and skimming the surface, trailing continuous Ss. He had once heard his father relate Mr Darwin's speculation to his own. Mr Darwin's tidal ascidians, his father suggested, had begun as unicellular creatures. They had combined, he argued, with their kin to exist as a form of living surface. Thence, over the millennia, growing gills, fins and limbs, had evolved to inhabit three-dimensional space. Life was truly, from its basis, progressing through an experience of space ascending in its dimensionality. Clifford, meanwhile, had speculated on the experience of a flatfish as an exemplary planar being, a creature whose existence might be considered two-dimensional. Clifford considered the flatfish in contrast with a suppositious worm – a being of uni-dimensionality, contained, in Clifford's somewhat artificially composed picture, he thought, within a metal hoop of extremely narrow bore. The argument was by analogy: as the worm's experience compares to that of the flatfish, so must the flatfish's compare to our own. And, to progress, as the flatfish's experience compares to our own, so must our own experience compare to that of a suppositious four-dimensional being. As the ocean's mineral spray refreshed his face, Hinton could not help but share George's excitement at the darts and glides of the flying fish.

The flying fish might be recruited to this thought experiment, thinks Howard, free as it is to glide and dive within its own three-dimensional universe; freer, indeed, than is he on the deck, denied by brute gravity access to the fullness of his spatial environment. The three-dimensional universe of the flying fish is constrained by the skein of the surface of the ocean, a limiting film beyond which lies a distinct spatial environment. The ability to transcend that surface, muses Hinton, to break through from one world to another that contains it ... And yet, the more he turns it in his mind, the more inadequate the analogy seems. A part of the scheme is missing. Higher space is not simply beyond some planar surface divide, but is also through, encompassing and within, as if the fish were at any point of the ocean able to breach the surface: as if the open atmosphere suffused the darkest profundity.

"Tuna," brays the Captain, appearing at Howard's side on the deck. "An ingenious way to flee their hunters."

George turns to Howard.

"Are they really flying, Papa?"

"They glide, more properly," Howard replies to his son. "They propel themselves into the air and hold their fins rigid."

"I think of them as sailors," states the captain. "Sailors of the spume."

"Will we see them again?" asks George.

"Perhaps not. The northern waters become too cold. Would you like to inspect one?"

George baulks. "I don't want you to catch one."

"There's no need for a line. You'll see this evening."

--

A torch is affixed within a lifeboat, which is lowered and dragged, sending spray behind it. The wind abrades their cheeks. Keane himself directs his crew, George by his side, commanding the rope handlers and pulley wranglers with Thompson watching in interest. Reverend Hayes stands by with Hinton, the ladies retired, Eric and Willy distractedly playing with some jacks on the pocked and gouged deck, Sebastian sound below.

"You are a writer as well as a teacher, Professor Hinton?"

Hinton surveys the man, assays his curiosity, judges it genuine enough.

"I have published some brief romances, Reverend. They are not broadly read."

The Reverend chews on this.

"Romances like those of Mr Stevenson?"

Hinton leans on the rail as he responds. "They are in support of a plan of work. A form of thought mechanics."

The Reverend puffs himself up. "I am a great enthusiast for swashbucklers. Are yours full of bright adventure?"

Hinton understands this line of questioning: he has experienced it before. He has long since deviated from the polite answers, preferring accuracy.

"One concerns the distribution of pleasure and pain among the inhabitants of a Persian valley. Their ruler allocates each according to the principles of the science of thermodynamics. It might not be to your taste."

The Reverend maintains course, ploughing across the line. "I have read much of Scott. Scott has fallen out of favour, recently, has he not? Mr Stevenson brings him back, I think. The popular romances of today are more feminine in their approach. Are yours in this manner?"

What kind of a mind, wonders Hinton. Such as does not wish to entertain change, certainly. Wilful ignorance, even to utterances freshly made. And yet change is the very condition of life.

"I have completed the manuscript of a romance while in Japan. It tells of a transparent woman. It is called *Stella*. I hope that my publisher may take it on." He sees her particularly now, he thinks, he sees them both in the same frame, in the same form. He observes not Mary alone, her worn features his own care; but Maud also, the lost Maud, the passion for which he had shattered all convention, the soul for whom he mourned. A wife. They do, in some way, share the space. Not because he places them there – his agency is not sufficiently vital in this confluence of womanhood – but because their kinship has emerged from an event shared, a groove in the aether, a particular channel that was carved out and now, as distant as they may be in geographical terms – and how distant that might be he could never know, the location of Mary being the only term available to him in the calculation – they were connected in the higher realm, paired twists of equal frequency.

"A transparent woman, no less! With a voice voluminous in inverse proportion, I'll wager." Hayes thinks himself the very essence of wit.

Hinton will not stand for the violation. "Her voice is like a haunting, Reverend. She lives with the narrator for the duration of his travels. She is never far from him. She has been mistreated."

The Reverend pats himself down for tobacco. "It sounds very much in the manner of the more modern romances, Hinton. It will probably sell very well but I do not think it would be to my taste."

To Hinton's left, Keane has his crew lower the lifeboat, which they do with an arrangement of hawsers and whip-lines, tallyboards and traveller blocks, a nest in which the small row-boat rests, which takes it close enough to the sea before separating to let its polished hull slap the surface. "Do you want to go down, boy?" George shakes his head vigorously, not wishing to abandon the safety of the main ship. The lifeboat looks fragile in comparison to the *Tacoma*. Willy, however, fancies his chances. Hayes looks inquiringly at Howard, who tips his head in assent. If the boy wishes adventure, then why should he not experience such? It will allow him something with which to shock his mother.

Keane signals to two of his men, who shin down a rope ladder and into the smaller vessel. The Chinese crowd the edge of the deck to stare over, curious and anticipating. Keane helps Willy over the balustrade and Willy takes to the rope ladder like the little monkey he is, jigging down its length, using his body-weight as counterbalance to the swings of the ladder. Howard chuckles, Eric clings to his father.

With the two men and Willy aboard, the row-boat is let out on its tow-line until it trails the *Tacoma* by some twenty feet. The men light lamps and set them in the middle of the boat: not only can Howard and Eric see Willy's excited face, underlit, from afar, they notice as he twitches at the projectiles that almost immediately begin to fly. The flying fish hurtle into the boat at a rate of three or four a minute. One of the sailors presents to Eric a specimen cradled between his cupped hands. Eric leans out to take it, the silver of its scales phosphoresced by the flickering wick of the lamps. He feels its sleek, metallic muscularity between his palms, and it flips immediately out of his grasp, whacking to his feet. The sailor retrieves the panicking fish while his mate ships the newer boarders back into the ocean.

"They are drawn to the light," explains Keane. "The men, on occasion, fish this way. We can haul hundreds in an hour and no need for nets. The flesh is ... the flavour is strong, so they are eaten that night." A yelp from the lifeboat, where a flying fish has arrowed directly into Willy's temple.

"An occupational hazard of the sport," chuckles Keane. "We do not typically man the boat." He signals to the two men who begin to draw the boat back towards the *Tacoma*, pulling in the rope. "We'll have him back up that ladder. Game lad."

Howard acknowledges the compliment. "An adventurous spirit." Willy's grinning face is illumined by flickering lamplight as his vessel is winched in to the mothership.

--

In the cabin, as he plants a kiss on the heads of each of his sleeping sons, Howard indulges himself. The smell of the top of Willy's head he recognises from his own pillow, something heady, deeper than he's comfortable with. Perspiration on the turn. Sebastian's has something of straw to it; light, windblown, a draught of perfume: none of the murk he has gifted to William. Knowing the fallacy of it, he wonders idly whether these scents indicate something of the personalities of each. Certainly, Willy is wilful, prone to explosions, musky of mood; Sebastian carefree and less fixed. The kind of thinking favoured by the likes of Galton, a predetermination in the body, an evolutionary inclination, allowing insufficiently for mind, its transformative capacities, its ability to act upon the world and to remake it in its own image; speculation made concrete. And why not? George's head has an orderly scent, he thinks. Correct. It is indicative not of mood but of thought. George's systematic mind prompts the release of systematic odour. Is it thought one smells? If so, Eric's scent must be extravagant and wild. Eric hardly stays still long enough for his father to smell him. Perhaps Mary knows. How would one ask such a question? Have you smelt the boy's head recently? How does the boy's head smell to you? She would fear a collapse. She would read his inquiry as an indication of addled thought, the beginning of a descent such as suffered by his father in the final months of his life. He can never communicate such imaginings. Perhaps he might make a comic tale of it! A jeu d'esprit! Tribes of boys associating through scents: the musks, the orchids, the machines. A story fit for the newer magazines. Yes, he will propose it in America.

--

Keane opens the catches on the chest and Sebastian peers in. Cushioned inside lies a brass torpedo, finned like a flying fish. Keane takes it out and hands it to the boy. It is heavier than he could have imagined! Heavier than a scuttle, or the iron tools Father kept in his outhouse. How dense it must be! And cool to the touch, so cool, a chill emanating from within. Sebastian inspects it. Behind a thick glass panel, three enamelled dials are set in the polished body, recording tens of miles, units and quarters. An inscription beneath these reads: "Walker's / patent / harpoon / ship's log." On each of its five tail fins is engraved an anchor.

"Thing of beauty. Gives us the speed of the ship," Keane tells the boy. He leads out of the cabin and onto the stern deck. He fastens a line to the taffrail. "Throw it in and let's get a reading."

Sebastian drops the instrument from the stern, watching it disappear beneath the heaving immensity with barely a splash. The reel runs at a buzz before pulling taut.

Keane watches the line. "How long shall we drag it for?"

"Six minutes?" offers Sebastian. The captain puts a hand on his shoulder.

"Clever lad. Why six minutes?"

Sebastian looks up at the captain, pleased with himself. "Multiply by ten for miles an hour."

Keane slaps him on the back. "A Professor in waiting. In the meantime, though, a dead-reckoner."

--

Howard distributes to each son a pencil and a sheet of paper. He sets the boys an exercise: to chart the course of the *Tacoma*. Sebastian is dutiful. He copies from the charts Keane shows him, making the best approximations possible for a six-year-old hand. His islands are misshapen, his scribbled course commences Southwards before turning abruptly East. He draws the lines of longitude thick and black, as if geographical features of the ocean. He sketches the ship itself and must redraw it every day, a series of *Tacoma*s making their journey across his approximation.

Willy has become frustrated. He cannot make the thing work. He has asked Howard about the flattening of the sphere but can make no sense of his father's explication of the Mercator projection, of the distinct techniques emerging in that moment which might unpeel segments of the sphere to reduce distortion most appropriately to record a passage across the Pacific North. Willy attempts to flatten his map over the globe on the bridge and copy what he can read beneath its crumpled surface. It proves a forlorn task. He rips his paper in two and abandons the game.

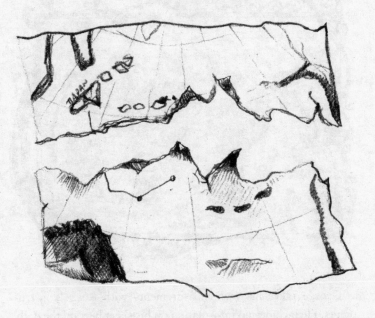

Eric has made a fiction of his map. Here is Hispaniola, there Atlantis. Here is the fabled north-western passage through the Arctic ice floes, with a small Frankenstein's monster pursued by a smaller Victor. Here are terrible whirlpools, there sea-monsters and great white whales. A ghost-ship, with a pirate's ensign. It bears scant resemblance to the world as it is lived and traversed. It is beautifully embellished in curlicues of design.

George takes his own measurements with Keane's instruments. He includes no information on his sheet beyond the daily position of the ship, recording time and compass reading. Despite this detail it appears to his father that he has misunderstood the required scale, has commenced the course too far towards the right-hand edge of his sheet which, sure enough, he reaches at day eight. George simply flips his sheet and continues the course on the reverse side.

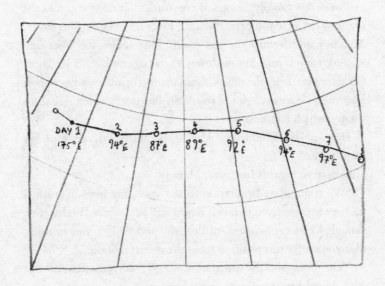

--

The names of the islands offer a peculiar poetry, open-mouthed and catching: Attu, Agmatinak, Adak, Kiska, Unalaska, St Makarius. They appear from the mists, rough-grassed in rye, volcanic slag rivers running from steam-crowned peaks to the sea, tarry black residue slicking into slack-grey swell. Fluted cliffs caving towards profundity. Sebastian marks each island on his chart, copying from the maps Keane allows him to read on the bridge, 1890 Admiralty editions giving tides and rocks in the vicinity of the Aleutians.

"These charts are useful to us here," Keane tells him, "where we can navigate by land. Out at sea they offer us little. We use this." He shows the bridge guests the Pacific Coasters' Almanac for 1893: the lyrical Ephemerides in minutes and seconds, giving positions for the mythological creatures that course across the night sky: Ursae minoris; Piscium; Hydrae; Leonis. The moon, Mercury and Venus: the sun itself. Tide tables for Sitka and Kadiak island, nine hours slower than Greenwich Mean Time. Guidance on using the tables. Guidance on using breeches buoys; how to navigate cyclones in southerly latitudes; which signals to use for which conditions.

Howard is delighted. "The stars above us, govern our conditions!"

Sebastian regards his father blankly.

"We triangulate in relation to the stars, my boy! In truth, I had never considered that this might still be achieved in this way, though I know, of course, of Ptolemy and Halley. But to think that you derive our position from the celestial bodies."

"The moon and the sun are the easiest," corrects Keane. "But it's a form of triangulation, aye, that seems right enough."

Howard shakes his head in wonder. "You must allow for the curve of the Earth?"

"The tables allow for it already. I have to calculate for parallax."

"Of course!" exclaims Howard. "The cosmic distance ladder! You can have no idea how far distant from each other at any given moment – many hundreds of thousands of miles – are the projected lights of, say, Venus and Mars. The art of navigation is a true expression of our civilization as a species: a practical application of the truth of geometry."

Keane is disinterested. He wants only to ensure that his course is charted and cares not for the theories he inherits. Howard must think to himself of the wonder of the sextant, the astrolabe, the cross-staff: ancient technologies for reading our position on the surface of this tilted sphere. Technologies that predate even the realization of its rotation! Of its orbit of the sun! As late as Kepler we knew not how these trajectories across the heavens were interwoven. No wonder a creator was assumed. The cosmos, its Platonic certainty, that must have been impossible to conceive as chance: the patterns repeating with complex variations. Those variations now coded in the logarithmic tables printed in this Almanac by the US Naval Observatory. The work of men at telescopes in cities enabling the work of men at sea in steamships. A correlation of shared labours across distinct fields of operation. A form of symmetry, should one choose to see it, encoded in an altruistic and abstracted work.

The truth is, thinks Howard, we are triangulators, geometers, by dint of binocularity. Perspective is imposed upon us by our physiological arrangement. We allow for parallax! In all things.

--

A marengo sea. Kittiwakes, bluethroats, egrets.

Keane points out a small steamer in a pass. "The fur-traders still have the run of these islands. Russians as much as Americans. Brought from Russia in '67 but they're still here. They marry the natives, make a nest out here, have a few pups, hunt the otters, amass a fortune in fur then back to the mainland and drink themselves to death. Should be a law against it."

William, Japanese-reared, yearns for geological drama. "Will Mount Makushin explode?"

"She blew in spring. Ash falls for a month. Fine grit in everything. Goes in your mouth, sticks to your teeth."

Keane takes to the role of sea-dog.

"Let me tell you a story. Some friends of mine went ashore on one of these islands. Fancied some of the fur money for themselves. Escorted by the natives in canoes. Went ashore, took pow-wow in one of those whale-bone huts, brought some alcohol for the locals – Russians were happy, Indians not so much. But they want to show them something in return. Something important. They lead them up the mountainside, past all these tumbled rocks, into the mouldy hills. They point at a cave in the side of the mountain. My friends don't want to go. What's this about? Are they bandits, these natives? No, they insist, inside Mr Yangee. Inside. My friends go in to this place. Smells like hell. Sulphur coming up through the rocks. Hot as hell, too. Towards the volcano. Wrong way to go. Dark, dank, stench like Beelzebub. My friends push on till the cave opens up enough to stand. Their guides say, "Here, Mr Yangee, Look here." What's this poking out the sides of the cave, all this crumbling rock – lava set to stone – what are these white extrusions, reaching out? They're bones. Look closer. They're finger bones. Pick away, there up above, a leathery face, mummified. To the left, another, blackened skin mask. The whole cave, lined with them, gnarled, leering at you. Feathers through noses. Ancients of these people. Their ancestors. Mummified like in Egypt, but lava in place of bandages. My friends were honoured! Honoured guests, meeting grandy and grandau. This was not their thinking. They were given the history of these people in preserved flesh, in that hellish hole in the mountain, but they only wanted out."

--

Under the cover of a storm, Eric has slid a piece of paper under the locked door of George's cabin and retreated to his own. The bucket slides across the cabin deck and the gastric odours cause George to retch once more. This motion is hateful, inescapable. Why did they have to make this journey? What sort of a job is so important to Father? He wants to be with Felicity, he wishes to explore the forest to the north of the monastery. He does not wish to be thrown, nauseous, from pillar to post for the entertainment of his little brothers. He has been experiencing fevered dreams; buccaneers and privateers have caroused across his disturbed imagination, baiting him, threatening him, and he has fled through marsh-like atmospheres, dragged ever backwards, impeded impossibly. He has awoken panting and smelt his own bile. He tips his head to one side, ready to convulse again, and sees it on the floor. A crumpled scrap, in its centre imprinted an ink-black spot. Panic rises. He wishes to rinse his mouth. He quashes the panic: he knows full well dreams cannot manifest. But can this have slipped from his dream? He recalls a black spot, he recalls it all too well, pressed into his hand by a leering Silver, a leer of such magnitude that it split the monstrous face in two across the beard revealing a fleshy mouth, devious and red ... He retches again and snatches for the bucket, tips his vomit onto the floor of the deck, moans weakly for Mother and awaits the next swell. It must be that bleeder, thinks George, that rotten brother of mine. It must be him, surely, this storybook trick, this taunt. It mustn't be that mate. The mate is not as wicked as he looks. An eye patch does not a pirate make. The captain would not allow a pirate on his ship, for one, reasons George. A pirate would not wish to serve, for two. Unless he plans for mutiny. Father would resist, thinks George, and I would help him. Eric would be useless, and Sebastian, of course, too small to help, but Willy might be some assistance. Mother would be capable, she might lay traps. In fact, Mother would know whether or not the mate was a likely culprit. But it was Eric, certainly. A black spot. A nursery game! He crumples the paper in his fist and makes to lob it away but there is nowhere he might throw it. He returns to his reading, his thoughts smudged by that black spot, sucked into its unity, becoming reflexive.

--

Mary sits in the corner of George's cabin, stitching. She sits sentinel over her firstborn, interrupting her hobby only to slop out and to soothe his brow with gentle strokes of the back of her fingers. As she sits on the edge of his bed, he is barely conscious of her presence in his fever. Mary is confident that the sickness will pass, induced only by motion. She is conscious, too, of an unexpurgated sigh in her core, a dissatisfaction with her set of conditions, self-imposed. It is momentarily released in her attention to her stitching.

She returns her focus to that activity as she settles again in her corner tub seat. Her mother had instructed Mary and her sisters in the use of sewing cards as a form of direct contact with mathematics. Not for the Boole girls the knitting of infant caps or shawls for great aunts. One commences with the plotting of points in a grid and joins these points with the thread, each line both bisecting and augmenting its fellows, tangents on the cards combining to form curves and parabola. She works presently towards a cardioid design. The work is rhythmic and builds towards satisfaction, its angles perpetually softened and arced until a perfect form is achieved. She is minded of how distinct it is from the view of geometry, derived from Kepler, in which the masculine cube sits first and foremost amongst the Platonic forms. Her mother had realised that this generative act of producing arcs was both instructive and inspirational. Mother is and has been right, she thinks, about a great deal, if not in her attachment to Howard's father, a fateful friendship whose implications still play out in all their lives.

The rectilinear be damned. She will have her sublime, practical curves.

3.

The time ball at Greenwich – a sphere commencing its ascent from an octagonal structure at twelve fifty-five, rising to the point of its rod at twelve fifty-eight and falling at one hour past the meridian precisely – emits percussive waves of time that wash laterally around the globe at equal rates in opposite directions. When the westerly meets the easterly – one hundred and eighty degrees from Greenwich – a twenty-four-hour period must evaporate in the collision of the waves. The antipodes are not continuous.

Fifteen days have elapsed since the *Tacoma* left Yokohama on a Monday. When the ship arrives at Tacoma, the port in Washington State for which it is named, on another Monday, George explains to his brothers that owing to the fact that they have been travelling with the rotation of the Earth, following the sun, at each degree of latitude they have gained four minutes precisely. Sebastian does not question, knowing his brother to be a reliable informant on such matters. He scribbles this down in truncated form on the chart he has recently updated. Willy squares his shoulders at the news. Eric is largely ignorant of the conversation, concerned instead with a deck of cards.

From their berth on the *Tacoma* they move as a unit into a cabin on a locomotive of the Pacific North-West Railroad. George recovers his spring immediately on attaining dry land: for the eldest brother the sea journey has been a torture but now he might enjoy the lengthy railroad trek. He marvels at the engines that pull them eastwards, pistons, beams and rods; wheels grooved onto tracks.

The family are settled into a compartment of beechwood racks and upholstered benches, marginally more spacious than their steamer cabins. Once settled, they roam to explore the first-class carriages and meet fellow passengers. After Missoula Howard is befriended by an eager young man who wishes to discuss with him Japanese customs. The man is travelling east to begin his sophomore year at Harvard. In conversation, he proves himself gently inquisitive. At each new piece of information gleaned from the conversation he tips his head in something near delight: "Ah!" The man is called Singer. His father works for the United States Naval Signals. Singer senior runs a new department of Observation and Information Gathering, aligned to the Diplomatic Mission. The United States needs to be less insular, Singer junior argues, hence his interest in Japan. His father has been experimenting with surveillance techniques and has placed the son under observation. On occasion he receives correspondence from his father asking how he enjoyed such and such a bar, or advising him to take certain precautions against disease, so much does his father seem aware of his activities. Why, he wouldn't be surprised if one of his father's agents weren't watching him at this very moment, noting the conversation! Howard raises his eyebrows. "Ah!" Howard notes a man reading a newspaper towards the rear of the carriage. Has he once turned the pages? Howard remarks that it must be a novel experience to feel as if one is watched at all times, thinking that Singer might benefit from working with the cubes. "Have you heard of the fourth dimension?" he asks. "Ah!" proclaims Singer. "I have read about it in the Theosophical journals." Howard inclines his head to one side. Theosophy? The old charlatan Blavatsky? So much has changed while he has been in Japan.

--

The College of New Jersey is in some ways what Howard had expected: a pygmy Oxford. It deceives itself of its modernity, an undergraduate wearing a long beard and quoting from Thucydides, but its buildings betray it. The newness of the stone. No ancient rocks, here. No medieval grain in the wood. A freshness beyond its freshmen, its customs a shadow-play of the gaudies and formal dinners of his own student days.

He must integrate into the social life of the faculty, undertaking a chore Mary does not feel obliged to indulge. He accepts all invitations, to colloquia and inaugural lectures; to informal dinners and symposia.

Before the commencement of the fall term he is invited to meet his colleagues in mathematics. They congregate in a corner of the senior common room, in the wooden angle between oak-panelled walls. Professors Duffield, Fine and Thompson; Dr Chittenden. Fine studied for his PhD in Leipzig and holds the practice of meta-geometry in little regard. "After he had been chased from your shores, my countryman Slade arrived in the city, much to the excitement of a number of elderly colleagues in the university. Hot-bed of spiritualism, seances everywhere. Wasn't a table that didn't tap! Zöllner, a curious old bird; lived with his mother, you know. Terribly misshapen face. Unhappy about Jews. Brilliant astronomer – inventor of lenses, stereoscopes. Great believer in spirits. Slade had him strung along. Spirits from YOUR fourth dimension, Hinton. Polarising light. Inverting crystals. Tying impossible knots. Got old Fechner along to run the rule in support. Blind from staring at the sun. Testimony of a blind man. Great believer. Wundt, also, psychologist. Less so."

Hinton is careful not to sound defensive. "I read of it in the dailies. There was some interest. The British spiritists were much bound up in the knot."

Thompson chips in. "It's a problem inherent in the practice, though, surely? Invites the metaphysicians in."

"It has been so remarked," concedes Hinton. It is an interview. He is on trial.

Duffield has the charm of the senior man of letters. He cares not for sensitivities. "I read your paper on poiographs. A curious piece of work. I am unsure what it achieves." Howard knows better than to challenge his opinions.

"It was the work of a younger man, Professor. A staging post in my thinking. I find that I no longer value it."

Duffield looks elsewhere. "Ingenious, nevertheless. The infinite regression of co-ordinates. Quite counter to the mainstream of thinking." His subordinates have fallen quiet to allow the senior man the stage.

Hinton sits up straight to acknowledge the compliment. "Thank you, Professor. It was a first step in the direction of my current thought."

Duffield assiduously avoids meeting Hinton's eye. "Yes. That too is curious, I see. Not precisely the direction in which most meta-geometers work."

Hinton shifts. "I find myself less inclined towards the projective methods than towards a manifest system of thought."

"But to what end?" Duffield stares at the ceiling. "This is abstraction, and useful as such. What can we hope to gain from fixing it in matter?"

Hinton fixes Duffield a serious gaze. "I contend that it is a property of matter, Professor. That in fact the finest molecules are higher-dimensional. Some physicists are of the same mind. Clifford, for one."

Duffield ponders this briefly. "Clifford died some years ago, did he not?"

Hinton is prompted towards great sincerity. "He has been

dead for some years, yes, but his work was visionary. I would recommend his *Common Sense*."

Duffield is losing interest in the conversation. "I see. Well. Your letters of recommendation come from similarly great minds."

Hinton keeps pace with the inquisition. "I have known Professor James for some years. He was an acquaintance of my father."

Duffield now examines a wooden panel. "I've known William for some years too. His genius is overstated."

Howard maintains his course. "He has been a support and a friend to me."

"Quite. You have been in Japan for how many years?"

"We left London in 1887."

"And why Japan?"

Howard almost stumbles. "I was offered an appointment. As the headmaster at a school."

"You were very courageous to traverse a hemisphere with such young children."

"My sense was that we had been offered a rare opportunity. Had we not travelled when we did we might never have been able to. My eldest son was approaching the age at which his education would begin in earnest. I was concerned not to disrupt his studies."

Duffield now studies a curtain, now the view beyond a window. "But did you not disrupt them in Japan?"

"They were, I hope, well-instructed. I travelled to Japan in advance of my family to ensure that all arrangements were in place. We engaged a most capable governess for the children. They miss Felicity a great deal. The children's mother and I are poor substitutes."

Duffield seems satisfied enough. "You must introduce your wife to the faculty wives' luncheon club. Well, Hinton, it makes you quite the exotic for a Princeton instructor. I trust you will share with us your wisdom on matters of Japanese culture. An informal lecture, perhaps?"

"I would be honoured. I became particularly interested in Buddhism."

"It has become quite the mode in certain circles. Are you a sportsman?"

"I would not describe myself as a natural athlete though I have enjoyed sports."

"We have a faculty baseball team. You should come to practice. Are you familiar with the game?"

Howard sees the game in his mind's eye: spheres, arcs and dynamics. "It is akin to rounders?"

"It is. You'll try out, I hope? It is a sound way to form acquaintances."

"Certainly. I would be fascinated to learn a new game."

"Let me introduce you to Jennings. Our secret weapon. Hero of the negro leagues. He's training our pitchers this season."

"Thank you, Professor."

The professor makes to leave. "It has been good to meet you, Hinton. Chittenden, will you show our new colleague around and outline to him the extent of his duties? He will chiefly teach the freshmen for his first year."

An eager student, Chittenden nods vigorously. "Certainly, Professor." The senior party leave in a curtain of robes. Chittenden visibly relaxes, a tautness departing his face. He turns to Hinton with some relief. "You survived the interrogation."

Hinton tilts his head. "I was expecting that I would be required to give some account of myself."

Chittenden nods. "They are high and mighty." He leans forward conspiratorially. "I must confess, I *am* most interested in *n*-dimensional work. It seems to me to offer many possibilities. I am preparing a paper myself. I studied under Newcomb at Johns Hopkins. Have you read his paper on the flexure of the sphere?"

Hinton furrows his brow. "I have not. As I explained to the Professor, I have tended towards distinct techniques."

Chittenden does not mind. "It is a remarkable piece of work. The implications are astonishing. Allowing for a space of n to the four, any object in n to the three might be inverted. Its interior made exterior."

This is intriguing for Hinton. "Indeed. This would be analogous with the case of the cube."

Chittenden raises open hands before him. "It is an incredible speculation. But it surely shows that the theory does not match to the reality. It sounds messy to me."

"I'm afraid I don't follow your reasoning."

"I mean, if applied to the human form, Newcomb's flexure would yield appalling results."

Hinton is given pause by this remarkable suggestion. Chittenden continues.

"The organs themselves must be inverted. The process of flexure, taking place, as it does, within a space in which such processes are mundane, would not disturb the integrity of the structures. But imagine if the human were returned to three-space after such flexure?"

"Indeed." Hinton pictures in his mind the inverted human, its liver, colon, heart and lungs expressed. He divines the n-dimensional musculature and skeletal system. The abductor hallucis unfolds. The scaphoid opposes the piriformis. Infraspinatus describes an arc. The buccinator reverts, effloresces. The radius repeats the form of the serratus anterior. The gemellus beckons and dartoi implode. Deltoids twist and spur. Depressor anguli oris rises and over-arches. Extensors become erect; flexors ossify. The lateral pterygoid imbricates the latissimus and the risorius oscillates itself throughout.

Orbicularis oculi deliquesce and the sacrum deviates from the norm. An obturator metastasises. The rhomboid is extrapolated. The trapezius blossoms. Pectoralis major blooms. The masseter bisects the scalenus. Tensors vibrate at Röntgen frequencies. The subclavius harmonises with the zygomaticus minor. The navicular maps onto the mylohyoid.

Chittenden summons his return: "What are you working on presently?"

Hinton steadies himself. "The current line of my research is directed towards the implications for our thought, should we accept our higher-dimensional natures. How our lives might be thought to be ordered according to such conditions."

"Ah! Perhaps you will elaborate?"

"I have been much occupied by the phonograph of late. I wonder if Edison's invention might not provide for us a model of our own existences."

Chittenden's enthusiasm is genuine. "Please, expand."

"Are you familiar with the functioning of the phonograph?"

"I can picture it. There is a cylinder and a needle."

"Indeed. An indented metal sheet is moved past a metal point attached to a membrane. The metal point transmits the vibrations caused by the indentations and furrows in the metal sheet to the membrane which reproduces them as waves of sound. Imagine if our lives were plotted as the grooves in the phonograph, and the history of nations, stories of kings, down to the smallest details in the life of individuals, were phonographed out according to predetermined marks in the space-filling aether."

Chittenden is agog. "I must confess, Hinton, this is some way from my domain."

Hinton edges forwards. "Given these conditions, I believe that there might be grounds for my earlier speculations, viz that all minds are connected in the higher realm."

Chittenden simply blinks. "This is rare speculation."

Hinton scratches his head. "It is not very mathematical, I concede that."

Recovering, Chittenden attempts a clarification: "You are, in the first instance, making an argument about predestination?"

Hinton is pleased to have been understood. "I am. That our actions may be determined. But what, I wonder, of our inner lives, which do not so correspond."

Chittenden dredges up a memory. "I wonder if you have heard of the experiments to measure the aether drag. There was one in Cleveland a few years back."

"I have not."

Chittenden has something useful to impart. "Perhaps you were abroad at the time. They proposed to demonstrate the presence of the aether by measuring the speed of light in perpendicular directions simultaneously. The experiments were, I believe, inconclusive. The aether remains. Or it does not." Chittenden indicates the options with his hands. "We exist in an ambiguous medium!"

"Indeed." Hinton drifts away once more, his consciousness bobbing in the swirls and eddies of the more expansive but doubtful aether-filled space. He is aware of Chittenden talking but not of the sounds he makes.

James Hinton to Margaret Hinton, May 16th 1855.

My dearest Meggie,

I have sad news to tell you: our dear father fell down the pulpit-stairs at Cheltenham and broke his arm, his left arm, happily. I enclose you mother's letter. You will see he is progressing favourably. I remember how, when your poor father fell down and injured himself, you felt so vividly how very, very dear he was to you; and this accident brings the same feeling to my mind.

What a loss his death would be to us, and how we should miss his sweet, grave kindness! Even Howard would mourn for him, would he not? But I hope there are many years of usefulness and happiness before him; only he must be content with doing less; he always exerts himself beyond his strength. Will it not be pleasant for us to wait upon and cheer the old people if they should be spared so long, when they are quite laid aside from active life, and only able to sit and meditate by their fireside? I delight to think of my old father so; I think he will make a glorious old man.

I am glad to have such a good account of the children. It must be glorious for Howard to be revelling so much in the open air, it is so natural and proper for a child. I feel almost as if we had no right to confine him to a London home unless we are absolutely obliged. That is why I am so willing for you to remain away; for I am sure you feel with me that our comfort and enjoyment are as nothing compared with the securing of a healthy, happy, and powerful life for our children. Do you not see, as you watch his little soul expanding beneath the sun, and amid all the beauties of nature, that he cannot attain the full stature of his manhood cooped up here? You know I was a country boy, and would have fresh air and fields, and all the sweet influences of natural scenery for my children.

Your loving husband,
James

4.

Howard has become enamoured of baseball. The balls themselves, occupying the entire palm, almost too expansive, are wondrous things. Engorged spheres, lighter than a cricket ball yet almost twice the diameter. A raised red stitching binds together a leather outer in two figure-eight sections, a masterpiece of projective thinking. He bisects one and observes its cross-section: an entire Earth in a palm, layers of leather and magma, crust and calfskin around a rubber core.

He delights in the "mitts" – what an understated name for such marvellous accoutrements: prosthetic leather hands, also engorged, as required by the dimensions of the ball. The bats are unfussy: great clubs of oak. One weighs them happily in one's hands. The game itself, a cousin of rounders, but increased in all dimensions, allowing the batter a greater number of opportunities. It furnishes intensities of rhythm; explosions and longueurs, drifts and attacks.

He attends every game he is able. He studies the laws with the zeal of the converted and can soon correct natives with his knowledge of regulatory arcana.

--

They had known in Japan that George's eyesight was poor. He had been measured for a set of wire-rimmed Japanese spectacles, made in the way of all Japanese goods, with great care and craftsmanship: their lenses polished to allow as much as possible for his extreme near-sightedness. On arrival in America, the boy's sight was formally assessed by a Princeton optician employed by his mother, a displaced Southerner who drawled misses and ma'ams. It was ascertained that George could not accurately pick out a five-inch letter on a board at six yards. The optician called the boy purblind. Knowing how well he had fared under the tutelage of his governess in Japan and fearing for the boy's further education in the system of the American public schools where they could not be certain that his disability would be accounted for, Howard and Mary elected to continue to tutor the boy at home. Eric and William would start at school at the commencement of the academic year and Sebastian would be cared for by Mary. Howard ordered from Swan Sonnenschein at cost price a selection of text books from their backlist, making full use of a contractual perk to which authors were entitled. The resulting list was non-canonical but would, combined with their own personal libraries, allow for a fuller education than would many of the great British schools.

Howard would teach – naturally – mathematics and the natural sciences, with distinct lessons for physics and chemistry. Mary would teach geography and history. They would share the teaching of the classics and would structure a syllabus of reading to be undertaken by the student in his own time of great works from the history of literature.

Howard determined to assemble a laboratory for the fulfilment of his teaching duties. He ordered from London a chemical cabinet: Statham's students' laboratory. For George, the finest gift he had ever received. Fourteen bottles with corked stoppers, a further eight with cut glass toppers for the reagents. A Boy's Own Laboratory.

--

A makeshift diamond in the park, bases marked by crumpled vestments. George takes first base, a study in focused anticipation; Eric, second, languid and distracted; Sebastian, startled, stands guard at third where his brothers assume he will have less work: each wears his outsized mitt. Willy shifts his bat from hand to hand in a rolling, smooth and perpetual motion. Howard will pitch, having commenced a study of the science of the art of the hurled ball. He would like to observe also from the position of the backstop in order better to judge the deviations from inside and out. Were he able to split himself it would be a distinct advantage: multiple points of observation would allow for the assessment of relative swerve, above and beyond the practical consideration: someone will have to fetch the missed balls.

Willy steps up to the plate. Howard tosses up the ball and catches it himself. His eyes meet Willy's. Willy appreciates him flatly. Howard senses that the boy feels no doubt: he will heave the ball into tomorrow; beyond, into the further future. Howard envisages the extending arc, projecting from his arm, interrupted and sent into a fresh parabola; Willy, the primary engine of change, then trotting around the bases as his two elder brothers chase the ball.

Howard winds back his arm, taking it past his ear as he has been instructed, raising his front leg bent at the knee, before sending it forwards to propel his weight in that direction as he brings his arm back past his head and shies the ball towards his son. With disdain, Willy regards its flight some three yards wide of the plate before him.

George sets off, jogging, to retrieve the now distant ball. Howard wonders if Mary might be impressed upon to sit at the backstop.

--

There is a particular way of thinking that emerges through boredom and is uniquely generative. In the process of the active distraction of one's own mind one is forced to imagine and to construct fresh lines of thought, which then bifurcate in unexpected directions. One is able to follow chains of reasoning not typically available to the concentrated mind. Environmental distraction in such cases can be both useful and desirable, thinks Mary, catching a reference to Menelik in Abyssinia and reflecting that the lecture had started hopefully enough, with an appeal to the newcomers to the New World from Old Europe that resonated most powerfully with her, encouraging her companionship with the speaker, celebrating – differing here with Mr Stone, who thought it a mad cry – Voltaire's "down with the scoundrel!" an expression of distaste addressed to Christ himself, a sacrilegious cry she could enjoy.

The passage on "life-systems" had seemed promising but she had relinquished any effort to follow the argument with the doctrinal hectoring that followed: Augustinians, Lutherans, Socinians; she wished she could care which were favoured factions and which were not. He's against the Anabaptists, of that I'm certain, she thought, and almost certainly against also the Pagans, Islamists, the Romanists, perhaps even the Modernists. She was less certain about the Modernists, thinking that in the prefatory remarks he had styled himself a Modernist.

Silence was yet more conducive to thought, she knew, having experienced such profound silence at the temple in Japan. As she had practiced meditation she had worked towards allowing conscious thought to slow, to pause, as was expected, but in those first experiences before becoming so able to calm that mental activity, the surrounding sounds, of exterior happenings, of the creaks and moans that reside in buildings themselves produced perhaps by draughts, insects or larger animals, had prompted in and of themselves butterfly flits of thought. Her attention hooks suddenly as someone's devotees are reported to have run naked through the streets of Amsterdam, but it is just an Anabaptist's devotees, and their naked gallop is mere proof of Calvinist superiority, so she allows again Mr Stone's words to become background to her own, unvoiced and polyamorous.

It rushed upon her, a realisation: that she no longer experienced physical contact with a single soul. Since Sebastian had become studious in his march towards independent adulthood he no longer wished for the comfort of embrace. It had happened so swiftly. The older boys had long ago withdrawn. All were conducting a dance in which they reeled towards the corners of the room, a dance she led by example. She had not danced since her children were born. She had loved a ceilidh as a child, been quite the spry wee thing; could remember the focus with which she had laced the dance shoes, the plaiting not unlike curve stitching, an over and under, cords and eyes. She would dance in America. What else to do with all that space but to occupy it with one's body.

It was so pleasant to be able to think like this on her own, to be able to find space for her own imaginings even if she had to hide in Mr Stone's lecture to secure for herself this freedom. To wander the autumnal avenues of Princeton seeking out lectures was no great chore and to vacate the home essential. There were chapels she wished to explore, wall-hangings she had glimpsed through the windows, tapestries of such scope and reach and optimism. The novelty was refreshing and she would drink it deep, a cedarwood draught of this new world.

--

"See, I hold it like this and when I pitch it cuts down and moves away." Jennings demonstrates his action. Hinton observes with narrowed eyes.

"The rotations you impart are counter-clockwise. If viewed from above."

"If you say so, Professor. All I know is the batter got to reach if he wants to hit it and he got to see it coming if he wants to set himself right. So I show him the ball like this before I pitch it every time." Holds up the grip. "He don't know which way I'm gonna go, fast ball or curve ball. I move my wrist like this" – linear motion – "and it cuts away. Or I can slow it up like this." Looser, more circular.

He moves his hand over the ball as he shows it, caressing its movement.

Hinton drifts. He inhabits the surface of the sphere. A mite Hinton treks across its pocked leather surface, sighting the vast ranges of stitching. He is oblivious to the rotations of his spheroidal home. At the foot of the great cliffs of thread he rests, plotting his passage between the ridge of red cord, lying upon the surface and gazing at his heavens. He sees objects pass across the theatre of his sky in accordance with some unfathomable cosmic law. A cataclysm sends his sphere upon a new trajectory: intense compression of his world in that moment of the meeting of opposing forces, the spheroid crushed into oblation but resurging.

"'*Ita nil numquam natura creasset.*'"

"Begging your pardon?"

"The curve is the true creation."

"Am not really reading you, Prof."

"The change of direction. I should have thought of it."

"There's some say there's no such thing as a curve ball."

"I can imagine so. I have, myself, at various times argued for predestination. We might prove otherwise with my cannon."

"You think so? Only saying that it ain't everyone believes it makes a difference in the game."

□

"And you think?"

"Ask Patterson at Chicago. Struck out every single inning. I got six pitches. Fast ball, split-fingered fastball, fork ball, knuckle ball, curve ball, change-up. Knuckle ball moves two ways, not much, but enough. Curve ball goes out then in. Patterson can't pick any of 'em."

The ball is a vessel, leaving a wake. It disturbs. It forms turbulence. Its rotation is like a rudder, the section of the spheroid rotating in the same direction as the flow of the medium causing its curvature in passage. All creatures so pass through life. *Momen mutatum.* We must realise this. "So too thy calculations in affairs of life must be askew and false, if sprung for thee from senses false." He had false sense once, no doubt, but now?

"I know my knuckle ball, pitch it right, strikes every time."

--

A catapult.

Linear velocity is key.

Newton's equations can determine ballistic motion.

Hook's law gives the elasticity of the rubber: $F = -kx$.

He explains torsion to Sebastian as he winds the stick at the rear of the breach to draw back the sling. The child releases it

FTDOOINGchump

The ball strikes the ground some ten feet before the sheet screen he has erected. They return to the jottings. The distance of the cannon from the batter must remain constant so they need to achieve greater velocity. The potential energy of the rubber is $\frac{1}{2}kx^2$.

They   experiment   with   greater   torsion.

FTDOOINGkhomp

Can they purchase rubber with a higher e l a s t i c i t y ? Hinton inquires. The answer is no.

They return to the jottings.

In the week Hinton discusses the matter with Chittenden. Has Howard considered

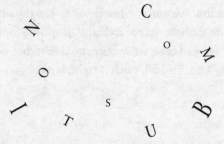

asks his colleague? Might not the tube, after all, be thought a component in an engine?

He recites some sentences of Carnot to Sebastian:

"Everyone knows that heat can produce motion. That it possesses vast motive-power no one can doubt. From this immense reservoir we may draw the moving force necessary for our purposes. Nature, in providing us with combustibles on all sides, has given us the power to produce, at all times and in all places, heat and the impelling power which is the result of it. To develop this power, to appropriate it to our uses."

Chittenden procures for him a copy of P. Bashforth's "Treatise on the Motion of a Projectile", including his Ballistic tables. These prove most fruitful reading.

He follows the reasoning, that the resistance of the air varies exactly as the square of the diameter of the projectile and as the cube of the velocity. Bashforth, experimenting with muzzle-loading guns, set up screens at regular intervals of space and an electric chronograph to record the successive instants at which the projectile passed through the screens.

Hinton sets up three screens at intervals of fifteen feet apart in the gymnasium. Using a chronometer purloined by Chittenden from a physical scientist, he times Jennings's pitches from plate to batter: 0.45 seconds. Jennings is bemused by the paper screens – he can no longer see the target at which he would shy his pitch, but Hinton entreats him to snap his arm nonetheless: he is after the initial angle of projection. He procures a clinometer by means of which to determine this. It is higher than he might have assumed, at 5 degrees. The ball makes holes in each of the screens. Hinton realises that by this method he might record the arc of the curve balls.

Bashforth, revising Newton, determined and tabulated the times taken to go from one screen to another. Since the second differences of $0, t_1, t_2, t_3, ----, t_1, t_2, t_3, -----$ being the times of passing each screen, are nearly constant, the equation connecting space and time may be written in the form $t=as+bs^2$. If v is the velocity of the shot at time t, $V=\frac{ds}{dt}=\frac{1}{a+2bs}$. Let $v=V_0$ when $S=0$, $V_0=\frac{1}{a}$.

Willy becomes interested when he hears of the purchase of gunpowder from the general store.

A great flame follows a little spark, as the Italian poet wrote.

Willy looks vacant and distracted while Hinton speaks his workings aloud in an endeavour to think them more clearly. Sebastian is rapt, though must not understand a word.

If the weight of the ball were 5 ounces the resistance of the air acting upon it would be $-2bv^3\frac{w}{g}1$ lb. Bashforth gives extensive tables of the coefficient of resistance Kv where Kv is defined by the equation $f = \frac{d}{w}^2 K v \left(\frac{v}{100}\right)^3$ in which d is the diameter of the projectile in inches and w its weight in pounds.

AKKKTOMPF

The combustion is more powerful than Howard had imagined; the volume of powder has been overestimated. A cthonian stench fills the laboratory. They peer over the edge of the upturned table. Willy charges towards the target before which lies a blackened mass, a pocked meteorite smoking infernally. Howard must restrain the boy from picking it up. The cannon is a smoking proboscis.

The target is charred where this projectile has struck it. The accuracy is good.

He adjusts the volume of powder, considers inserting a charging plate but dismisses it as too complex.

HAKKTOMPF

The charge is now correctly calculated but the ball itself is once again badly charred. Sebastian calls them cannerballs. Willy, admiring the evidence of destruction, spirits them away, Howard knows not where. George has heard the explosions. Howard describes the process thus far. George suggests channelling the exhaust from a rifle into the tube, thereby removing the need for a plate and the risk of the ball coming into direct contact with the agent of combustion. This suggestion has great merit. Much to Willy's excitement, Howard procures a breech-loading rifle.

A week of evenings sketching. He takes his assemblage to the engineering school's machine shop. They praise his scheme, though cannot conceal their amusement. He knows he must appear foolish, monomaniacal even. They agree to undertake the clamping, bending, sawing and welding. Their work is exceptional: great precision is employed, the location of the tripod on the assemblage adjusted to allow for the barycentric shift of the whole.

He considers rotation. The problem has become intriguing. He dives into his papers and neglects his teaching.

Newton wrote to Oldenburg "I remembered that I had often seen a tennis ball, struck with an oblique racket, describe such a curve line. For a circular as well as a progressive motion being communicated to it by that stroke, its parts, on that side where the motions conspire, must press and beat the contiguous air more violently than on the other; and there excite a reluctancy and reaction of the air proportionally greater."

Robins in a paper read before the Royal Society in 1747, spoke of "the hitherto unheeded effects produced by this resistance; for its action is not solely employed in retarding the motions of projectiles, but some part of it exerted in deflecting them from their course, and in twisting them in all kinds of directions from their regular track; this is a doctrine which notwithstanding its prodigious import to the present subject, hath been hitherto entirely unknown, or unattended to; and therefore the experiments, by which I have confirmed it, merit, I conceive, a particular description; as they are themselves of a very singular kind."

Euler, later: "Hence this proposition appears indisputable true: that a spherical body which besides its progressive motion in the air revolves around its centre, will suffer the same resistance, as if it had no such rotation. If therefore, such a ball should receive two such motions in the cannon, yet its progressive motion in the air would be the same as if it had no rotation."

And then, of course, Tait on golf balls; old Tait, out on the links near Nairn with his son, the champion, measuring distance and dynamics. Slice and spin. Twist through the air, using the resistance of the wake. How then to apply such to the breach of the cannon? He inserts two threaded screws through the muzzle, such that their interference with the path of the ejected ball can be calibrated minutely.

tthhRHAKKTuuuk

The test ball is scarred, its leather ripped open and gaping.

There must be another way. He models fingers of rubber-coated metal, digital prostheses to caress the ball on exit.

There is a word from Lucretius that comes back to him persistently. The clinamen. It describes the generative swerve of the atom. A minor deviation from a direct path, a small arcing, from which *all* proceeds; that which makes a lie of pre-determination.

There was something of this in the model that had occupied his earlier thinking: the corrugated metal disc of the phonograph moving past the point attached to the membrane, the earth and all its inhabitants responding to the indentations and grooves of the aetherial medium through which it passed. He had grasped the curve in that model but had struggled to understand the deviation from the channel.

--

Howard takes the boys to Brokaw Field for the game against Harvard. Harvard are the weakest of the three sides playing the league. They are reported to lack batters. Princeton have been on top this season but Yale may yet challenge.

Seated on the lower bleachers, Willy and Howard watch

intently. Eric is distracted with his dice, throwing them again and again into the earth. George squints but can make out nothing of the game. He imagines how it might in fact take place. Sebastian clings to his father.

Easton is pitching for Princeton. Varying his pitches, as Jennings suggested to Howard, he limits the Harvard batters. The first batter strikes out. Batters two and three manage to find his final pitch and make a run for first base but none can hit him cleanly. With these batters trapped at first and second Harvard's fourth batter strikes out attempting to give his men a run home. The fifth follows. The inning continues in the same manner with not a single Harvard man able to connect with Easton's pitches.

Between innings, Howard spots Duffield and approaches. Duffield – wearing his gowns of office, as ever – looks Howard up and down and introduces him to his companion with what seems great reluctance. The companion is a scientist and naval man: Singer. Hydrographer. Hinton pictures him writing with water rather than ink. The image is pleasing.

Singer has a weathered face. A small triangular nick has been removed from the edge of one ear. "Singer was in the Orient also, Hinton."

The man barely looks at Howard. "You have travelled in the Far East?"

Howard attempts to muster enough social enthusiasm for the three of them. "I lived in Japan for five years. It was quite the adventure. Where have you been?"

Singer tips his head. "I've seen many different stretches of water from the bridges of many different ships. Don't often get to dry land. Didn't miss it. Preferred my view."

Their conversation is interrupted by an inebriated freshman in the black cap and sweater of Harvard. This man sways, his eyes coming into and out of focus. "This game. Harvard?"

Duffield ignores the drunk. "Hinton, I hear you've been working with Chittenden?"

Howard watches the drunk sway this way and that. "A pet project. A baseball training aid, in fact."

The Princeton inning commences with a sound hit, the ball scudding to right field and the batter sprinting to second base.

Duffield stands stiffly. "This collaboration is a happy entertainment but I would ask you not to distract Chittenden from theoretical work."

Hinton is again taken aback by Duffield's bluntness. "Of course, Professor. In truth, we do not spend much time on it."

The second Princeton batter makes a beautiful connection, the rounded *thwock* sounding to the entire field. Willy runs after the ball, Eric in pursuit. Sebastian clings to his father's leg. The freshman bends double and vomits on the ground, splashing Sebastian's shoes. Duffield views him with disgust. The third man is no longer there. What was his name? Singer?

Willy emerges from behind the bleachers holding the ball. Howard begins to feel tense. "William, please return it to the field of play."

Willy looks at his father with contempt. "I fetched it."

Howard feels great discomfort. "William. The ball does not belong to you."

Duffield regards William with the same level of disgust displayed towards the freshman.

William is breathing heavily. "No one else went after it. Apart from Eric."

Eric emerges from behind the bleachers with a bloodied nose.

William looks petulant. "They've started playing again. They don't need it."

Duffield looks as if he is about to pass comment, then turns on his heel and marches away. The freshman, wiping his mouth, looks at Howard and sees his yellow carnation. Leans over and grasps it from his lapel. "Princeton man?"

Howard feels a burst of nervous energy in need of release. He turns to the drunk, grabs his lapels and sweeps his legs from beneath him, placing him on his back in the dust. A cheer erupts from behind him as Princeton men salute their professor. Howard quickly gathers his sons and leaves.

--

Hinton stands precisely sixty feet and six inches from a home plate that has been placed on the sprung boards at the north end of the gymnasium. A hubbub of competitive excitement spills from the packed bleachers to east and west. The faculty staff have taken the front two rows, lending the event the appearance of a ceremony, berobed priests closest to the crown. Duffield appears already wearied by the experience, Chittenden grinning beside him. Hinton himself has dispensed with his gowns in favour of an athletic attire: white shirt and plus fours.

He ponders commencing with "Dearly Beloved," because here today they are gathered. He signals to the porters who close the doors to the gymnasium and the hush agitates from within the throng, overcoming as each particle is carried by the motion towards silence and the closure of the system. The man from *The Globe* readies his pen and scribbles.

"I would like, first, to offer my immense gratitude for your attendance here today at this inaugural trial of the world's first mechanical pitcher." There is a cheer from the west, a group of rowdies Hinton recognises from the matches. "If you will forgive the imposition upon your patience, I should like to describe to you the thought processes which brought me to this juncture before demonstrating for you the machine." There is an audible groan as the rowdies realise they are to be lectured when they had hoped to witness more of what has been rumoured: batters taking cover as fiery projectiles are launched towards them at eighty miles or more per hour. Hinton has anticipated this; it is a necessary part of his theatre.

He details his first encounter with baseball, elaborated, of course, for the audience: his English foolishness played up, his use of cricketing terminology in place of the correct native language of the game which he knows full well: batsmen for batters; wicket-keeper for backstop. He affords his audience some laughter at his expense in his account of those early laboratory sessions with Sebastian as his assistant: baseballs flung from one end of his makeshift workspace to the other by assorted slingshots and catapults, the father and son taking turns to duck and cover as the projectiles flew thick through the air. He recounts how it occurred to him that practically whenever men wished to impel a ball with velocity and precision, they drove it out of a tube with powder. He details his experiments to gauge the correct charge, picturing his scorched face following one such failed attempt and Mary's temporary restitution of his eyebrows by boot polish. All provide hilarity enough to excite his audience before he switches pace and proceeds, carefully and patiently, into the technical description of spherical aerodynamics and the motion of a baseball through the air, owing heavily to Tait and Rayleigh. All the while, his prop, his bazooka upon a tripod, stands next to him while his supporting cast loiter with bats near the plate.

Suddenly, an agitation near the door. The porter is restraining a man wearing a uniform bearing the mark T&T, the most prevalent of the local couriers. The courier insists upon access. Hinton walks towards the porter. The hubbub returns among the crowd as those in the bleachers nearest the door strain to see the cause of the change in proceedings. Hinton plays the placator.

He calms the porter and receives the delivery from the courier. He returns to the centre of the gymnasium and clears his throat.

"Gentlemen, I can only apologise for this interruption. If you would all be so kind as to indulge me with your patience one more time. This fellow insists that this delivery is of the utmost urgency. His condition of delivery was that I read this missive immediately. I realise how unconventional this must seem . . ."

Hinton rips open the envelope and scans the contents of the document within it. He scratches his head in bemusement. A carefully calculated pause. He exclaims: "Hah! Indeed!"

Some grumbling from the assembled crowd. He tries the patience of too many important men with these theatricals.

"If you will bear with me. I . . . I am at pains to explain what this is. It appears to be . . . I think it perhaps best if I share it with you directly . . ."

He readies the manuscript.

"My dear Hinton,

"I write to you from the future. From the year 1956, to be precise. It has come to my attention from this distance in time that you are in the process of trialling a most extraordinary device, a device indeed whose ancestors we use upon a daily basis. I write to you from my seat in the 52nd level of the Nova York Cavea on this day, 17th July 1956. The time is 11pm and the game between the Washington Cayleys and the New York Kelvins is entering its ninth inning. The pitch some fathoms below is bathed in the blue light provided by the elephantine fluorescent tubing that overgirds our fine stadium.

"The umpires, suspended above the game by dirigible balloons inflated with a rarefied form of coal gas, are signalling to the Cayleys to speed up. Previously, umpires made use of gliding wings: we called them umpire bats, back then, and not only because they were so poor in sight! These wings proved impracticable, however, with the spectacle of umpires colliding with the over-arching fluorescent tubing or falling from the sky due to poor aviation skills all too common in our lower leagues. The new laws introduced at the 1942 Universal Congress on League Baseball banned the use of umpire wings. The dirigible umpires are more easily able to maintain a constant altitude.

"How might umpires be freed from the plate, you may well ask, from your temporally restricted point of view? Well, the calling of strikes has been entirely automated for some twenty years. A chronophotographic gun aligned with the strike zone triggers an alarm whenever the batter misses the ball. His failure is sounded through the radio-receiving helmets provided to all spectators. Mine has just buzzed to indicate the dismissal of Betser. He's not had much of a season!

"There was an experiment with balls cored in aluminum" – Hinton stresses the American pronunciation, shaping his mouth to sound the vowels – "in 1935, though this too was deemed unsuccessful due to the frequency with which such balls were struck beyond the confines of the stadium. The cellulite catching mitts introduced in the same year are, however, very popular.

"Perhaps all that will be familiar to you from the game of baseball of 1894 is the Hinton-patent cannon which has saved the elbows of pitchers for two generations now. The batters, it is true, still behave in the same way: a team of electrical automata from Chicago were entered into the 1944 Universal Series though they proved to be poor catchers of the ball and were retired the following year.

"It is because I have been reflecting upon the efficacy of the Hinton cannon that I thought I should make use of our transchronic courier service to inform you of your brainchild's success. This form of mail, utilising stabilised aether grooves for transmission of printed messages, allows us such opportunity.

Ever since the realisation of the fixity of time's passage and its reversibility under specific conditions, we have enjoyed many such communications. But I digress.

"The one addition to your cannon since your own time has been the n-dimensional bracket attachment developed by your student Rosenfeld. This imparts upon the ball a twist that sends it into the fourth dimension. That surely confuses the batters more than anything we have yet witnessed! A higher-dimensional bat has yet to be conceived and games must play out over several weeks as we await the return of pitches that have travelled beyond the perception of mortals and into that realm of which we can only dream.

"All that remains for me now is to wish you well, Professor Hinton, in your current demonstration!

"Yours sincerely,

"An enthusiast."

In his imaginings, the termination of his presentation had been forestalled by laughter. He looks now at the crowd and sees hanging jaws, bemusement, even among his colleagues. He smiles winningly. Chittenden shuffles. A young man shouts: "Let's see the thing." If they want the whizz-bangs, he concedes, let them have the whizz-bangs. He loads. The batters cower.

HAKTOMPF

James Hinton to Charles Howard Hinton

18 Savile Row, June 29, 1869.

MY DEAR BOY, *Thank you for your letters. It interests me
to read them. I like to think of you as turning your mind to
such subjects. Still, as you know, I think the knowledge of the
phenomena, that is, of what the senses can perceive, is the best
basis you can lay, and that the superstructure is of secondary
importance till a good basis is laid, though the exercise of reason,
especially with good strong criticism afterwards, is a very useful
thing.*

*I am glad you like the idea of studying geometry as an exercise
of direct perception I think it must be specially valuable so; and
I am very pleased that you think it practicable and useful. The
habit of looking thoroughly and minutely into things, alike with
the eyes and with the reason, so as to cultivate the power of seeing
their qualities and relations, and not merely trying to infer them,
must be a most excellent one. It will be very valuable to you.*

*I do not, at present, see very much in the formula you quote
from Professor Boole, but perhaps you will be able to make me
when you show me the book. It is true the advance of thought
has consisted in simplification, and must do so still; but then,
before this can come, there must be a perception of the apparent
complications; so that there are two processes, a recognition of
apparent variety, multiplicity, disharmony, and a resolving it into
unity and order. We must have both, and if the first is not ample
and exact, the last is petty and fictitious. Write to me and tell me
about the school and your companions; what boys you know,
and what they are like. I am glad you are an early riser. I used to
be one also; there is no plan so good.*

Your loving father,
James

`5.

Ralph Radcliffe Whitehead rushes not for gold but for freedom; not for wealth in matter, but for wealth in soul. He has renounced his inheritance in Yorkshire for a Californian idyll, in Montecito, the hills beyond Santa Barbara. The Oregonian idyll was unsuccessful. The Italian idyll a disaster. He wears a linen smock and heavy cotton work trousers, Byron masquerading as a farm labourer. Jane, his second wife – his Ruskin wife, not his Oxford wife, met while the first was still in tandem – wears a simple Portuguese dress. Two days' journey from the mountains, the Hinton boys run wild among vines, scenting freedom, scrubbing each other's faces in dust and berries, spotting woods at the foot of the vale. Even Mary has shed her Minneapolis woollens.

The four recline at a table on a veranda, both handmade by local craftsmen of Ralph's acquaintance; they share a jug of rosé wine, produced co-operatively from the small-holding Ralph and Jane occupy which now they overlook, framed against the nimbus-streaked azure. Those grapes, crushed by their own feet; their own ankles stained purple in testament to their labour. Howard wonders at the journey made by this son of the industrial North, shoeless; further, perhaps, though no more circuitous than his own.

Ralph is the benevolent host, surveyor of an Edenic valley. "Howard, it was with such sweet pleasure that I read your letter. That you were also in this great, so hopeful nation. So fortuitously met, my old friend. Mary, your husband was such a captivating soul at Oxford. To a Northerner such as myself he seemed the very essence of sophistication! He counted amongst his friends many great intellectuals. Why, Ruskin, The Master himself, found in Howard a captain."

Howard enjoys this playful tone. "Northerner, indeed. You boarded at Harrow?"

"That is true," acknowledges Ralph. "And returned to Saddleworth every Michaelmas break, as well you know."

Howard knows well that Saddleworth is a mill at which the Whitehead family employ three hundred in the production of felt for the lining of piano keys and hammers. That old man Whitehead now seeks to sell, his only son having renounced that path for the ways he learned at Oxford. There were those at Oxford who were jealous of the Whitehead wealth; those who thought the boy Ralph a dilettante. Howard had not known Ralph well at Balliol until Ruskin's plan thrust them together. "He was a fine man, Ralph. He would have been considerably moved to see you follow his example."

Ralph acknowledges the compliment with a gracious tip of the head. "There were so many of us who did. What Toynbee has done in the East End. That is no coincidence."

"Toynbee's work is impressive," concedes Howard. "There was a great need for such work in Whitechapel."

"Who else was there?" continues Ralph. "Montefiore, Rawnsley, Wedderburn, Collingwood ..."

"You were students of Ruskin?" asks Mary. Howard suppresses his shame at this absence of knowledge and what it reveals. Howard has inherited so many acquaintances, so much of his father's world.

"We were. He had addressed the Metaphysical Society on occasion. Father was interested in his writing on art. But Ralph was much closer to him than I. You went with him to Italy?"

There were those among the disciples who had followed Ruskin to Venice, to Rome, to Florence, to hear him speak yet further on Botticelli, on Tintoretto, to take the tour in the company of the ultimate guide. Hinton had taken a distinct path, to Berlin, to hear Helmholtz speak on the non-Euclidean space.

"Jane and I met there," replied Ralph.

Howard had known Sarah, the first wife, Austrian; rumoured now to be in deep decline in London. But such talk would not be civil in present company. "In Rome. We established our first colony in the countryside at Lazio. The Master approved, naturally."

"Along such lines as your work here?" asked Mary.

"Just so. Ah, it's not easy, is it Jane? We have learnt so much already."

Jane has no doubt: "There is no royal road to utopia!"

Howard nods. "The work of altruism is a perpetual challenge to those who pursue it. Living must be for others, though how best to achieve this . . . well, that is a question to which we might endlessly turn our minds."

Mary has no patience with this line. "I would hear more of Ruskin."

"His lectures were always well attended," responds Howard, chastised. "He was an orator of no little skill."

"Entirrrrrrrely true!" Ralph performs for the table, sweeping his arms wide.

"I have heard his voice described as harsh?"

"Not so, Marrrrrry. He spoke with a burrrr in his rrrs, as befits a grrrrrreat Scot!"

Jane grins at Ralph's mimicry. "Ralph is forever eulogising Ruskin. He is even now a disciple."

"I do not know how you dare mock, Jane! He was a singular teacher. One of a kind. You feel the same."

Jane knows what Ralph would have her say though wishes to play devil's advocate.

"I *have* felt this, though I must confess that I am no longer so enamoured of the Ruskin way as I once was. Perhaps we outgrow our teachers?"

Ralph is exasperated. The caprice of the woman! Howard nods. "He carried us all with him, whatever route he chose. He would start with some humorous remarks . . ."

"Ah, Rrrrrrrawnsley! How kind of you to join us today! I am afraid I cannot today speak on Carrrrrrpaccio, as has been anticipated. I have been unable so finely to slice my beef."

"He would commence from notes and then extemporise."

"The verrry rrrrocks, do you understand? The earrrrrth itself frrrrrom which we drrrrrrraw our toil."

"He would have with him original sketches by the masters on whom he would expound."

"Do you remember the mineral samples?"

"Indeed. Whatever he required by way of illustration."

"You recall the breakfasts?"

"In his rooms."

"Mallock would attend those. You know Mallock, How?"

"I thought he was a bore."

"But How, *The New Republic*! The scandal of our age! All our masters taken down. Ruskin thought him the most useful critic of us all. I think his work will last. There is much there if only you are minded to dig within it. I have his recent novel, *A Human Document*."

"The same may be said for any work. I'm not sure that I remember him as fondly as you do, Ralph."

"It's how you dig, is it not?"

--

The boys run to the woods, hearts pounding. George, studied and angular even in a jog; Eric languid; Willy, a genuine athlete, easing past them both; wee Sebastian, straining to keep up, trying each style on for size, and appearing instead to be in retreat. They hurtle through thickets, shielding faces from stray whips as they go, hurdling fallen logs; steeplechasers in a pack.

The thumps in his head, iron saliva and raw lungs, Eric all but collapses at a clearing beside the river. Willy is already engaged in testing the depth and strength of the flow with a large stick, one arm looped around the trunk of an overhanging tree. George arrives, his breathing steady and controlled, looking over his shoulder after Sebastian; simulating care for his youngest sibling, fortifying his pride. Sebastian yells from some way back: "Wait! Wait! Where are you?"

"Here, Seb. By the river."

Eric is inspecting a tree; perfectly hollowed out by disease, its bark remains as a shell and through a crevasse a young man can slide inside. Once inside the trunk, there are just sufficient ridges on which to place feet to climb within. Eric's head pokes through another crack some ten feet above the ground.

"George Hinton. You will obey the tree-king!"

George looks up. "How did you get there?"

"Look, it's hollow. It's a den."

George approaches the tree with Sebastian in attendance. He peers into the hollow and tests the bark with his hands.

"This is magnificent. It's sound. It's the perfect hideout."

"It's like Robin Hood," says Sebastian.

"It is, isn't it? It's an oak too."

Over the next hour the boys take turns to climb it, the older brothers helping Sebastian find the footholds. George suggests constructing a shelter alongside. They drag branches, Willy proving particularly adept at finding barely portable logs and making Eric carry them with him, giving them a sound base.

Sebastian approaches George. "Georgie, I've had an idea."

"Seb, we should all work together on the same plan."

"I know, but, you remember in Japan? Father's climbing frame?"

"The one Eric fell from? You remember that?"

"I think so. I remember climbing and I remember Pa telling us where to go. Like – Willy, X2, Y4, Z3, George, X1, Y1, Z1. We could build one like it."

Eric and Willy have an argument and Willy hits Eric with a branch. Fun over. Eric is bleeding from a wound in his head. George mops it with a handful of sphagnum moss concerning whose antiseptic qualities he lectures Sebastian. Willy, despite being the aggressor, sulks by the river, throwing stones into the centre of whirling eddies, hitting moving targets.

--

"Did we meet before the Dig?" Ralph is glowing, suffused with fine memories.

"I'm not certain. It brought so many together." Howard, too, becomes contemplative.

"The Dig?" scolds Mary. "I hope this evening is not to be conducted entirely in an undergraduate code."

Howard explains. "A project at Hinksey, a village near Oxford."

Ralph continues. "Ruskin dreamed it up. He decided we should put ourselves in the service of a work that would help others. Honest labour for the finest minds of our generation. No more lounging in punts, or idly playing croquet on the quadrangles. We should assist the community. We should make of ourselves stone masons! The living exemplars of his theories of art and labour."

"He had already trialled street sweeping at the British Museum," Howard notes.

"I remember Downes came from that to Hinksey. How he missed Coniston."

"Downes?"

"The gardener from Ruskin's grand house. The old man brought him down as overseer. He was quite the figure, pot-bellied and gruff."

Ralph laughs. "The only man there who knew what he was doing!"

"He taught us to handle a pick and shovel."

"We had to dig through a grassy slope, make the road to pass through it."

"Rock-breaking, also."

"Do you remember when the old man came himself? Looking like a dark pillar in his frock coat."

"He tried his hand with a pick."

"Downes wanted to take it from him! 'I'm quite able to manage it myself, Mr Downes.' He wasn't able, not in the slightest."

"Running the barrows over the planks, that was the hardest of it."

"To think we volunteered."

"Some of us were appointed."

"Ah, of course, Captain Charles." Ralph mimes surliness.

"And then Ruskin disappeared to Italy. Great works, you understand."

"Do you recall Wilde?"

"I recall reading him claiming to have been part of it. I do not recall him participating."

"Nor I! He wasn't there!"

"I suspect the great Decadent felt imagined solidarity with the jeered. Ever the posturer."

Jane needs to interject. Mary appears distant. Jane wonders that Howard does not see. She has little doubt that Ralph does not see. "Jeers? Mary, do you want to come inside? I fear the gentlemen are running away with the conversation. What on earth are you talking about?"

"We were road-builders for Ruskin," explains Ralph, tempering his glee. "Navvies. The project was to rebuild a road that had fallen into disrepair. To redirect it and make it more direct. A royal road, for sure, Jane. We operated in teams of twenty on two-day shifts. Balliol men to begin with. Howard captained the team I was in. It was true labour but the most worthwhile I have ever undertaken. It is no underestimation to describe the experience as transformative."

"And who jeered this?" Mary is curious. There is little to mock in such endeavour.

"Our peers," says Ralph wistfully. "Oxford men of a type. They came to watch us work and to mock our efforts. Lying there smoking."

"Some rustics also," corrects Howard. "In that sense, it was a collective effort."

"It mattered little. If anything, it grew our solidarity."

"There are always those who will wish to belittle true change."

"By Wilde, you mean Oscar Wilde?" asks Jane. "He participated in this?"

"Perhaps so, perhaps not." Howard deviates with his head. "He was at Balliol while I was up, though only yet becoming notorious."

"Pater's coterie!"

"Mallock put paid to that."

"His work is terrifically funny!"

"Mama! Willy is killing Eric!" Mary leaps up at Sebastian's call, little doubting that murder is possible in paradise; that Cain might split the head of Abel with the self-same rocks that might give others worthwhile labour. Howard reclines yet further with a patient shrug.

"Your boys are elemental!" essays Jane.

"They are boys, certainly," records Howard. "They will survive."

--

Jane has accompanied Mary to the children and Ralph invites Howard into the drawing room to smoke. He offers imported cigars. There is elegance and simplicity in the plain wood furniture. Howard declines Ralph's offer of a glass of Tennessee whiskey and settles into an upholstered chair. Ralph commences a disquisition on literary matters. He would press Howard on his relations with his publishers. He has some writings of his own.

"I doubt whether writing in the spirit and form of modern literature – especially French – is not too ambitious for one who is in no wise an artist. For literature too is art, do you not think, and the only kind of criticism which is worth having is that of such men as Ruskin and Arnold and Pater whose criticism *is* literature."

He awaits a response and Howard nods assent.

"Still, there is the humbler function of those who can appreciate such men and help the crowd get nearer to them. That might be done in the Sunday edition of a daily paper. That might be done by me."

Ralph fidgets. He wishes for intimacy. He does not know how best to broach what he must say.

"Howard. I had heard of your difficulties in London."

Howard does not move or speak. Ralph waits for a response but Howard does not acknowledge in expression or word what has been said. He acts as if Ralph had not spoken. Precisely that:

acts. Ralph waits for some intimation of the difficulty of this subject but it is as if a paralysis has overcome Howard, so completely frozen is his posture, that Ralph begins to doubt that he has said anything.

"I simply wanted to say that I am sympathetic to your plight. Lord alone knows we all err."

Still, the perfect deafness to his words. Perhaps Ralph senses a confusion in the eyes, betraying some form of internal struggle, a breaking down of deep logics, but Howard makes no movement. Ralph offers him a carved wooden ashtray. Howard takes it.

"Thank you, Ralph. Tell me more about these grapes. They are an Italian varietal?"

Ralph can do nothing but acquiesce to Howard's refusal of the exchange.

"They are, How. Primitivo. They grow well here." The conversation is progressed and the inquiry negated, cancelled from time.

--

Mary takes hold of Jane's arm. "Jane. The injury can wait."

Jane, immediately suspicious, recoils. "What if your son is hurt? The little one was terribly upset."

"They will find us. It is nothing more or less than what happens on each and every day. They enjoy the drama." Mary indicates a bench by the side of a stable. "Please, sit with me."

Jane moves uncertainly towards the bench. Sebastian has disappeared behind the stable.

Mary smoothes her skirts. "Tell me what it is like to live in such isolation. We are in cities now. In Japan I very much enjoyed such peace."

Jane looks anxiously in the direction in which Sebastian has fled. "It is less isolated than it seems. We have a steady stream of visitors. Ralph collects Bohemians."

"You enjoy this company?"

Jane turns her attention towards Mary. "I like the musicians. They bring joy. They are easy with themselves."

"Go on."

"They do not waste endless hours in disquisition about their art. The art itself has voice. I enjoy that. I enjoy filling the space with sound. I tire of the endless discussions of the idea of creation, all the theories of the stones, of labour. The musicians simply act. You can't theorise a fiddle!"

Mary nods her assent. "I understand this. There is insufficient music in our lives."

"Do you play?"

"As children, we had a governess who gave us piano lessons. We have not had an instrument in the house for some years. We travelled a great deal in Japan. I suppose that the composition of verse is the satisfaction of my yearning for music."

"Japan is such an exotic land. How did you live there?"

"There were many like us, foreigners, settled in the most part around Yokohama. That made the change simpler. It was only in the last years that we began to understand more of the land and its people. I hope one day to return."

"I believe I am content here," says Jane. Mary smiles. Together, they sit, uninterrupted for a period. Mary studies shadows as they edge across the dusty stable-yard, the complexity of objects reduced to cool shade. The gnarled branches of the tree, impossible adequately to hold in one's mind, each leaf unique and yet each familiar. Nature's teeming generosity of difference, reduced and flattened by the sun to a gloom of absence. We must never be satisfied with the shadows of our beloveds but must attempt to understand their fullest form, even if that must involve pain.

James Hinton to Charles Howard Hinton

18 Savile Row, March 24, 1870.

MY DEAR BOY, How long I have been wanting to write a letter to you; but I have let other things, which always seemed to want doing, make me defer it. It was too bad, but I suppose I knew in my heart that letters between us were not very much needed. Each knew so well what was in the other's heart.

I am glad you decided for yourself about the confirmation, and also I am glad you decided not to be confirmed. It might have been in many respects good, but I think you did right not to consider the advantages it offered equivalent to its being connected with a mode of religious thought and action with which you had not perfect sympathy, so that you could not throw yourself into it without reserve. I think, and I believe you will think with me in this always, that in all that we call religion, the very first and chief condition is, that we should be utterly and absolutely sincere, open, straightforward, and free from pretence, and should consider nothing an advantage that has to be purchased at the least shade of falsity. In other regions, as of material advantage, though falsehood must always be a crime and a mistake, yet at least some visible results may be for a time secured by it, it has some excuses if no reasons; but in religion the whole meaning and worth of which lies in honesty, purity, holiness, and devotion of the heart, the least shade of insincerity, or of endeavouring to secure results, is as absurd as it is hateful. If religion means anything, it must mean absolute truthfulness. We may dream we can serve our fellow-men by pretences, but to think of serving God by make-believes is to insult Him. But, indeed, I know you feel this as much as I do, and I am sure that you will try as much as ever I could wish you to make all your life transparent, and to banish all the false pretences which fill our present life with evil.

If you wish to spend another term at Rugby, I think we must spare you; you will make a good use of it. We want you to come soon and live at home; because the opportunity won't last so very long, and it is time now you began to share our life. We want you to do so very much; but still distance does not prevent this, and that is the best sharing which best enables you to take up what we leave unfinished, and perfect what we do incompletely. I am sure it is a great age of the world for which you are preparing, an age in which the great question of the true significance of human life will, at least, begin to decide itself. I like to think of my sons and daughters having a part in that. It need not be great (as men call greatness), but it cannot be little, if it is honest and faithful. This is one question men will have to answer: Is it our nature to take the best care of ourselves or to live in giving up? I know how your heart would answer this, and I think the time is coming when all men will give the same. Your loving father,

James

6.

Grayson settles, eases his bones; the chair suffuses him. Prof Hinton looks whiskery today. The subject: Japanese Buddhism, Prof Hinton orating, flights of reverie, his travels in Japan, his conversations with monks, this seeker after the metaphysical truth, meditating on a wooded mountainside, the flow of all matter through him, no doubt, the aether pervading his soul. The monkeys picking at his ticks in simian acceptance. The Japanese travellers pausing to marvel at his calm. The old man atop a pole.

Grayson feels deep affection for Prof Hinton, his humming chuckle from the back of the nose, his absence and presence, the way he oscillates between the two, simply disappears for minutes at a time. Hinton has become accomplished in the daydream, he thinks; he has honed it, worked with it, as a master cabinet-maker learns his craft over the course of a sawdusty life; the Prof turns his daydreams over the lathe; he can drift like no other.

Also present: the Prof's eldest son, his head crooked over a pamphlet, some flimsy thing, heavy spectacles magnifying the pages. They say he has inherited the Prof's technical ability, no doubt because he is taught at home, attends all such as this event; the youngest son is said to be the one who has inherited the extravagance of Hinton's mind, who thinks, they say, the expansive thoughts, and he too is around the house somewhere. There are two other sons but no one in Minneapolis has seen them.

He comes with a legend trailing him, the Prof. Tales of derring-do at Princeton, not to mention the travels across the States with his cannon. They say he threw – bodily threw – a Harvard man over a fence. This rapscallion had commented upon the Professor's rosette and Hinton had given the comment such short shrift that he took the matter into his own hands. Was thereafter known as "Bull" on account of his considerable physical strength. They say he rowed in the all-conquering eight at Oxford; counts among his friends Oscar Wilde and H. G. Wells, John Ruskin and Professor James and various others of the greatest minds in the world. They whisper that he can see into the fourth dimension, though no one truly knows what that means beyond what they have read in Wells: that it makes you invisible! Turns you inside out!

The cannon has been demonstrated at Minnesota and what a thing it is. You wouldn't want to face it. The crack it makes as it launches the ball towards you at eighty miles an hour. There was a veteran faced it in Denver, they say, took cover and refused to come out. Sent him back to the skirmish. Struck out the entire team at Yale.

There are tales of his classroom antics, his belief in the physical engagement with geometry. He makes the men picture in their minds spatial grids, asks them to fill the imaginary grids with imaginary objects and to locate themselves in relation to those objects. There is a chair in $x1, y1, z3$. Baxter is in $x1, y2, z3$. Where is Baxter's hat? He has a three-dimensional chess set of his own invention and each year invites his brightest students to play. None have yet figured out the rules, though he intends to patent the game nonetheless.

He was swindled by Princeton, they say. Thought he'd secured a deal on his contract, pension accrued to him after five years instead of the usual twenty. Failed to read the small-print, that his post could become redundant at three, dependent upon publication. Has failed to publish – at least, in the recognised journals. Princeton is run by businessmen now, they say. They encroach upon the higher thought. All will be economical.

A handful of faculty hearties, attendees at every opening, every social, the emeritus crowd, ring the right of the drawing room; some disciples like Grayson – he nods to Bachelor, whom he recognises from his calculus lectures – are sitting with backs rod-straight in intense anticipation. A fable of Zen Buddhism spirals from the Prof. He is an admirer of this form, of its asceticism and its insistence upon deep contemplation, upon arduous meditation that aims for nothing less than the voiding of the self. This self-lessness is close to his own thought, he explains.

The greatest of the Zen thinkers in Japanese legend was Ikkyo. Ikkyo had surpassed all others in the depth of his thought, Hinton says, had reached a point where he saw beyond all half-truths to their points of origin; saw the inner meaning of all. He was disciplined, clear-minded, and renowned for his idiosyncratic utterances. Ikkyo had gathered around him many disciples but only one was able to follow him. This disciple was his equal in enlightened matters. Together they laughed at the superstitions of Goruraku, the place of paradise, and Ojinoku, the place of punishment. They maintained that these were echoes of the truth, whose absolute truth was incommunicable in the words of man. That verse might approximate it, but only that, and meditation sense its shadows. The two discoursed at great length on such matters, each providing fellowship and affection to the other. And then, suddenly, the young disciple died. Hinton says this lightly, with a wistful smile. As his master, Ikkyo performed the funeral ceremonies. He performed the traditional rituals of cleansing but when he came to the part of the service at which the priest should wish the spirit of the departed a safe journey he could not bring himself to say the words in which he did not believe.

At this break in proceedings, it was told, Hinton says, that the corpse of the disciple stirred and said: "I came into the world without any assistance and am capable of leaving without help."

The great master of Zazen, Ikkyo, replied: "You neither came from anywhere nor are you going anywhere." Hinton continues: when he, Hinton, asked the monks who had related to him this story of its origins they said they could tell him nothing; all they knew was that it was written in Chinese characters in an ancient book held safe in the temple's inner sanctum.

Hinton does not explain why this story has meaning for him. He seems to drift again. Grayson attempts contemplation of equal profundity. Am I a disciple of Ikkyo? Do I, too, come from nowhere and depart to nowhere? How might I void myself? He closes his eyes, focuses on patterns of orange floating within his darkened vision. Sees specks. Focuses on the specks. These move within his closed eyes.

Hinton is telling the tale of a book. His last. He had prepared the manuscript and was working with an editrix of great skill and experience, one Mrs Wilcox. He had asked Mrs Wilcox to edit out anything that did not make the work more beautiful and Mrs Wilcox responded to his wishes with great vigour. Together they cut much from the book. Mrs Wilcox was not a literary woman but she was very efficient.

After they had edited the work he had 290 pages. On the 294th he had written his acknowledgements in which he simply wrote of his gratitude to Mrs Wilcox for editing anything which did not make the book more beautiful. He had to travel to another city to give a talk and he left the manuscript in the hands of Mrs Wilcox asking her to forward it to the printer and to liaise with the publisher.

When he returned from his travels she had sent the book to publication and it was printed with 293 blank pages and the final acknowledgement. Naturally, he was most upset, said Hinton, but it was too late to recall all the copies of the book which had immediately been distributed to subscribing libraries and those of his readers who had placed advance orders. Hinton says that he was deeply concerned over the matter but that over the ensuing weeks he received more letters about this book than about any of his other books. The letters were of two principle types: on the one hand, readers would ask for a full refund and offer to return the book at their own cost. Hinton had expected this, he says, and was more than ready to accept such terms, though he had no idea what he would do with such books once returned to him. The other type of letter surprised him, he claims. Typical of this type of letter was one in which a man wrote to say that the book contained more wisdom and beauty that any other book he had read that year.

Once again Hinton slips into a reverie. Grayson wishes to inquire but feels he cannot. Is this tale true? Or is it a parable? Perhaps it is a joke? Does Professor Hinton intend us to laugh? As Grayson examines the Prof, his head dipped so that his whiskery moustaches occlude his mouth, he cannot tell if he smiles or frowns. The Prof raises his face and commences once more. He says that in Zen, novitiates who wish to become priests are obliged to participate in the deep study and observation of practices for a period of five years. At the end of this five-year apprenticeship, the novitiates are summoned by the high priest who will give them the final and conclusive key to their enlightenment, initiating them into the path of true knowledge. At this point, all that was earthly is forgotten: the two monks are no longer teacher and student, novice and abbott, but equals in their religion. Hinton says that it is the tradition that to symbolise this newfound equality, the novice should strike the priest, an act that had it occurred during the apprenticeship would have been punishable by death. At this stage, however, it is expected.

Hinton says that a young novice of his acquaintance, of meek temperament and limited intellectual capacity, was at this stage of his initiation unable to bring himself to strike the abbott.

This novice was expelled from the temple. His fellow initiates, understanding their brother's predicament, interceded on his behalf. The abbott acquiesced and allowed for the ceremony to be repeated the following day. The initiates went searching for the monk and found him just as he was taking drastic steps, about to fall from a cliff into a raging river, attempting to take his own life. They managed to catch hold of his robes just as he toppled from the edge and returned him to the monastery. The following day he underwent the ceremony once more and on this occasion understood completely the requirement to strike his master.

Grayson marvels at the Prof's reveries. How he must have seemed to the monks, this gaijin, as he calls himself, who studied their ways and learnt their myths. How they accepted him into their midst. One can understand, thinks Grayson, for he himself exudes a peacefulness of mind. Hinton has been murmuring, working at his thoughts with his lips, bringing forth his next homily. The Zen monks, he says, compose death poems. They wish, he explains, to produce the composition as close to the final act as possible and as a result many wait too long and die before they are able to compose their final words. They aim to capture the peace that comes immediately before death. And yet, he explains, despite their years of contemplation, their knowledge and belief that a man is only truly at peace when at one with the notion of his own end, many do not want to die. Many become distracted, he says. Though some are capable of beautiful verses, hymning their friends, nature, capturing simple moments, others are more robust. He had heard recited to him one such poem. He speaks it first in the Japanese. Grayson attunes his ears to the alien syllables. *Jisei to wa sunawachi mayoi tada shinan.* Hinton pauses, reflects, and translates. Death poems are mere illusion. Death is death.

--

When a child she had attempted to construct a music that was all cadence. She had so desired the cadence – the perfect cadence – that she did not wish to wait for the close of the piece. She had yearned to be so enraptured throughout, had attempted to stay close to the keynote throughout. She still thought such composition might please her.

Her writing of verse had begun for itself but had slipped free of her grasp. The gatherings at which she had spoken and read to certain friends and close acquaintances had encouraged her. There were those in attendance who had wished her hobby to be made public.

In Japan her writing had been pure. First marks. Close to the tonic chord. She thought it had become since, in its proliferation, less pleasing; had strayed too far from cadence. Here, in this expanse, this profusion, it could not be contained in such determined lines as it had been. It wanted to be more.

Two moods dispart my soul.

Today which shall it be.

The mood of bitterness?

The mood of reverie?

While formally distant from that which she wished to place on the page – the perfect cadence, the soul-nourishing resolution – she found these word combinations allowed her to excise thought structures that were a discomfort. That was simply how the act of composition operated. She had not anticipated that her words would be carried to the poetry editor of the *Los Angeles Tribune* who would comment that "it is possible that the reviewer's mind is not properly attuned so as to recognise and comprehend the real worth and feeling of Mrs. Hinton's poetry." She had not attuned her poetry to any mind but her own so why should another mind expect to be attuned to it?

She had dedicated the volume to her husband. And so

Hear how the sense doth shrink
As from a crevasse brink
At the slightest swerve in tone.

She had read to George when he was tiny but when the boys had come so quickly – Eric and William so soon after each other – no number of nurses might have given her the freedom to read as she wished to each. There was need to rest, to feed, to nurse, to put to bed, each at different times. What time for reading? No doubt this lack of reading was significant. Eric never troubled himself with it, gifted in mental arithmetic as he was. She encouraged his interest in numbers, providing him with an abacus at the age of three; she attempted to nourish the natural space awareness, providing the boy with Froebel's gifts, cubes, cones, plates of wood. That had surely helped the child into awareness of the world. He had never interested himself in books, though.

In bitter pangs the babe was borne;
By greater pangs the child was reared.
Not yet the mother's heart, though torn,
Was scarred and seared.

As for William
'Tis written in the book of fate
That each must follow his own star,
And all must wait.

Certainly the greater expansion and adornment of her words was necessary in the greater expansion of the place. Even the rooms were of a grander scale here. There was simply so much more land. She had great affection for the Japanese love of simplicity, for their accommodation to a lesser space. Here, in the new world, they endeavoured to fill and tame space and still the space itself was excessive. The buildings were too large.

She had considered, not for the first time in her life, religious retreat.

You ask me why I did not take the veil.

Howard had asked her that. It was a curious question for a husband to ask his wife, was it not? She had contemplated vows a great deal in her youth. There had remained in her a wish for children that outweighed her reverence.

Emotion is a vice like drink.

Howard: dedicatee. He had never heard her read. She was not sure she could have read before him. He could not have heard.

What monster sin is this who comes by night,
Hugging his permit from the deathless past?

James Hinton to Charles Howard Hinton

18 Savile Row, December 3, 1872.

MY DEAR How, I am very proud of your Balliol exhibi-tion, for I know you have worked very hard for it; although it is not worth so much as the other one, I would rather you stopped at Balliol. Do not do yourself harm; you will be tempted; but it is unwise. It is contrary also to good for others. Willy comes out like a real student.

I am very glad you have done so well, and particularly glad that your old friends at Rugby find pleasure in your success. To me it is more still. As a reduction in the expenses of your education, it is a distinct facility for doing things which else I might not have been able to do; and I thank you much for help-ing me. Of course, also, it will render you more able to be free to do the work that your heart may be set upon, by rendering it possible for you to be more free from the need of earning money. It may not, however, be particularly advantageous for you to be able to do this, because I have found having to devote myself to earning money, the very greatest help and advantage in my best work, and this most when it looked least like it. One of the chief lessons of my life has been that what seems most hindering is most helpful.

Your loving father,
James

7.

Burgess is arrestingly short. Howard has never met a man of such diminutive stature. What he lacks in physical presence, however, he manufactures through the quantity and quality of his repartee. Since the publication of an essay in *Harper's Magazine* to which he received numerous responses, Howard has engaged in a correspondence with this energetic young writer, a tyro who has achieved some fame as a humorist in the small magazines; as an author of nonsense poetry and as a society commentator. He is, in the written word, a wonderful companion.

Gelett Burgess has travelled in Europe and heard Wells speak. He is an admirer of Hinton's work and shares this enthusiasm with its author. Howard has insisted that Burgess lodge with them on a trip to Minneapolis for a talk to the members of the Humorists Society. The man has emerged from behind his written words, dynamic and dandyish, and immediately assumes intimacy. There is no need for the passing of pleasantries. In the spin of his company one barely notices his height.

Burgess launches into a disquisition on his adventures in the occult groups of his native San Francisco, only lightly glossed in recent correspondence. He has become a follower of Clarion, that great city's most noted Theosophical thinker. He lists her qualifications as if reciting a psalm.

"She has read Leadbeater's *Astral Plane* and holds a subscription to *The Vahan*, which is posted from London. She has followed the suggestions to the letter. She has fasted and meditated for forty days and forty nights in the Nevada desert and returned ... enlightened. She has made contact with distant intelligences. They have strange and exotic names. Amla Shamoor. Sayara." He pauses, to allow the twinkle in his eye greater time on stage. "She is imprecise, certainly, I have heard it said and it is true, but such is the nature of this contact. She awaits instruction. She yearns to be revealed. I see your quizzical eyebrow, Howard, and I raise it by a power of two ... while it is not her claim that she is in any way messianic, she will not deter her followers from reading the clues she plants and making the obvious conclusion that she is at least messiah-like."

Howard cannot bring himself to engage in the game.

"This strikes me as distasteful. There is an awful hubris here."

Burgess scoffs.

"How long have you lived in America, Hinton? I'm not talking about a non-conformist gathering. We're all great religionists. We're believers in the dream. We start our own churches if we're not getting close enough to the gods in the old ones. Why wait for someone else's paradise? Make your own, man!"

Despite the taunt – Howard has discussed his own religious upbringing in prior correspondence with Burgess, his refusal of communion – he will not take the bait.

"Higher knowledge is not the work of mere imagining. Application is required."

"Forty days and forty nights, Hinton."

"On what ground does she found these assertions of holiness?"

"And others! Letters, ashes, notes, cotton, flakes, scents, powders, *all* precipitate in Clarion's presence since her fastness."

Burgess now gestures broadly, enraptured as he orates.

"She can apport objects at will: not that any have witnessed such acts, but she assures us, nay, she simply relates to us, that this is so."

Hinton recognises the mockery.

"This is jugglery, surely. You don't believe yourself?"

"Perhaps I want to," acknowledges Burgess, with a shrug. "I, too, wish for enlightenment. I am getting away from my tale, however. There is a reason for my relating this to you specifically, Hinton. Have you read Leadbeater? He has read you, without any shadow of a doubt. He sees clear comparison between the astral plane and the fourth dimension of space as you describe it."

Burgess pauses.

"Leadbeater has witnessed your tesseract in the astral plane."

This last line delivered in a dramatic basso. Hinton simply blinks. Burgess awaits his response.

"Should I be reading him? Is his work . . . useful?"

Burgess is encouraged. "He claims to have access to many planes beyond the mundane. The Devachanic, for example. He can see the fine granularity of three-dimensional objects, he says; truly, he has earned great powers. And our Clarion likewise now lays claim to these."

Howard states simply: "I must confess, Gelett, I am confused. My experience of higher spatial thought is not that one simply enters some kind of geometric wonderland. Your Clarion sounds like a charlatan, a Slade or suchlike."

"As well you might be unconvinced," concedes Burgess. "But Howard, I truly wish you would accompany me to a lodge meeting, I promise you that you would not regret it. You would have authority on the matters Clarion and her acolytes speak on. And should you find her pronouncements lacking, well then, there would be opportunity for great mirth, and mischief, should one be so minded."

The point of the conversation achieved, Hinton feels deflated. "I am rarely any longer so minded."

"But I frequently am," responds Burgess with authority. "Besides, Clarion is truly fragrant! If anyone can lead me to the planes beyond the astral, pull back the veil, that anyone is she. She might not yet realise how she would transport me there but I should greatly enjoy her instruction in the meantime."

That evening Howard ponders the possibility. He might attend a meeting: he has heard so much talk of the Theosophical Society and their incursions into higher space that he should surely make a direct assay of its nature. He makes the arrangements with Burgess. Mary will not miss him.

--

Hinton and Burgess are welcomed by a housekeeper and led through a garden, in which is set a palm-lined bathing pool, to heavy wooden doors framed by a stone-pointed, ogee arch. "Ersatz," judges Burgess.

The doors are swept apart and the pair led within the house, a palace of Moorish design, intricate zellige tilework adorning the ceilings in hexagonal patterns. "Imagine the expense! Moroccan craftsmen in Oakland!" Through this vestibule into the meeting room, where an audience are already assembled in ranked seating. Orders of service sit on the cushions of these chairs. Hinton surveys the gathering as he and Burgess assume their seats. Some twenty men and women, fashionably, nay, extravagantly attired. A gentleman in the front row wears spectacles of pink glass; the matron to his right an Indian wrap dress; a couple wear matching tartan suits; another lady an Inverness cloak. Howard feels troublingly sober.

Burgess indicates the order of service: "We shall have to wait to hear Clarion commune with Her Masters. We are to be treated first to a reading of poetry by Mrs Elsebeth Hardinge, a short paper on the Sandpainting of the Tibetan Mandala to be presented by Adrianne de Montfouchault and Dr Conrad Black's demonstration of his Harmonilux, 'an invention of the greatest interest to all those of a Theosophical mind'."

"Is the programme normally so full?" asks Hinton, his interest piqued.

"There is so much wisdom to be discussed, Howard!" Burgess cannot contain his mischief. Sarcasm has so overwhelmed his habitual tone that his ironic remarks are indistinguishable from his serious. He has become an instrument of glinting ambiguity.

The audience comes to a hush as an elderly woman takes a position standing before the ranked seats. "*Namaskaram*. I welcome you all most graciously to this assembly of the United Lodge of the Universal Brotherhood and the American Theosophical Society."

"We are several schisms beyond a manageable name," whispers Burgess to Hinton.

"We are able to present this evening a wonderfully full and stimulating programme. I am honoured to have been invited to open proceedings with my own work. I thank you in advance for your gracious attention for this hard-won composition."

"An epic, no doubt," sighs Burgess as the Indian chanting commences.

--

The man wears plaits in a beard of wind-blown, fence-caught wool. He flourishes from within a suit of maroon and gold brocade. He carries a violin bow. The lenses in his spectacles are tinted pink. "Albino harlequin," giggles Burgess. "An albiquin!"

He takes the bow and rests it against an iron-green, quarter-inch-glass plate clamped to a wrought-metal stand. The surface of the plate is dusted with a film of fine sand.

"The figures were discovered and described by Ernst Chladni, a great philosopher of Theosophical bent *avant la lettre*." Great gravitas given to the French pronunciation. "This instrument was his invention."

He works the catgut along the side of the glass and the sand shifts upon the surface, coalescing into lines and arcs. Hinton holds his breath in astonishment. He has read of Chladni's work but never before seen the figures produced.

"The geometric forms, as you will see, mimic the mandala."

The form is indeed geometric: a cross with four ellipses at its poles, outlined by symmetrically oscillating lines. The albiquin increases the vigour of his bowing and the form flows into a fresh organisation like a sentient liquid, assuming, as if in contradistinction to its fluid nature, a perfectly rectilinear grid.

"These vibrations indicate the harmony of all things, such as we may witness in the thought forms visible on the Devachanic plane. Through these patterns are made visible the underlying vibrations of the ultimate unity."

The albiquin gives his liturgy in sighs, transported to the pulpit and beyond by his production of tone and pattern. He shifts down in pitch and tempo to produce a form of reduced complexity: four arcing lines and one straight across the diagonal. Hinton overcomes his transfixed attention to inquire.

"Do the patterns alter in different media?"

"The patterns are universal: the manner in which they are produced is indeed dependent upon the material made to resonate."

The assembled onlookers emit whispers and wonders as the forms and tones morph between lines, corners, curves and circles. The eternal beauty of nature. Harmony in all things. Yantric devotion. Ancient wisdom. Carvings upon temple walls. Stones and crystals. Vibratative frequencies. The ultimate truth of the Orient. Cures. The mind itself oscillates. Fine granularity. Atlantis. Boehme. Thought forms. The removed masters. The realm of the seven dimensions. Ascension.

"A looblum. Poppycock, right, Hinton?"

Burgess speaks too loudly and Hinton can barely conceal his embarrassment.

He mutters, shuffles. "The figures are quite striking, Gelett."

"Sure, but they don't mean anything. It's just music, right?"

Just music? Hinton takes the taunt seriously. "The fact that the forms that are assumed are so symmetrical . . ."

"I'm surprised at you, Howard. A man of science. Of mathematics. Geometry appears on the plates but geometry is no more than patterns."

Burgess wishes to joust. Hinton pulls him to one side to limit the glances of the others. "This is physical science, Gelett, waves represented in physical form. The patterns are cross sections of the waveforms produced by the vibration of the plate. The space-filling sound is here made to dance in the plane. I see . . . parallels."

"Yus. You are seduced by the huckster."

"Gelett, you are familiar with my thoughts on the matter of higher being. That there is accessible to us all a higher form of thought and that we may truly be extended in dimensions beyond the three we physically occupy is, to my mind, an absolute surety. I see no evidence of higher being in this particular entertainment, diverting though it is. I do, by my nature, wonder that what we witness is a reduction into two dimensions of the three-dimensional form of sound. Imagine, then, how such form might appear in the fourth dimension? What beautiful, symmetrical complexity must sound possess in higher space? I would see the three-dimensional sand-dance of the sound forms. This dance is what enters our bodies and we might well attune it to our minds. And this dance may yet be the projection of that higher form of which I dream. Perhaps this is what we glimpse in the work of a Beethoven or a Mozart. Or yet more in the music of a Mahler or a Strauss."

Burgess remains unimpressed. "Or in an albiquin frotting at windows." Returning to their seats, the friends separately consult their programmes. Burgess breaks first. "Well, if you liked that, you'll adore Clarion. She's the top of the ticket."

"I await her arrival with untrammelled curiosity."

Await no longer: a deep, almost choking throb of perfumed air – ambergris, rich pickled orange – precedes the great mystic. Something has landed on Burgess's nose: he blows away a feather with under-bit lips and it floats forwards over the heads of the sisters; others still fall through the air of the room, their source not apparent.

Clarion sweeps between the chairs in a sashay of creamy silks, feathers falling around her. Her hair, even in plaits, falls behind her to her waist. Without any evidence of feet or ambulation she has arrived at the chaise longue at the front of the room, upon which she seats herself, tucking her legs beneath her skirts, curling in feline comfort. She appraises the room with beatific gaze.

Clarion's beauty is unseemly, decides Hinton. One swims, unable to locate a point of orientation. Her features so symmetrical they defy the eye to measure them, seem to extend to infinity, each plane more perfect than the next; each intersection a treasure of natural organisation. If the Almighty were a lapidary he could not achieve such. Her skin is preternatural: never has he seen any surface, artificial or natural, appear so dulcet. It yearns to be brushed so lightly with the tips of the fingers that they barely impinge. It would not do actively to touch: such a surface is most properly intangible. Blushing cheeks and strikingly green eyes; pale pink lips in puckish smile. Hinton becomes conscious that his breath has become short. She has taken it away! By her presence! All else momentarily falls from his mind. He feels as a cub, a calf; wishes for nothing so much as succour. He is infantilised by this Helenian beauty.

The members are duly respectful, perceptibly leaning towards their figurehead as sunflowers towards the source of their nourishment. Clarion raises her chin, proud of her neck, as if she too inclines towards something higher, revealing a throat of elegant extension. All await. It commences as a squeal. Hinton glances around him for the source. It rounds into a sustained note before collapsing into the heavy rattle of flatus. Hinton realises his mouth is open. Despite this awareness, he struggles for control of his jaw. The members are enraptured. Two rapid bursts, fully colonic. Prrap, prrap. A sigh from the lady in the cloak. Clarion's eyelids flutter over her shut eyes, her gaze rhapsodic. A huffing, such as might be encountered amongst a herd of cattle. Clarion's eyes light open: she looks as if to speak and rounds her mouth. A roaring belch, unrestrained, the aesophagous distended. How? Hinton flounders. A diuretic? She must have . . .

He smells the intestinal gas, the clear tang of allium as it enters his nostrils. The members have noses raised, inhaling deeply. Hinton turns abruptly to Burgess whose twitching grin betrays mischievous delight. All along! Burgess snakes his head as if straining to catch a sweet air. The ruptured distension of puckered flesh, a rubbery sound, but moist. Vapour of rude soil. Bog-like. Hinton fears a medical emergency but his is a lonely distress. There is no joy in the room to match that felt by Burgess, from whose hard-clenched eye a stray tear begins to roll. Something summoned from deep within, a vomitory of bilious sound. It becomes inhuman. Hinton experiences epiphany. This *is* supernatural. This *is* a gift. A visitation. Though it is a mistake to think that it is spirit that speaks through her, he realises. It is brute matter; it surges forth through Clarion, demanding to be acknowledged, only for these members to miscall it.

--

"So now you know how she has the name." Burgess has the air of a victor ludorum; he displays the satisfaction of a game well won.

"Does she speak at all?" Hinton remains distracted.

"Not that I've heard. But what need words, right? When one is so ... fluent."

"Never before." Hinton shakes his head.

Burgess gazes heavenward. "I think I believe in her."

Burgess loops his arm through Hinton's, comradely after the escapade. As they make their way between the trees a voice calls at their backs.

"Professor Hinton! Sir!"

It is the albiquin. He approaches Howard and bows in the Japanese style. "Dr Conrad Black. You are Hinton."

"I am."

"I am familiar with your work."

Hinton is wary. In this context such familiarity might be something entirely distinct to that hoped for.

"I have another device I would demonstrate to you. I believe it of urgent import to your project. You must come with me to my lodgings. They are not far from here."

Hinton looks to Burgess. "We have time before our train?"

"We would be intrigued," says Burgess. "We are, after all, seekers after the truth."

--

A superfluity of objects, filling space. Buttes and stacks of books emerge from the floor, haphazard bibliostratic formations; jars and ceramic containers, many broken or cracked, catch drips from assorted apparatus established around the ledgework of shelves; tin and lead boxes packed deeply with yet more things, found things, a scavenger's hoard; pine cones, mottled eggs, mammalian skulls, children's toys; sheaves of paper, listing.

The albiquin has cut various channels through this hoaching to a clearing. In the centre of the clearing, a machine. A dentist's chair the basis; accoutrements about the head rest.

"Would you care for a drink? I might suggest an infusion. I have a well so you need not worry about the colloidal silver here." Burgess declines. Hinton ponders until he feels Burgess's elbow in his ribs and a rapid shake of the head.

"No, thank you. It is most kind. This is your invention?"

"It is a prototype, though I believe it has already yielded results." The albiquin ponders his invention as if it remains a mystery even to him. "It enforces a vertical stereoscopy. The periscope lens is, in effect, a third eye. By imposing the altered perspective of this third eye over that of one of the extant eyes we must reconcile the vertical parallax as well as the lateral. A lens also is built in to magnify the second eye."

Howard takes hold of the contraption. It is not well made. He sits gingerly. He places the helmet upon his head but it is too loose and the weight of the scope rising above it threatens to topple the whole. The albiquin jumps in with assistance, fearing his invention might fall.

"Allow me to adjust the headstrap."

Howard feels the leather pulled taut around his cranium and the device locked into place. The albiquin guides him into the chair. "It is advisable to be seated." The eyepiece is swivelled around on a hinge.

Immediately he experiences a doubled and distorted horizontal vision.

Immediately he experiences a doubled horizontal vision.
His brain does not reconcile it at all.
His brain does not reconcile it.
Face upon face, thing upon thing upon thing. It is nauseating.
Face upon face, cloud upon cloud. It is nauseating.
He requests the albiquin help him remove it.
He requests the albiquin helps him remove it.

"You see now that it enables a higher dimensional vision. I will patent it. Your endorsement would be a very great value. Perhaps you will advertise it in your books?" The albiquin frees the chinstraps and Hinton feels a lightness in his neck, as if his head itself wishes to rise.

"It is a rare contraption, though I am unsure that it quite correlates . . ."

"That's settled, then," interrupts Burgess. "My turn for a spin."

Burgess has already taken his seat for the voyage and gestures towards the albiquin to hurry along.

☐

James Hinton to Charles Howard Hinton

Kentish Town, April 1, 1874.

MY DEAREST How, We have made the great change. I trust in God that it will be for good. I think it was a true desire for good that moved me to the resolve; and nothing more encouraged me than the kind and generous and loving way in which my children, as well as mamma, entered into my hopes and aims, and chose less of this world's advantages in order that those aims might be carried out. It was a trouble getting out of the house. I could only feel one thing – a hope that I might never have so much furniture again.

As you may suppose, I feel the change. Already the whole Savile Row life seems like a dream to me. It is as if it had never been; so much so, that even the old Tottenham life seems nearer and realer. But perhaps this is only temporary. But the feeling that has come is not one of great depression, which I should have thought natural I only had a few hours of that but one of great seriousness and solemnity. The excitement of my recent life has passed away, and I want to pause and think, and be spoken to again by God, in quietness. Then I have had a sort of unrooted baselessness of feeling, as if I had no place in the world, and especially a feeling of total and utter impotence, as if I never had been or should be able to do anything again. This has been very strong, but it is passing away; and as I was reading some of Matthew Browne's essays yesterday I felt quite a passionate gladness come over me that my business now was with human life.

Willy will come to you to-morrow. After he has had a little rest try and get him to work, and help him a little. You can do this in his natural philosophy. I believe he will get through. I tell him I believe in him; which, indeed, I always did and do. It is impossible to look in his face and not believe in him. Mamma has gone to grandmamma's at Bristol. Your loving father,

James

8.

Minneapolis has been exchanged for Washington. Six years completed, Howard has accepted that he is not cut out to be a university instructor. The American university is run by businessmen and Howard cannot be made profitable. He plans to take the civil service examinations. He crams in the evening and writes in the morning. He considers taking up golf the better to enter networks of professionals.

Mary's sister Alicia has made the great transatlantic voyage. Alicia is Howard's closest among his in-laws. His former collaborator, no less, his conspirator in the cubes. The only student who would set herself to them, learning the Latin names with a dedication of spirit. She would stay while they were at Uppingham and spend hours moving them through sequences. The pupil has exceeded the teacher. She has extended Howard's method to describe the four-dimensional analogues of all the Platonic solids. She has imagined a new realm of forms. Her visit is a cause for celebration and the exchange of family news. Much has, of course, passed in correspondence but Alicia's visit brings detail and discussion of the matters not fit to be entrusted to paper: scandals and sadness.

Mary quizzes her sister while Howard listens. Aunt Lily has finally married Wilfred, and they have assumed the name Voynich. She is experiencing a return to earth following the reception of her first, *The Gadfly*, a runaway success which the Irish poet George Bernard Shaw – an enthusiast for its revolutionary themes – is to adapt for the stage. Her most recent romance,

Jack Raymond, has not so pleased either critics or readers. Howard wishes to know: do Henry Holt publicise Lily's books? Did they arrange the Russian translation? Is Bernard Shaw a prig, as he has heard? Alicia provides answers as best she can while Mary rolls her eyes.

Sister Lucy remains gravely ill. Alicia and Mary weep together, Mary realising in a moment that she will never again see her sister. A succession of Harley Street doctors has been unable to help. She remains at home in Notting Hill with Mama, no longer able to instruct at the School of Medicine. Howard does not wish to intrude in this moment. His own family becomes a way of moving the conversation forwards. Alicia has become an intimate of Howard's sister Adaline.

Since Howard's brother-in-law John died the previous year, Adaline struggles also. She worries particularly about her daughter Ida, who has inherited her father's gift for painting and studies art at the Slade, where she has fallen in with a gypsy. Ada does not know what to do. Mary sympathises, Howard becomes recalcitrant. He retreats to his study, allowing the sisters a degree of privacy.

--

"Mother is difficult."

"She is easier to love from this distance, certainly."

"I see her infrequently. That has fallen to Lucy." Alicia shakes her head. "I refuse to feel the burden. It would make little sense for her to grow attached to me. I am content in Liverpool. William has a sound appointment. I will not return to London. Ethel is the very gadfly of her book. She will not settle in England. I suspect you may see her soon."

"You will tell Mother how I miss her?"

"Was she always so difficult, Mary?"

Mary is contemplative. "I do not recall. When we moved to London we were straitened. Mother was very concerned that she might provide for us all. That is why Ethel remained in Ireland. I do not underestimate that decision."

"She was mourning Father?"

"Mother did not discuss Father with me. I was still a child, after all. Even later we have not discussed Father. She seems more interested in his name than in his true memory. The Boole name for Mother's books."

"I remember falling sick with a chest cold. She made me bathe in ice water three times."

"She has her beliefs."

"I often wonder, did she care for Father when he fell ill?"

"Such thoughts serve little purpose, Alicia."

"It must have been strange for you, Mother's intimacy with Howard's father."

"It is what brought us together."

Alicia looks meaningfully at her sister. "I wish Mother were not so at odds with the world."

"It seems to fall to some of us. Howard feels this too. He wishes for greater acceptance for his theories. It is such a pleasure for him to meet with you, to know that there is one at least who has profited from them."

"I have profited. I keep notes. I have made models. It gives me great satisfaction. Howard's methods are outside of the convention and yet there is much geometric benefit from the direct appreciation of space. It is unfortunate that there are so few who recognise this." Alicia looks sternly at her sister. "Mary. I must say this though. I do not regard the Hintonian moral theory as sound. I find my nature quite disinclined to the self-openness Howard hopes will come from the higher spatial experience."

"Your geometric work is enough, I think."

--

Over dinner, Howard wishes to discuss matters of the mind. He talks of the cubes, of the problems he had in producing them to a sufficient standard; of his correspondence with Sonnenschein complaining about their quality and the price at which to sell them. He has received few inquiries. He worries that they are not worth the candle. Alicia insists. She tells Howard of her work with a Dutchman, Schoute, with whom she has corresponded. She reassures Howard: without the cubes never would she have been able to work towards the polytopes; Howard's own tesseract, for example; the hyperoctohedron; the 600-cell whose cross-sectional model she had constructed using techniques learned through working with his marvellous vision. Her shading, even, owes to the cubes, her recruitment of colour as a qualium through which to indicate dimension. This talk is a great kindness. Howard is soothed; his life's work, for the duration of their conversation, not quite the failure he has come to imagine it. He outlines his plans for the new collection of essays and the colour plates: Alicia is ecstatic, in her own way. Yes, this is certainly what his readers will want. He hopes so. He hopes more than he knows.

Mary brings Sebastian into the room, on his return from his athletics club, to wish his aunt good night. The child who left England as a babe in arms is now a young adult. Alicia fusses and Sebastian replies politely. How rapidly he has become a man. Alicia inquires after her other nephews. Where are they? She has seen only Sebastian. Howard answers to the best of his knowledge. George is in Mexico. The mining companies use him. His skills in assaying, learnt in the laboratory, and at mining schools across America, are well-appreciated by speculators. He works in Mexico in the breaks and returns to his studies at the University of California in the term times.

William, Howard reports, is at college. He is not a strong student, though capable enough when able to apply himself. Eric, Howard is disappointed to inform Alicia, has not been heard of for some months. Eric left college without notice. They are concerned for him – Mary particularly. She has begun to attend mass at an Episcopal Church, which Alicia must know to be out of character – but he is, after all, an adult. It is his life and he must divine his own path through it.

Solutio, ablutio, conjunctio, fixio. Earth, water, air and fire. North, south, east and west. Four sides of a square. Fourfold. Isosceles triangles: base down, divided across the horizontal, apex down, divided across the horizontal.

Howard is the alchemical sun, Mary mercury, the closest in orbit. Maud is the moon, orbiting some other body, elsewhere.

--

Eric falls, but he does not reach the ground. The distance between his position and the ground can be halved, infinitely; parcelled into ever smaller units. So too can the time that elapses between his fall and the impact his body should make on the flattened earth beneath the climbing frame. It is halved, halved, halved, halved, halved, halved, halved ...

Eric remains forever the falling boy.

Eric travels between the west coast and the east, running the railroads, working on farms, picking up odd jobs, but he never reaches his destination. Each coast serves as an elastic limit for his travels.

He writes to his brothers for money. George declines, Willy does not respond, Sebastian sends money that derives from George in any case.

Ma and Pa know nothing of Eric's child, a daughter born

out of wedlock with sweet Sinead in Poughkeepsie: a second-generation Irish girl, barely five minutes out of the Bowery and believing her trajectory towards hope and decency. Eric told her he wasn't the marrying kind even as they explored together sins of which he'd only heard whisper, but pretended to know, and of which she, he was certain, pretended to be innocent while possessing a facility that was far from innate. The Sisters of St Ursula was his inclined solution to the difficulty in which they found themselves, but when she took it into her head that Eric was from a grand family, a Princeton family, there was no dragging Sinead to a convent. She carried the child to term and dreamed of raising it with its father. Eric's actions during that period had caused him to change his name: he no longer went by Eric, but preferred instead his middle name Bjorn, convinced that he could pass as a Swede. Sinead would not find him, nor would her brother, because neither would be seeking a Scandinavian named Bjorn. He heard from mutual acquaintances that she had returned to the Bowery with a wee girl named Rose. He felt it best to maintain a distinct orientation: he went West and South, to Chicago.

He had not told Ma and Pa because he suspected, though did not know, that Ma might take it upon herself to bring Rose and Sinead into the fold. She could be like that. Though no longer Catholic, brought up that way. That way was there for all of them, sure, but he was more of the agnostic type when it came to the great questions of ethics. Pa had at one time been quite the ethicist, but no longer. He felt his own path more aligned with his father's. He headed West, and South. Bjorn to roam, he liked to tell folk, bedding into his new name. He worked days here and there, small labouring jobs, put together small parcels of cash, then found games where these parcels could be multiplied.

--

Faro played fast and loud was his weakness; he liked to ride a roaring tiger, as they said. He loved the table when there was a crowd and here, now, there was a crowd, each part urging the other on as the draw came out fast. He slaked himself with porter, sweet and strong, probably worse than brandy, he thought.

Eric was working the odds each time, didn't need to look at the case, as the feller flipped the beads zipping across their runs. Twenty-three cards down, all the kings, three deuce, threes, eights; two twos, sevens, jacks; one each four, six, nine, queen. Plays on five and ten, four in twenty-nine each, or one in seven, close as you like, best odds on the table, and a hedge on the odd. Eight drawn, dealer takes.

He could work the odds without the case but he knew that didn't count for much if you couldn't find an honest table, was what he was thinking, but what he did was double up, buck each five and ten and switch the hedge to evens. Too many ways for the banker to goof the draw, he was thinking, too many ways, when the last deuce came out and the shrieking of the lush next to him in his ear as the bank paid out on her odd bet.

They couldn't be pushing two a time in this game, he thought, placing his marker carefully on the heart of the five, something telling him that his luck had to change. He watched the box with slit-eyes, concentrated upon it, insisting to himself that he was looking out for a spring action, or a button; in truth, hoping to control the draw with his mind. Out comes the ten, sure as shit, telling him to pack up and go home. Damphool. Oh, how he loved to play this game, this mean tiger, this whipped cat. One more double up, four bucks now, more than he'd spend in a week on food, this time he'd play it safe, get it all back, four bucks on evens, his time had come.

The three was pushed. He should have known right then it wasn't a fair game. Cards must be cut, the dealer feeling the way to goof him with fingertips attuned to the specific serrations and rough edges. Went all in to dig himself out and called the turn wrong. Disgusted with himself, cleaned out to the lint in his pockets, he slouched out of the bar.

Don't stay down, was what he thought. Plan A was already in train by then, he thought, so he'd simply switch back to that. His stake this time had been borrowed from his old dorm buddy back in Kansas City so he decided against paying any more visits to that group of friends, naturally. In truth, had been planning to put any winnings into Plan A regardless. Had grown impatient. Wanted some of what George had: independent earnings. George had it right: mining was the game, that was clear enough. Rushing to Nevada. Rushing to the West. Wherever people were in a rush there was money to be made. He'd decided this was a superior area in which to focus his energies.

--

At Salt Lake he finds a guide, second generation Nevada native. Dirk knows the route to Tonopah like to his own bed; been taking folk out there every week since the news of the strike the last year. Says they have two headframes up and running and claims offered at 75 per cent. Eric is going under Bjorn. Says he wants to buy a claim. Two weeks' trek, with stops at Wendover, Ely, Warm Springs and fishing holes to drink and dip. Supplies of dried beef and coffee, feed for the burros. Journey has too much time for talking. Dirk tells of plans for a railroad already being talked of. The ore coming out of those claims rich enough to pay for it.

At Tonopah, Dirk introduces Eric to a man named Jim Butler, owner of the entire claim. The deal is by the square foot, twenty-five per cent reverting to Jim. He doesn't have the wherewithal to mine the entire claim, he says. This way, anyone willing to work gets rich and he gets richer still. Eric says he wants a thousand square feet. If Jim will take a down payment on one hundred, he'll mine that and come back with money for the rest. Jim says fair enough, likes a man willing to back his plan, but he can't hold the claim any longer than one month. Eric spits in his palm, shakes to seal. Spends three days digging with substandard equipment but it don't matter – the stories are true, high grade ore as good as lying there on the surface of the earth, yellow metal like sparks in the stones. Spends his evenings with men come from as far as Pennsylvania, Oregon, freed slaves from the South, singing campfire songs, old time religion songs, biblical figures – Saint Elizabeth, Doubting Thomas, the ol' tempter himself – scampering through his dreams and taunting him with gallows jokes.

Fourth day, packs his burro with ten kilos of the best rocks he can find, meets up with Dirk on his next trip out, makes the journey south east to Las Vegas where he knows a man with a jewellery store. Puts his samples on display, big sign stating they come from Tonopah. Causes a stampede to the camp. Hundreds wanting this kind of ore. Returns the following week, Jim Butler all sold out, men begging to buy out his hundred square feet. Eric sells that day at five hundred per cent profit.

Returns to Vegas with a fresh plan already cooking. Takes out an advert for the Tonopah Trading Company, selling stakes in mining territory. For sale by correspondence. Fifty per cent returns guaranteed. Raises – within the week, mind you – enough cash to buy stakes ten times what he's had. Returns to goldfield, finds Jim Butler and offers him partnership. Jim Butler says he don't need no partner but there's a feller starting up at a claim called Mohawk looking for capital investors. Just further along. Eric sets off, finds this man, Adamson; shows him the money and the Mohawk Prospecting Company is born. Returns fifty per cent to investors within the year selling claims alone.

Same process repeats, price of shares increasing each round. Voca, Red Top, Bullfrog, Manhattan, May Queen. Wildcat investors buying 1,000,000 shares at 25 cents, 35, 70, 1 dollar, 3 dollars. Adverts in the papers, Mercuries, Echoes, Heralds and Dailies. Listings on San Francisco Stock Exchange, New York Curb. Eric, by now, a reputation for picking the fields. No longer gets his hands dirty. Jim Butler, his own stake sold on, senses the truth. Tells Eric: "Son, you are so crooked that if you swallowed a ten-penny nail and vomited it would come out a corkscrew." Eric takes this as the highest compliment he's ever been paid. He's still going by Bjorn but sometimes, in his cups, lets slip his real name. Kinda frequently. Eric's enjoying his success.

That summer the May Queen stock is bought almost entirely by one investor, name of Ballatore out of Atlantic City. Eric doesn't care: he's a democrat, he'll take anyone's money. May Queen strikes out. May Queen's a poor claim. Eric is unconcerned, he's made out. Sitting in the saloon bar of the Grand Hotel in Vegas, peacock in his fine threads, he's approached by a smart young lady offering a fine opportunity if he'll come up to her room. Eric not discriminating between business or pleasure and hoping for a bit of both follows the young lady. The door to the room shuts behind him and he's face to face with three men not minded for pleasure. Eric starts to talk quickly, shooting his mouth, and the one standing nearest slaps his face. Eric is outraged: a rabbit punch to his kidneys follows and Eric realises too late what this is about. Lying in his own spit and blood in an empty room two minutes later, it's the name Ballatore that has lodged, and the timescales. He's got a week.

--

There's only one damphool now, thinks Eric. Damphool American speculator, he used to think. The whole shitshow round his ankles he knows full well who's the damphool. He needs to disappear.

He's just an advert in a newspaper, Eric tries to tell himself, not even believing it. He's just the words on the page, they can't find him again. So why has he not been to the office since the hoods turned up? How come sitting in Sally's diner in a side of town he's never spent any time in seems such a good idea? If the print is all he is, why does he feel charged like a Van der Graaf generator, static arcing from his fingertips through the space he inhabits, lighting him up for everyone to see, conducting everything towards this one body, this one form, this one specific place?

He needs to disappear. Hiding would be no good, hiding would be damphool too, that would be reducing the space in which he was operating, limiting it, but foiling wit with just the same fear, only concentrated. No, he needs a new space, one that isn't or hasn't been his. He needs a space where he's different. He likes some of the stories the old man told, how you could move out of one space and into another, that would sure work for him right now. Maybe he should telegram the old man, get some advice. It's been months. He can't draw Ma and Pa into this, though. They might come try to help him and be seen. He can't do that. Too great a margin for error, the odds all off.

There was this one story the old man told with some Professor who started stepping out of space when he wanted to get away from people. He'd be walking down the corridor in the library, see someone he didn't like and he'd exit stage everywhere. It looked like he went narrow, first, down to a line. If you saw him from the side it was like a cross-section. Then that thinned up too, till there was just a strand of him in this space. Then that shrunk right down to a point before popping away to nought. Pa said this Professor was like a ghost only alive and he could move into the space somewhere else entirely. It was godlike ability – omnipresence – though truly available to mortals. Only thing was, you had to sit down with Pa's cubes and learn all the Latin names and no one, 'cepting aunt Alicia had the time for that. Damphool cubes.

Fourteenth infantry regiment recruiting for some adventure in China. That would get him the hell out of Dodge, no more Ballatore trouble, but it did not feel right. He'd always felt the need to head west rather than east. He'd make for the prospect.

--

He tried the journey to Bullfrog without a guide. At Carvers he was warned of weather coming in from the west so traded a hunk of silver for some furs. Spent an evening in the tavern lounging next to the player piano, an untuned machine. He could pick out the notes that played wrong but could not tell what they were. Could not tell the lady who came to keep him company, Ellen, working for the tavernkeeper. She took him to a room and listened to him try to describe the notes that were not playing right. He wept for his lost family, her sympathy neither expected nor given. She brought him a hot toddy, called him a child: just an observation. Tucked him up in his long johns. Sheet under his armpits he swigged pechuga from a canteen, feeling his thoughts sour with the spirit.

In his twisting dreams he slid on his belly through hotel corridors, came to rest in a boxing ring, threw dice, his old bones, won a rose from a woman with the face of Felicity but it wasn't her in spirit, not at all. Woke in the night, grinding his teeth, pinned by his sheets, the wind rattling his windows. Panicked himself free, flopped to the boards and rummaged through his bags to find his dice where he'd packed them. Sat there, in his long johns, throwing dice. Kept rolling pairs. Goddamn Willy. Damhim. Left the room leaving five dollars extra for their trouble. Walked out into snow. Snow in Nevada. Thought to walk the remainder of the route, leave his horse. That horse did not know his mind, was the problem. Will of its own.

Yomped for some miles lugging his pack, teeth still gritted, worrying at problems wouldn't unfurl. Pa's theories? What was that damphool stuff? Could that stuff help him? He'd give a nugget of gold for action at a distance. Needed to experience the thoughts of another. Could never get behind that logic, so much woowoo. Conjoined souls from extrapolated lines. Draw them in the snow. Pinprick points. Heard a thump in the sky looked up to see crimson cloudbursts in place of birds. Shook his head till his eyes rattled. Only thing numbers was good for was more numbers. Odds proliferating, chances multiplying, limitless potential, no feeling in his toes, boots gummed up.

At a shack he begged some snow-shoes. He thought he had frost-bite but the mother told him he was just cold and stop skitterin like a maid. He climbed higher, sure the claim was nearby. From memory yes but his memory not being much good at this altitude. Stumbled to a cranny in the rockface by the path to shelter a squall and it felt tight nice enclosing round him warm lithic embrace he settled right into the womby bones of the mountain sure as wouldn't find him no matter not for grifters up here in the hills. Place to stay preserving one's warmth among the furs and mosses. He did not know how he had withstood the strain, such woes as are beyond man. He realised it was his company, his shadow, that had so assisted, that had borne him through the raging gale, through the stress and strain, struggle with might, struggle with main. The one who walks alongside. His footsteps alongside. Eric met a man who wasn't there. Together they journeyed apart. Eventually Eric wished him to come out from his side, his beside, and to be front, affront him. This he did and Eric saw himself and he looked into his eyes and he saw great depth and beyond, further than eyes can see, and he was matched with this one, they were the same one, mirrored, same, inverse twists perhaps, and when they came together they cancelled each other leaving nought but residue.

James Hinton to Charles Howard Hinton

Kentish Town, 12th April 1874.

MY DEAR How, I am glad of your little note. You must send to me now all you write, because I shall have more time to enter into your pursuits, which I have long desired; and also you must give me some lifts in mathematics. I must attend to them a little. They are so interesting and so full of suggestiveness.

I have been going on a little with Mrs Boole in our desultory way, which nevertheless has its value, at least for me. I got a little inkling about the conic sections, and then we came on to the calculus. It is very jolly; and I find it quite like what I thought it. The four forms of it are such fun. The Fluxion (what I call the honest or nature-form) as plain as the day; the Infinitesimal, which keeps hold of the infinitely small quantities and neglects them (which roused Newton's ire even to madness, and no wonder); the refined Infinitesimal or Differential, which takes the ratio only; and La Grange's, which tries to get round the whole thing, but, as is said, doesn't quite. These are splendidly interesting, quite apart from mathematics; they are a study of human life; nor does one need to know anything more than algebraical notation to enjoy them I won't say thoroughly, but exquisitely. And my ideas about a new teaching of mathematics become both clearer and more confirmed. I should say this way: What is taught in our schools (to boys) is not mathematics, but a little fraction of the history of mathematics, and not even as a history. It is just as if, in teaching astronomy, boys should not be taught anything of what Copernicus did, but trained just a little bit in the tracing on paper the apparent motions, and formulating them, and should simply hear of Copernicus as a man who did some

*wonderful thing which great astronomers could know about.
That is exactly as our teaching of mathematics does in respect
to Newton, and with just as good reason. What Newton did
was simply what Copernicus did to make the thought true
to nature, putting aside the non-perception that infects our
native vision, and makes us deal first with fictions of our own
constructing. Now, I would have every child trained a little in
the epicycles before it heard anything about what Copernicus
did; and so in geometry. But of course the earth's motion is the
beginning of astronomy; so is the fluxion of mathematics. And
this should be our teaching of it: "This is what Newton did for
us: he revealed to us nature, and this is how it was done first;
but the dead or fictitious mathematics came before, and must
have come."*

*Then the lessons of it are infinite, for you see what Newton
showed us was not speaking of realities and true values anything about magnitudes and spaces (much as that is in one
point of view, but it has no glory, by reason of the glory that
excelleth; these were just the clay given to create a statue in
anything will do); but what he did was, to show us the ever-
lasting art, the art of Life, of letting go and holding on at once,
of having in effect, of raising from things into powers, from
physical to spiritual.*

*This is what he taught us. To look merely at the lines and
values is as if in a book one should look merely at the letters.
It is his process, his act that has an infinite value and significance. That is being true to nature, always and everywhere.*

*Then look at the dependent variables. What it is, is the rela-
tion of the external law to the law of the soul the variation of
the former with the latter; the mutual varying, indeed. It is Life
it teaches us. And so it is all through; the child must have these
things put before him quite afresh.*

But I suppose, perhaps, it is not "wise" of me to put these thoughts before you now. Only, I can't think of that, because, you see, you are my dearest friend, whom I want to know all about me ... Your loving father,

James

10.

Following his success in the exams for the civil service Howard has been invited to the Naval Observatory. He had expressed a preference for work that would be primarily mathematical in nature and has been delighted to be appointed to the staff of the Nautical Almanac: he recalls, vaguely, examining the publication on board the *Tacoma*. The Almanac requires mathematically competent computers as a matter of urgency due to an expansion of the equipment and the construction and installation of new telescopes.

The role of a computer is essential. The computer is a gear in the machine. The computer operates gears in the machine. He has been issued with tables, although is permitted some freedom in expanding or contracting these. He is to calculate the locations of the red star 12 Ceti within the celestial sphere for the forthcoming year. It is a minor task that will fulfil only one line in the Almanac but 12 Ceti is a star of use to navigators due to being visible to the naked eye. The computations are a relatively simple matter requiring knowledge of techniques of spherical trigonometry, calculus and differential equations. He is comfortable in these methods. He is offered the use of a counting machine and accepts – a slide rule is only accurate to three decimal places and he is required to compute to six. He is furnished with a copy of Charles Henry Davis's translation of Gauss.

--

A tennis court is marked out on the lawn to the north of the main observatory building. It is in the lea of the dome housing the 12-inch telescope. The eastern wing of the building houses the library. The main building is slightly to the east of the centre of the Observatory circle, which is the clock-house. The clock-house is the centre of the Transit House Complex, which includes also the east and west transit telescope buildings. Just north of this is the newly built dome for the 26-inch telescope.

A game of mixed doubles takes place on the court. Two men and two women bat between them a sphere. One of the women imparts a spin upon the sphere with her forehand shots: each time the ball kicks on from the ground it baffles her male opponent. Her male colleague imparts a sideways spin on his serves which has a similar effect. The male opponent becomes increasingly agitated, despite his best efforts at maintaining a sporting attitude.

Hinton observes with interest as the male opponent swipes at a ball that bounces away from him, loses his grip on his racquet, which flies from his hand on a higher arc than one would expect, rotating through the air and making sudden and traumatic contact with the forehead of the female opponent, who swiftly falls to the ground. Hinton reacts more rapidly than the shocked players to assist the fallen woman. The racquet has made a cut to her forehead that bleeds troublingly. Hinton staunches it with his handkerchief held in his left hand as he supports the woman with his right arm. The three players approach, the agitated opponent hurdling the net.

"Marie. My God, Marie, I am so sorry. The racquet slipped."

Her partner is outraged: "You're a fool, Updegraff. You had lost control of your own actions."

Updegraff rounds on his opponent: "Belt up."

The second female player steps in. "Thank you, sir. Marie, can you speak?"

Marie's voice is tremulous. "Yes. Yes. Yesyes."

"Can you stand?"

"Yes, yes."

Marie makes her feet with the support of Hinton and the female player. Doubt has begun to enter her expression.

"I'll take you to the nurse, Marie. Thank you, Sir. Thank you."

"Of course."

"Yes."

--

Inside the dome for the 6-inch telescope, Hinton is shown the apparatus used for making the observations from which he, as a computer, will calculate the tables of correct motion. Before the telescope sits a mercury basin which can be rotated at constant speed to produce in the mercury a paraboloidal form, making of it a concave, reflective surface. The telescope may then be pointed directly upwards towards the zenith to determine the constant of the nadir. Smaller, fixed telescopes are used for adjusting the line of sight.

The clock-house is the radial centre of the Observatory Circle, but the centre also of a network broadcasting to several cities. Within the clock-house, an astronomer reads time from a sidereal telescope, pressing a handheld key to record the passage of stars over micrometer wires, consisting of threads of spider's silk laid across the lens in fixed period. The signal from the key records the pulsing of the seconds, setting the master-clock. From this the Observatory's chronometer is set, and by comparison with that chronometer, the mean-time clock. From the mean-time clock to the transmitting clock which gives a telegraphic signal at exactly noon. The telegraphic signal causes the activation of fire alarms.

The ticking of a telegraph; the firing of a gun; the ringing of a bell; the discharge of a flashing signal; the dropping of a time ball.

Time is a commodity. The Western Union Telegraph Company has wires in the State Department building. It steals time, transmits it to its main office and thence throughout its network.

The trains are regulated by Observatory clocks.

--

He is left with the two male tennis players.

"What a folderol."

"That was entirely preventable."

Updegraff offers his hand to Hinton. "Thank you, sir. Forgive me. Milton Updegraff."

"Howard Hinton."

"I do not recognise you. You are new to the Observatory?"

"A computer at the Almanac. My appointment has just been finalised. I have been making a tour of the facilities the better to aid my understanding of the operations of the Observatory."

"Whose appointment are you?" asks the second man.

"See, for God's sake, don't embroil him."

Hinton replies uncertainly. "I have corresponded in the past with Professor Newcomb. His paper concerning the flexure of a sphere in space of n to the four. I was subsequently initially approached by Professor Brown when a post became available. But Professor Newcomb and I have corresponded."

See whispers: "Stay close to Newcomb."

Updegraff is appalled. "Christ." Howard is confused.

"I beg your pardon?"

See speaks with urgency. "He's the emperor. Brown is the consul. There are moves."

"I do not think my role has much to do with the daily work of the Observatory."

"You're a computer, you say?"

"I am. I am to review the tables for Ceti 12."

"One of the asteroids? Perhaps you need not concern yourself. The naval people are the ones to watch." He picks up the balls and turns to his friend. "I'm done here, Updegraff. We should check on Marie."

--

Recumbent upon the board-backed chair, Hinton places his eye to the lens.

He thinks of the horopter, the mapping within the structure of the eye of the points in space exterior to it. The mirrors within the telescope reverse also: space inverted and inverted again before the accomplishment of its reconstitution within the image-making processes of the brain. A space spun endlessly, a space never of fixed dimensionality, nor of scale. A negative immensity blossoms within the mind, pricked by points of light.

For Kepler these celestial objects orbited within a fixed scheme, modelled upon the Platonic solids: the demiurge was nothing if not a geometer!

--

Flustered by his most peculiar exchange with the tennis players, Howard has wandered through the Observatory premises, a gentle parkland punctuated with fine buildings. He has settled at a bench in a white stone portico and has been staring at the sky, pondering the stars he must now chart, their distances and the times taken to traverse those immensities.

The voice comes to him gently. "It is a fine day to take in this view."

Howard watches a gull fly across the vista. "It is, Sir. The sky is not fettered by cloud."

Howard senses the man nod. "Although, as I understand it, the blue is itself a form of cloud."

Hinton turns towards his interlocutor, who remains fixed in profile, sitting two feet from him on the stone bench in the portico. A pugilist's nose and ridged brow, wire-framed spectacles from beneath which the man squints at the sky over the fields surrounding the Observatory. A greatcoat in grey wool draped over the man's broad shoulders, its collars turned to protect against the wind. Only this narrow vector of face is available to his view. Hinton feels an uncanny nagging.

The man turns to him. "Tyndall, correct?"

"You are a scientific man?"

"Not so much, although I maintain an interest."

Hinton looks back to the view. His companion has appeared by his side without notice. Indeed, he could not recall the man arriving at the bench, which had been vacant when he had arrived. Certainly, he has been deep in thought beneath this beautifully spacious structure, an open-faced columnar veranda: something like a Doric temple, a shelter, a place of earth.

"You have an interesting family." In a tone so unremarkable that for seconds Hinton does not register the incongruity of the content. He turns again to see the profile fixed once more, notices the small section missing from the ear that is turned towards him.

"You know my family, sir?"

"I do. You also know mine. You met my son once, on a train. But that is by the by. Your family is the interesting family."

A flood of nervous, glandular energy.

"Should I know your name?"

"I hope not." The man examines his palms. "The Japanese lent us a lot of ships in China last year. British-made ships. They're good, but they're starting to build their own. Do you keep in touch with your Japanese friends?"

Hinton does not know what to say. After a pause for an answer, the man continues.

"Your middle boy, he's gone off the rails, as they say. No longer hopping the railroads. He's settled with a travelling troupe. But he's not the interesting one. That eldest boy of yours. Clever man. He's the one has his father's brain apparently. Mining in Mexico. I would ask how often you correspond, but it's once a month. We're friends with Diaz but if you hear anything from the North we're always interested."

Howard shuffles. "I fail to understand."

The man turns to face him.

"Plenty of time for that. The one really worries me is your sister-in-law."

"Alicia?"

"Ethel. Friend of Stepniak."

"Ethel? Ethel is a novelist."

The smallest flicker of the eyelids.

"Ethel is friend to anarchists. Greenwich five years ago."

"I don't follow."

"Martial Bourdin. The clue was in the name, unsure why he wasn't picked up sooner, truth be told."

Hinton searches his memory for clues. "I do not know the name."

"Anarchist. Failed bomber. Friend, also, of Stepniak. Your publisher. Sonnenschein. German Jew. Friend, also, of Stepniak. You will see that I imagine a form of network. You as relay."

Hinton cannot abide this any longer. He places his hands on

his thighs and leans forwards. "Might I have your name? I am certain I should know it."

"No need. My job is to observe the Observatory. You have no need of my name. You sat in the time seat up there?" He points towards the clock-house. Hinton follows his indication.

"Where they read the sidereal clock?"

The voice turns to a hiss. "Correct. I would not have an anarchist in that seat. Able to recalibrate the national time."

Howard is defensive. "I think you mistake me, sir."

The man tips his head. "Perhaps. That's why we're having this conversation." And suddenly his tone shifts. He is genial once more. "You play tennis?"

"Pardon?"

"You should. It is a significant game. Angles. Reactions. Responses. Cut across the grain of the ball."

James Hinton to Charles Howard Hinton

Jamaica, 1875

My Dearest Howard, Good loving, eldest son, happy yet much to be pitied, my joy yet a source of so much sorrow to me when I think of what I might have done and been for you – I write to you now the deepest, most serious, earnest, most heartfelt letter I have ever written. It is a letter of confession, of council, of entreaty. My boy I have erred. Do not you walk in my steps nor listen to my voice. I mean about human life and its laws and methods. I have made innumerable mistakes in blindness and self-confidence. Let them be at least a means of keeping you more wise. Do not believe or trust any one of my thoughts about it now. Perhaps they are not all false utterly, but that must be for a long future to judge and assuredly they are utterly one-sided, partial and blind. I have been very very foolish, puffed up with folly and making disastrous blunders. My boy, I did not read the Bible. I did not, or but seldom and lightly prayed. You know it was so, you have even felt as I know partly what I more intently but not too intently feel now. If you are kept wise and happy that will compensate me in part (but what can really compensate in this world poor mamma yes and your sisters too!) for my terrible errors. Pray daily, earnestly, sincerely; with true heart-searching. Remember, he who trusts in his own heart is a fool. The heart is deceitful above all things and desperately wicked. Watch, for there is a terrible adversary within us at heart; & do not aim at far off things to which you are not called; but keep a true sincere affection and care for all those persons who are around you in the way of direct duty. Love, think of, study for, care deeply and truly for the interests of everyone whom God places in your path. That would have kept you, if I had done this I should not have made such terrible mistakes. I sought far off things and neglected near ones at hand and the first is bitter indeed. Dear son, do not

go to Mrs Boole, do not let her any more be one of yr friends.
Keep from all contact with her & do not say anything against
her but this I lay on you as an absolute charge. Do not be uncivil
but do not spend any time more in her company. Please do this
for me. Be as kind as ever you can to her children. But absolutely
and totally avoid her influence for ever. My son, I trust you will
be able before long to marry. Choose a good, quiet, amiable,
pious wife as much Mamma as ever you can (you have a perfect
model before you and I trust you will not err) & then go to her,
study her feelings, rejoice in her love, share her joy; the things she
loves and needs & do not bind her to your objects to her fatigue
and distress; not even to the least objects. Let her councils unite
with your own and live a united life; every action guided by your
joint wisdom – the wisdom of both will not be too much for this
difficult and deceiving world. Read the Bible earnestly. Proverbs,
Psalms, Gospels, Epistles. Know them, reverence them. The
world has not been mistaken in holding it so good and sacred
a guide. I do not say believe the inspiration, or have any theory
about them; turn away your thoughts from yourself totally. Do
not think about yourself, but love. You see I spent so much time
over those MSs in one way or another it was my own thoughts
almost always before me. I had no time for others. Be not highminded but fear. Do not think that you know many things, you
cannot. Do your own duty well; in the very best and completest
way and attending to it diligently in the fear of the Lord. And in
other things trust to those who know. Especially in money matters – let those who have studied this attend to them for you.

Do not speculate. Remember the world is full of people going
about trying to get their money from those who have any. Only
trust those you know with things that are not their business.

Mr Savory had a good plan of giving his money over to his
wife and she invested it for him . . . of course telling him.

I have made my boy all the errors I warned you against. You

will very likely find the same tendencies in you. Do not turn a deaf ear to advice. Take note of the least hints and search sedulously and carefully to see if they are not there. Do not be puffed up. Think other people's thoughts as likely to be true as your own. Especially they are likely to be much truer about things that are close to you & exciting to your feelings. While to them they are at a distance and matters of no special interest. Listen to the proofs; even to the gentlest suggestion – especially to those. Avoid, haste from, flattery; it is a fatal poison; little, little pleasure, full of pain and destruction. Do not think about yourself – but _live_; with a true heart – fervently. Be kindly affectioned. O How the Bible is full of beautiful precepts which if I had loved & kept my soul wd now be full of rejoicing, my hands full of gifts; my house full of light & gladness – instead of such darkness and sorrow. O How is it being demands grey hairs with sorrow to the grave & put such a rash blight upon all your young lives, do you at least forgive me. God's hand has been upon me, & my brain was overwrought so that I have not been capable of seeing truly. I sought to do so much, as you know.

Above all, Howard my son, reverence the purity of women. Let it be a sacred, sacred thing to you: reverenced, honoured in your inmost heart.

Avoid being in haste to make changes. Remember that there are many many things to come together; that seeds take time to grow and that the world obeys a law of _seasons_. It is not ours to know them – let your actions where they are designed to affect society in wide respects be done not private in your own way or strength but in large and wide consultation & with people _unlike_ as well as like yourself. Accept gladly all events & circumstances which would be likely to act as a check upon what you are disposed to do. Be thankful for that. For instance if I had taken Dr Cassell as a partner how infinitely better than selling to Mr Dalby. (Really, really, I had no right to sell. I ought not to

*have done it besides its being so stupid.) Recognise God's hand
in checks and limitations & do not be in haste to overstep them
or put them aside – God is guiding us if we will be guided. <u>Look
for his guidance always</u>: there is other misguidance soliciting us
also, especially if we begin to trust ourselves – look always carefully to see which is God's guidance, which is not; which is the
path of prudence, humility, near and direct duty; wh. of haste,
of pride, of self-choice. Do not trust intellectual power, neither
your own nor others'. It is not enough; it may be a lambent
flame, preying on corruption.*

*Reverence age. When you hear an old man praying for
another man that he may be guarded against pride of intellect
do not desire the danger. It is real & great enough. Consult
your fellows in great and doubtful things. Make a confidant of
your doctor, & <u>when you are advised to rest</u>, rest. Do not hurry
things together but let them come one by one, & see if a future
time is not really the best for some. For instance, how much
better it would have been for me to have collected the money for
printing my MSs & then have done it at my leisure, after I had
left practice (if I left it) or when I had taken a practicer.*

*And as to this whenever anyone comes in your way (espe-
cially a good striving earnest man) think if you cannot help him;
cannot perchance spare him some work, in which he and you
may eventually help each other. By this means you may perhaps ascertain angels' wishes as I should have done if seeing Dr
Cassell's wishing for work so much I had offered him a practice-
ship. It would indeed have been entertaining an angel for me.
Think of the humblest practical wants of all the people who
come about you & rejoice in helping. But don't do riskful things.
Be not highminded but fear. Even when you have saved money
remember that riches make themselves wings to fly away.*

*I trust and believe my son that you have too much of your
mother's and grandfather's blood in you to need so many of*

the principle cautions my soul looks back upon with tears as of blood, wishing, wishing, oh wishing so that I had followed them.

But, dear son, one mitigation there is for some of my follies, & that is that overfatigued and exhausted my brain rendered me unable to use my judgement. I ought to have avoided it; a little sense & humility would have enabled me to do so, & I might have retained for me invaluable things that I have lost.

But after a certain point I had not the real exercise of my judgement. Never let yourself get into this state; or being so listen to any least hint and abstain from all important action till you have recovered. If I wd. have listened we should have had a happy home still. One thing more, do not have needless transaction with people you do not & cannot heartily sympathise. Do that only with friends – soul friends, people whom it will rejoice you & do you good to have for friends and counsellors for ever. Be very, very sure of this.

Dear Mamma is still <u>very poorly indeed</u>. My terrible act, done in such ~~haste~~ a state of incapacity has given her I fear a shock she never can thoroughly recover from. Oh How, the agony is terrible to me and must be. Notice these things, dear, that I say – that you may avoid any such terrible cruelty – You see, boy, how after leaving my practice the excitement of my mind continued and increased instead of closing.

It was not my practice I needed to part with but my thoughts to lay aside. And by the by I want to say: <u>do not be too much in the habit of writing down your thoughts</u> – a very moderate amount of that is enough – my overbalance comes from that in the end & it keeps one a great deal too much in contact with one's own ideas instead of others'.

We may come back soon after Xmas. We want to do so very much. ~~Will you consult with~~ Will & Aunt Carrie & Marianne & Ada about a house for us. We think of a little place at

Lewisham e.g. for Willy to be with us where we can live very cheaply; but for Mamma to go first to Grandmamma's for a time.

It is a terrible penitence I have dear son. Learn to be not highminded but to care and listen to those who love you. Do not trust yourself, you have – must have – many many weaknesses, do not trust your own wisdom to guide you. Reverence this great structure of human society which so many ages have laboriously built up: look at the vast elements of good in it and honour and love them, & thank God for them & lead all your energies to extend and strengthen them.

And let our love be not in word but in truth and deed in doing the things those you love or should love wish or need: not in talking but in acting, thoughtful yielding, and working. Do not carry out your own plans regardless of cries of pain but stop for them – for the very least and slightest & tenderly carefully perfectly succour & help; give up your ways to God's as shown you by the wants & case & wishes of the least even of those present to you & around you. There you will meet him closest & truest – in those hearts and souls – O my boy you will have to forgive me indeed & love me in spite of what might well have broken it will you – always?

Turn utterly away from all I have written on social subjects: utterly, & put it quite aside. If you know of any copies of <u>Thoughts on Home</u> burn them, or get them burnt. <u>Be sure of this</u>. Never mention anything about them, or about me & my views. I made there a most sad mistake: bury it in oblivion, & destroy the records of it. Put away absolutely all sexual thoughts – tell Willy these things like a brother to him indeed. He will need one. Let him be, above all, your care. I thank God for all the gifts he has given you of teaching and helping the young. Use them to the very best of your ability & be always thoroughly cheerful sober & gracious too. Life is a terrible *thing; and its possible falls are terrible: never can anything (with God's grace garnered by prayer always necessary) guard us from them but sober quiet earnestness (prompted and guided by sincere personal tender love & practical quick gentle responsive care for those dear about us – care not for the bodily wants only nor even chiefly, & through this will you be strong & quick but even more for the soul, the moral good.)*

We may possibly be detained here. And you may perhaps have to do the executors' part for Father in the spring. I will write to you again about this.

You will find your life, How, a difficult, different task, thro' me, so be girt up to it: it will succeed well & be a great joy and bountiful in the end.

By the bye, keep by all means possible the boys from mastur-bation (if ever you have practiced it flee from it as from Hell). Help Willy in this also, he needs it much. Look after him your very best – Tell me by the bye how you must do about finishing at Oxford. Would one more session do.

Good bye my dear Man. Be sure you write to me often and do all I have said.

Your most loving father.

Mamma sends her best love.

My best blessing. God my God be wth you always act as tho' his face shone upon you.

Your loving father

James

11.

Hawkers and hucksters, sawdust on the ground inside the tents, hay bales outside them. Hirsute women, preternaturally bald men, outsized hermaphrodites, inked skin and greased limbs. Jambo points this way and that, identifying "freaks and fuckups", doddering, leering, spilling his booze. Willy takes swigs, pausing to watch games of chance to ponder how the rigging works – balls flying under cups, shirt sleeves dangled, directions never direct.

A poster outside a bell tent and a shouter to outstrip them all pronounce THE GREAT RUMPELSTILTSKIN: The size of half a man, the strength of two. A fighting challenge, all-comers, twenty bucks to the man can best the dwarf.

"Why don't you have a go, Willy?" says Jambo. "Lookitim. You can have that. You can take him down. That guy. He's as good as a dwarf, Willy. You're college squad."

William swigs and grumbles: "Beneath me."

"He's beneath everyone, Willy! Lookitim. He's a dwarf. So funny. Beneath us all."

William swaggers: "No, I mean, it's not right. It's like bullying. You know?"

"Aw, Willy," pleads Jambo, "my heart bleeds, it really does, but you could win us more booze, Willy. I'm clear out. I'm sad for you, but you gotta do it for me. For the suds, Willy."

"Why don't you do it yourself?"

Jambo simpers. "He might be a dwarf but he ain't put out to fight if he ain't no good. I'm no sap. I can't rassle for shit, Willy, you know that." Jambo cowers.

William approaches the hawking man, the BIG MAN, the shouter. "What's your boy like?"

"100% killer. His mother loved a mule, you hear what I'm saying? He got kicks, he got grit, he don't spit the bit. He's the Rumpelstiltskin. Spin your ass into gold, boy."

William swigs and thinks. "Twenty bucks?"

The BIG MAN sizes William. "Looking at you, boy, I'll give you twenty-five and one bottle this hooch. He gonna eat you alive, college boy. Chew you up like a vej-jay-table."

Jambo spits, but it's dry spit, booze spit. Comes out like a string.

Willy shrugs. "Reckon I'll give him a go."

The BIG MAN spins to the crowd. "WE GOT US A BRAVE MAN, LADIES AND GENTLEMENG. A challenger for Rumpel. This boy thinks he can win."

Cackling as the mass moves. "Boy don't look much." "Boy don't speak much." "Like fighting a child." "Which one?"

William pulls off his shirt.

Rumpelstiltskin. His fingernails and toenails, gnarled and filthy, thickened and twisted. Stubble on his chin like filed iron on a magnet, hair cropped to his head. Scar tissue and burn tissue, white ridges upon his scalp. Corroded, corrosive.

--

Willy twists his elbow towards the dirt, pins the dwarf. Can feel sharp nails in his ribs, doesn't care, anaesthetised by drink and adrenaline. He's the king of this man. The king of this ring. King dingaling. The bell tolls the round and he's whipped to his feet by the BIG MAN.

"A CHAMPION win. He's the greatest! He's the MAIN man in the ring. He's a good GUY. What's your name, son? What a win! Made the little guy feel the pain."

His arm is lifted to the air for him.

"Here's your prize, son. Take a swig."

William gulps at the liquor. Oh sweet Jesus. Jehosephat. Makes his throat tingle the way down. Grins at the hawker. Sweet Jesus and his sister Jane.

"That's the good juice, isn't it, son? That's the medicine. You'll get some cunt out of this. You're the MAN, son."

William wobbles. Grimaces. The BIG MAN slaps him on the back.

"It's strong beer, right? It's hard to take but it's good for you. Makes a man of you. Big man already, bigger after this. Makes your balls grow lower, son. Gives you meat, am I right?"

Clutches his genitals.

"That's it boy, makes your prick stand. Ripe for all that cunt. Kicking a dwarf. BIG MAN like you son. Real big man."

Leads Willy off, Jambo whipping drool from his face, shouting after: "Willy! Willy! Get the prize'n come back, right?"

The Four Brothers, a story by Lafcadio Hearn

Ueno Satoshi, the daimyo of Shioya in Tochigi province, had four sons: Ichiro, Eiji, Kichiro and Katsuro. The four were as thick as thieves: each continually tested himself against his brothers in a perpetual contest to impress his father. Each wrestled and hunted, shot arrows in archery competitions, and undertook errands and labours. Each became increasingly skilled as a warrior, though each neglected the fine arts and meditation.

One spring day, the young men were hunting in the woods on the side of Aoyama when they came across a valley they had never before noticed. Ichiro led his horse down the steep sides of the ravine and the brothers came to a quiet clearing by a small river. Seated on a rock in the middle of the river, the disc upon its forehead glinting in the sun, was a kappa, snoozing beneath its shell.

Eiji exclaimed in delight: "A kappa! We must capture it for our lord. He will reward us for our ingenuity."

The brothers agreed, though Kichiro warned them: "Kappa are very cunning creatures. We must take care in our approach."

The four brothers had heard of kappa in the folk stories the people of their province told each other. Kappa were mysterious beings, mischievous and tricky, and able to change their colour to conceal themselves against any background. They were the size of monkeys and just as agile on land and in the water, possessing thin legs and webbed feet and hands. They kept their possessions in a pouch upon their bellies and their bodies were covered by a thin, smooth fur. The stories told of how kappa would drain the milk from cows, by lying beneath them and piercing their udders with sharp teeth; and of how the dish upon their heads must be kept brim full of water from their home river.

The kappa on the rock was reading from a piece of paper covered in writing in a hypnotic spiral script.

On seeing the brothers approach, the kappa placed its paper within its pouch.

"What are you reading?" asked Kichiro.

The kappa chuckled. "That is not a very polite way to ask."

Ichiro bowed deeply. "Honourable friend kappa, my brother does not mean to be rude. He is young and impetuous. We are all curious, however. We have never before met a kappa."

"I have met many humans," replied the kappa, "and they are rude and selfish creatures."

At this, Kichiro became angry, but his brothers urged calm upon him.

The kappa continued, an unpleasant smile providing a glimpse of his sharp, small teeth: "This piece of paper describes the way to another world, a world more spacious than this one. It is a place in which things that are inside are brought outside and there are no secrets between beings. In this place all creatures live together peacefully."

"We would like to travel to this wonderful place," said Eiji.

"But you would spoil it, with your fighting and arguing," claimed the kappa.

"Were we able to find such a place, we would have enough space for ourselves," countered Ichiro.

"I can give you this piece of paper," replied the kappa, fishing it once again from his pouch, "but you will need to offer me something in return. What I would like is a human companion to assist me in my work."

The brothers gathered together to speak. Each argued why it should not be he who went to serve the kappa. Being unable to select amongst themselves, and each being unwilling to sacrifice this or that brother, they decided to take the paper from the kappa. They counted to four and lunged at the creature, falling all five into the river. Ichiro emerged first, clutching the sheet of paper. Eiji followed. And then Kichiro. But Katsuro and the kappa had disappeared.

"It's skin was like glass," said Eiji.

"It was gone before we reached it," claimed Ichiro.

"What will we tell our father?" asked Kichiro. They were terrified by what they had done and fearful of returning to face their master.

Ichiro held out the paper. "Perhaps the kappa has taken Katsuro to the place described here," he suggested.

"But we can't read it," sighed Eiji.

"There is a priest in Nikko who can read Kappanese," said Ichiro. And so the brothers set off in search of the priest.

At the temple, the brothers found the priest praying. They waited patiently for him to finish, before asking him to translate the kappa's paper.

"You have been misled," said the priest, reading the kappa's script. "This is not a set of directions, but a filthy kappa story. It describes a banquet of human children."

"How will we recover our brother?" asked the three.

"That is quite simple," replied the priest. "You must return to the kappa its piece of paper, with a sincere apology."

"How will we find the kappa?" asked Ichiro.

The priest was thoughtful for a while and then replied: "The kappa world is at all times very near our own. One must only know how to pass objects between the two."

Saying this, the priest began to fold the paper in two, in three, in four; then to fold it back upon itself, in two, in three, in four. This folding he repeated, and as the paper began to take on extraordinary form, it slipped out of this world. Before their eyes a limb appeared, unnaturally folded upon itself. It began to unfold, and as it did so, a torso followed, uncrumpling itself; a head, expanding from a dot; more limbs, in sickening swirls. Katsuro was reborn into their space.

The brothers celebrated to be fourfold once again.

The priest was commended to their master and his temple endowed for one hundred years.

The brothers never again took anything by force, and each learnt the skills of paper-folding and calligraphy; though Katsuro was thereafter only ever able to write backwards, and upside-down.

12.

Within the panelled retiring rooms of the Celestial Club, Burgess introduces Howard to the architect Bragdon. Bragdon has become enchanted by ideas. Architect by training and Theosophist by persuasion, he dreams of an architecture that may contribute to and encourage higher spatial being. Architecture should correspond to nature, and nature, as Emerson so succinctly observed, geometrizes. Given a fourth-dimensional nature, as he is persuaded by Hinton, by Helmholtz, by Zöllner to be the state of the matter, then a correspondent architecture should evince a higher-dimensional geometry.

The means of accomplishment of this are, to Hinton's ear, somewhat vague. Bragdon will incorporate tesseract motifs into his buildings. He will treat the solid as a plane. He will observe harmony. He has theories of his own, he tells Hinton. That sleep is fourth dimensional. That dream, therefore, is when the cross-section of the fourth dimension most closely matches with our own consciousnesses. He would have Howard endorse his theories. Howard, as ever, is at great pains to be polite, to acknowledge the homage to his own work without ever managing to commit. Burgess, a confidant now of several years' standing, notes Howard's awkwardness, his slight hesitations and the denatured form of his smile. Burgess withholds contribution long enough to amuse himself at Howard's attempt to agree, without agreeing, that genius is in fact a fourth-dimensional quality granted to very few thinkers. Burgess eventually comes to the rescue with some witticism and his own theory, well-tested over the years, that nonsense is the correspondent of the fourth dimension in literature.

Burgess and Hinton beg their leave of Bragdon and make their way to the Philanthropic Society dinner. Since his paper on the fourth dimension to the Philosophical Society, Howard has been welcomed into the Society circuit. Here, his ideas are given a hearing, something that he has not experienced within the academy, and he is grateful for it. He has been asked to make a toast for the dinner: to female philosophers! Burgess has joked that one must by nature be philosophical as a woman, given the particularity of the feminine experience: of motherhood, specifically. One would not wish that on anyone.

In his researches for his toast, breaking from his work at the Almanac, Hinton had installed himself in the Library of Congress. He had found himself distracted by the works of Hildegard of Bingen. He had never before read her. Immersed in the original texts of her work, he became dizzied by their power. Visions of fiery light, of the sparks of God. He found himself desirous of such visions; willing to accept pain to achieve them. He wished for them: a curious sensation, wishing for the apocalyptic. He satisfied himself with lifting a choice quotation and returned to work.

All through dinner he has endured a queer experience. Scanning the room, the seated, rubicund diners, he recognises every single face at first glance. Faces from his distant past startling him again and again. What is Chittenden doing here? That can't be that man from the ship, what was his name? The Reverend Hayes? On each occasion, at the second glance, the familiarity dissolves. Again and again it happens. An old student of his. Grierson or some such. The albiquin! Surely not. The toastmaster calls upon him and he stands, glimpsing the man from the observatory at the back of the room. Steeling his nerve, Hinton reads from his notes:

"My Lords, Ladies and Gentlemen, Learned and Generous Friends,

"It is with indescribable gratitude that I acknowledge the kind invitation to propose this toast. There are no subjects dearer to my heart than philosophy and the feminine.

"From Hildegard of Bingen, great visionary, seer of stars and heavenly castles, I offer an initial exhortation: 'Glance at the sun. See the moon and the stars. Gaze at the beauty of earth's greenings. Now, think.'

"And while you think, my ladies and lords, please raise your glasses.

"To Harriett Martineau, a great Englishwoman, for her translation of August Comte, as fine a work of philosophical scholarship as graced the last century.

"To Margaret Fuller, formerly of this very parish, whose *Woman in the Nineteenth Century* stands as a luminous work of genius.

"But above all others, to Hypatia of Alexandria, remembered as a character in Mr Kingsley's popular fiction. To her I offer thanks for the astrolabe, that most precious of ancient navigational tools; I offer thanks again for a commentary upon the conical sections, a geometer's pleasure; but above all else, I ask you to drink in celebration of Hypatia's realisation that there lies a greater truth behind tangible nature; that geometry itself is the paradigm of this transcendent truth.

"My Lords, Ladies and Gentlemen,

"To Female Philosophers!"

--

"Quite the toast, How." Burgess is typically animated. "Cosmic. Nice. I'm sure they didn't want too much meta-geometry. I think you pitched it about right."

Hinton can think only of the faces arrayed in the audience. As he had sat down, he had sought each out again only to find all disappeared. A momentary hallucination? Has he spent too long in the library? Read too much Hildegard? He yearns for external corroboration to settle his doubt-filled mind. "Gelett, do you remember the albiquin?"

"Hah! How could I forget! I thought we'd never get out of that place. Sure he was planning to kidnap us. My guarantee of your endorsement was all that saved us. When he produced the hashish . . ."

"Yes, yes, a most illuminating evening," hurries Hinton, before pausing to impart the seriousness of his inquiry. "Gelett, have you seen him since?"

"Thank gawd, no! Of course, I have kept him abreast of your changing address . . ."

"I'm being deadly serious, Gelett. Was he present this evening?"

Burgess now reads the tone. "You are worried, How? You're looking a touch peaky."

Hinton receives the implied reassurance and resumes their progress towards the entrance to the lift. Box follows box through the opening, rising at an equal rate. Howard watches three past to judge the timing and steps into the fourth as it passes. Burgess has hesitated. He continues talking behind his friend, "I'll take the next one I guess, How . . ." Hinton is transferred now into the mechanism as it takes its carousel of boxes ever upwards. He is to exit at the fourth floor.

Hinton adores this machine, its gentle, perpetual cycle of carriages rising ever upwards, looping over the top of the chain and descending at the same rate. It is calming, the eternal cycle of rise and fall; seasonal. Bragdon should see this machine, thinks Howard. This is most properly a higher-dimensional architecture. He feels its kinship with the phonograph disc. He revels in its name, acknowledging its heavenly progress: Pater Noster. His mind runs involuntarily on to prayer.

As the first floor passes he casts his thoughts to his own father. He feels his neck tighten. He recalls, as always, the same conversation. I have a friend, Father, who is considering taking a mistress. Given his father's work, he had justifiably expected the gift of license. Instead he received a conventional warning. The cost is greater than the benefit. Well might his father have known. Well might he have taken heed. This memory is parasitical on his mind. It worms at him. It has taken up residence and will not depart but fattens itself on his experience.

He feels a clenching at the base of his skull, an instantaneous blooming of pain from his upper vertebra into his cerebellum; a gasp that becomes a choke and a rapid blink as a shadow passes from this bunching, muscle in abject spasm, a collapse of sensation like ink dissipating in water. As he passes the second level he sees only those who would enter the paternoster step back in alarm before they sink beneath him, cropped by the contracting rectangle of the open cell as it meets the ceiling and continues to become the between of the floors, a layer of wood and brick that becomes once more space as he reaches the third level which begins to unfold, his body sinking to the base of the coffin, the mycelium of stroke spreading its tendrils throughout the organ of thought and eclipsing every last shard of consciousness with its moribund root.

Above the fifth floor, the paternoster inverts, and Hinton's body – base flesh – is flipped within the box – purest geometry – as it begins its descent towards the confused Burgess on the fourth floor who seeks his friend outside of the lift and the appalled women on the second floor and the alarm that will be raised to bring the endless motion to a halt.

Hinton's corpse will be removed. The lift will recommence.

--

Sebastian arrives at White Pines. Through the porch, with its rocking chairs. The door is unlocked as always, the community priding itself on openness. He calls inside and a voice answers. Ralph Whitehead shuffles down the stairs.

"Well I never, my boy. Come, come, a drink, we must have a drink."

Ralph leads Sebastian through the corridors, hung with tapestries, in at least one of which he recognises Marie Little's style. They pass handmade furniture, pieces that mimic the form of the trees from which they've been carved, curving and arcing. Pots on every shelf in muted glazes. Ralph fetches a bottle. He has been experimenting with making grappa. He misses it from his Italian travels. It is made from the skins of the grapes, so he can get his raw materials very cheaply. He is using a still that was formerly used to make potato spirit. Some Poles of his acquaintance. Musicians. The flavour is good, he says. Sebastian sips and when the sting hits his cheeks swallows quickly, gasping at the strength of the spirit.

Ralph chuckles. "It's good stuff, is it not?" He becomes immediately serious. "Sebastian, I have written to your mother, but perhaps you do not know. I was heartbroken to hear of Howard's death. I just don't know what to do." He appears forlorn. He appears older in that very moment. Sebastian has no doubt that he is sincere. Ralph gives a summary of the letter. He shares some stories of their youth together. Sebastian listens to the by-now-familiar tales of undergraduate derring-do. He has heard the road-building stories innumerable times. The list of the names of their great friends. How his father allowed various debauched gentlemen access to re-enter college through his window after the gates had been locked. How his father was a good man, a kind man, with a great mind.

Sebastian feels the tears at the bottom lid of his eye as a slight burden. He thanks Ralph for his kind words then stands and embraces him, realising it is the kindest thing to do. Ralph clings on to his back and sobs quietly, before disengaging and apologising. "And how is Mary?" he asks.

Sebastian responds truthfully. That he suspects that she is still in shock, thinking to himself that in all truthfulness it can be difficult to tell. That he and George have taken care of all family matters and funeral arrangements, thinking to himself that his mother would happily have done this herself. That the letters mean a lot to her, knowing that they mean much more to George and him. That he worries for her finances because Father was not very successful in that regard, knowing that she cares not for material goods as long as she has books. She does not seem to feel as much as he does. Her stoicism is complete. It always has been.

Ralph promises to send some money, it is the least he can do, him a wealthy man through no work of his own, and Sebastian admires his honesty. Ralph says he will be there for the funeral. Sebastian gives him the date. Says he plans now to see Marie. Senses a fresh awkwardness that is perhaps a concealed form of jealousy and makes his excuses.

He walks the path down from the main house towards the edge of the estate and the memories tug at his consciousness. He passes the old studio. That first Saturday night in the art studio; that was when he fell in love. With the place and with Marie.

Byrdcliffe was an escape. Ma and Pa enjoyed thinking themselves outside of rigid society, talking about aesthetics with Ralph and Jane and then retreating to their cabin to drink Ma's teas made from leaves. They'd paid some men to put their house up on the edge of the estate, Ralph letting them have the land for nothing. Went there every break, every time they could get to upstate New York from Columbia. He and his brothers could use the place whenever they could get there also and he dreamed one day of coming through the door and finding Eric sitting in the cabin with his feet up, some amazing story to tell. Sure enough it never happened like that but he still believed it might.

That one Saturday night, that was Bohemia! Artists from Europe and New York, Californian musicians; fiddle players and singers, dancers in dresses they'd woven themselves on the looms at Marie's house. They drank potcheen and smoked Virginian tobacco from clay pipes. The second night was the end of term costume ball. He went dressed as Huck Finn – easy on the costume! Willy, before he did his own disappearing act, was cavorting with a serving girl called Hilary. Marie had jigged towards him, a whirl of red and green, and issued her first instruction to him: "Dance with me, young man. I enjoy your poor clothing."

As he approaches The Looms he wonders how Marie will have him act on this occasion. Will she invite him to consider his own tracks across her polished floor? Will she encourage the contemplation of a pattern formed between two branches at pains of a flick from her switch? Might she make him crawl on his hands and knees, all the while speaking in her favoured drawl? Or serve him a home-made broth and chastise him for failing to recognise and adumbrate its ingredients? Might she enact before him some intricate ceremony of her own devising, forbidding him sound or movement?

Did Ralph enjoy Marie's strictures? He knows Ralph has enjoyed Marie. He knows The Looms is built outside the strict limits of Byrdcliffe on the express wishes of Jane, who would not allow Ralph to be alone on the estate with Marie while she remained at Arkady. He is completely mystified by this woman, twenty-one years his senior yet so perfect in her innocence, so needful of regulation, so sweetly strict towards him yet so submissive in their conversation that she calls him her big brudder. He cannot help but wonder if it is normal to be so bewitched by these strange behaviours. He has been surprised at his own pleasure in them. But Marie is a wonder, a tall, commanding, fainting wonder, robed in cloth she herself has dyed from berries. Whip-like in form, with a long plait down her back; her voice insufficiently strong for the instructions for which she uses it. His little sister.

--

They lie on the bank of the lake, adjacent. She takes his hand in hers, little breaths on his neck, her grip decided. She moves his hand and he can feel her smile against him. His hand is placed on warmth which keens into his palm, urging it to return pressure. Her breath is pleased. She picks deliberately at his flies, a whimsical concentration pursing her lips. He watches her as she works without regarding him. His pego is loosed and springs towards his belly, ticking. He fights the urge to twitch his hips. With her lips, she provokes a heat that builds so that he must catch his breath. The breeze excites his freshly wet skin. She takes herself from his palm in urgent and decided fashion and moves one knee across his thighs. Never has he felt such heat, an internal sirocco spreading through his midriff and spending itself through tight pulses into her. He wishes for nothing less than consubstantiation, to merge his flesh with hers so that limb might seep into limb in carnal sympathy.

He lies, eternally tame, as she douches at the lake's edge. The insufficiency of speech presses on his mind: nothing he can say could describe the yaw that has opened within him. Does she sense this? She simply redresses and beckons him, with a giggle, to do the same. Splashes him from the stream. Laughs kindly at his clumsiness. Says to him: "Come now, big brudder, don't look so awful serious." He takes her hand and kisses it, hungrily, hoping again to speak without words, willing her to see his thoughts through his eyes. She looks him up and down and keeping his hand in hers, starts back towards her cottage, trailing her loyal beau. "You're an awfully attractive young man, Sebastian Hinton."

--

Marie and her Seb sit in The Looms, gossiping about residents of Byrdcliffe. All that freedom attracts "types", they agree, acknowledging that they themselves might also fit into this scheme: Sebastian, the railroad-hopping student son of a poet and a patent-examining philosopher; Marie, grand tourist, weaver of artisanal fabrics and mistress to too many. And here, in this wilderness log cabin, they cast intimacies into the log-crackling fire.

"Seb, it need not be said, but I was so sorry to hear of your pa."

Sebastian dips his head.

"You must be missing your brothers."

He bristles. "Why? Why do you say that?"

Marie backs away. "You mistake me. I didn't intend to upset you."

"You might not have meant it but you condescend to me, Marie. Young Seb, the littlest Hinton."

"Sebby, do not take it so, my sweet."

He sulks, and hates himself for it. "I'm the one who runs only so far as the family lodge, right? Hoping the others will show up here."

Marie attempts levity: "I thought you came only for me."

Sensing his over-reaction, Sebastian relents, ever so slightly.

"I do wish Eric would show up. It's been three years now. Ma won't even contemplate the idea that he's dead. Pa was concerned but did not know what to do. George is practical on the matter.

Each year, he says, the odds of him showing up recede. He believes that Eric was unhinged in some way." Sebastian pauses. "All I know is that he isn't sending the begging letters any more."

Marie is sympathetic. "You correspond with George?"

Sebastian raises a shoulder. "Sure. Georgie takes his responsibilities seriously, always has. Always been the big brother to me, despite his own travails. Which have been many. Georgie sends me money to supplement what Ma and Pa give." Corrects himself. "Gave. For books, he writes. Knows it goes on hooch. Doesn't mind. Regular as clockwork. He'll come north for the funeral. And then there's Willy."

Marie becomes husky. "I always liked Willy. He dances well. He's manful."

Sebastian rolls his eyes. "Everyone likes Willy. He's set in his skin. Same Willy from week to week, year to year. Hot-headed, loyal, straight-shooting. Would fight an army for you, if he likes you. Speaks his mind even when it's out of order with the rest of the world. Prefers it when it is."

Marie waits but Sebastian has stopped speaking. She prompts gently. "But he also no longer visits."

Sebastian shrugs. "He's been moving around, running the railroads. We all run the railroads, family tradition. Was talking about taking a correspondence course, learning to be a firefighter. Stopped by to see me in Jersey last year but haven't seen him since. I had been wondering anyway if I should go visit with him."

Marie looks earnest. "You should, Sebby. You should go find your kin. Seems to me like you miss them. You need them."

"I do miss him, Marie. I miss Willy."

The matter is settled. "Go find him."

1883 Marriage solemnised at the Register Office in the District of Strand in the County of Middlesex

No.	When Married	Name and Surname	Age	Condition	Rank or Profession	Residence at the time of Marriage	Father's Name and Surname	Rank or Profession of father
57	Nineteenth January 1883	John Weldon	28 Years	Bachelor	Electrical Engineer	Charing Cross Road	Arthur Weldon	Optician (Deceased)
		Maud Florence	25 Years	Widow	---	Belvoir Street, Norwich	Robert Wyndham	Gentleman (Deceased)

Married in the Register Office by Licence before me, Anthony Hart, Deputy Registrar, Charles J. Dorrell, Superintendent Registrar.

This marriage was solemnised between us   John Weldon   in the presence of   A. H. Maddock

    Maud Florence   C. B. Snell

13.

Prairie oysters. The chef stands over a vat of hot oil, scooping out crumb-fried treats. A young woman eulogises excessively. "These are delightful!"

Sebastian takes a poke.

"They're a natural aphrodisiac," cheers the chef. "Bone fide. Don't come any more natural than Ohio steers."

A young farmhand sprays words through a mouthful. "They're chewy."

"And yours are tender, I suppose? These glands are as fresh as the new-born day. Collected this pale from the Northrop ranch this very morning. Promise you stamina you will *not* have experienced." A giggle from the young lady.

The realisation is dawning. Well, what the hey, it's just another part of the animal. He eats chitterlings and enjoys them. These are chewy, for sure, but he's had worse. No need to be squeamish.

He ate brains with Pa the last time they breakfasted at Princeton.

Sheep brains whipped up with two eggs and fried in a skillet. Creamy, buttery, giving and forgiving: food for the soul and the mind! Sweet, crumbling biscuits, mellow, floury; rich, rib-sticking gravy. Pa had rhapsodised the incorporation of the neural matter, fantasised greater empathy with the ruminant from which it came, visions, transportation, the sharing of the ovine consciousness, the way only his father could. Sebastian thought desiring communion with a flock animal an elevated form of stupidity, though remarked to his friends at the time that it was still legal in certain states and positively encouraged in Arkansas.

He felt a particularly keening guilt when he made jokes of his father. The old man was such an easy target, so sweet of nature, so unworldly. Sebastian's friends adored the old man and laughed all the harder at the tang of filial impropriety to Sebastian's pot-shots, knowing full well that they could not rag at their own tyrannical papas in the same fashion.

"Hey la bas. You wan hear you future?" A young woman sits on the step outside a caravan advertising fortunes told. Sebastian is a rational young man but he is vulnerable to such notions. He steps up.

"Yes, sure. How much?"

She scans his appearance. "One dime only, young bra."

He fishes out a coin and passes it to her. He follows her into the caravan. It is stifling inside. There is room enough for a table and two chairs. She sits behind the table and beckons him to the chair in front. A deck of cards sits on the table.

"You have any questions you wan ax the cards before we start?"

Sebastian shrugs. "No. No, don't think so. I just want to hear about my luck."

"Sure thing. Thass what I can do." She takes up the deck and shuffles it with great dexterity.

"Alors. I give you twa cards. We gon find you future."

She deals out three cards face down. She tips her head at the first. Sebastian turns it over. The six of spades.

"Seese de eypey. You roday. You run the roads, jump the rails. You travelling man, mon frere." Sebastian ponders the accuracy of this card. She has simply made an assessment based on his appearance. He looks like a traveller with his knapsack. Most everyone at this carny must be some kind of traveller. A safe bet. He turns the next card.

"Un honneur. Le valet de batons. This feller is cooyon. How you say, he's a fool. You gots to watch out for him mon frere. Is he you? Or some other feller?"

Sebastian turns the final card.

"Seese de coops. This is about you as little boy, mon frere. Rememberings."

Sebastian's mind runs at remembering but all he sees are the cards on the table before him: all is foreground, embodied. There is no space.

--

He has walked the length of the carny. He has watched the bronc riders longer than any other act but seen some sights, sure enough. There is a possibility to the place: a sense that norms have been suspended. There is licence here, embodied in the misshapen forms of the carny folk who seem to act stranger than they are. He is unsure whether he finds the freedom troubling or optimistic. The one tent he has avoided seems like the only place remaining in which to seek his brother. A caller lurks outside counting bills. Sebastian asks if he can go in and the caller shrugs without looking up.

Inside is a tight press of rib and arm. Copper-lick sawdust and scried gizzard. A febrile air, booze tang and cattle funk, steamy backs slapping through the flap of the tent to unspent thrills. Hands on backs and palms on legs. Sebastian eases himself between bodies to witness what pens them in so.

A circle drawn in the sand: inside, a figure. Verses come to Sebastian from some instructor or other. Lo now, his strength is in his loins, and his force is in the navel of his belly. Behemoth, chained to a stake at the back of the tent, springing from its squat to lunge this way and that, causing the mass to lurch in retreat at his sorties. Its fist gripped around the throat of a cockerel, a cockerel that bursts into flurries of desperate flapping, its wingspan broad enough to swipe behemoth's abdomen. Sebastian's mind serves him now a sense memory, a nervous revelation, felt at the bottom of the lungs, experienced watching swine at Byrdcliffe, of the unbridgeable otherness of beasts; of the inhuman. This behemoth has a swine's eyes. It has a dog's jaws, teeth bared at the congregation. The crowd revels in the beastliness, so revolting and unworthy of them yet so queasily familiar. Behemoth raises the cockerel and with a sharpened fingernail opens its throat. Blood spits onto the sand and a panic of cockerel feathers bursts into the air. The gathered begin to shriek. Behemoth unclenches its jaw, brings the bird up to its mouth and with a canine flick of the neck separates its head and body. The gathered groan unapologetically. Behemoth drops the corpse, which drunk-dances towards the rim of the circle before tripping to fall. Behemoth drops the head from its mouth. Spent, the gathered guiltily recede.

On its haunches, bare-chested beneath the oil-lamp suspended from the apex of the tent, pitching now, spitting on its chain, behemoth picks feathers from its claret-clammed chin.

Sebastian approaches.

"Brother."

William looks up, quizzical.

"William. William Hinton."

William grunts, resumes his pluck-work.

"Hell's name, Brother. How you get to this?"

"You got a drink? Some fowls taste worsen others."

"Jesus, Willy. You haven't written. Six months at least." Sebastian suppresses the urge to shake him, scream in his face. How can he get through this? Get through to it?

--

Willy has led his brother to a caravan round the back of the tents. It's his home, he says, movable with the show. He was given it by the ringmaster.

Sebastian finds it oppressive. It is filthy.

"How can you live like this, Willy? It's demeaning, man. You're low."

Willy laughs, disinterested, rummages in a compartment under his seat and produces a flask. Pops the stopper and swigs.

"Lower than a snake's ass in a wagon rut, Sebby. You don't even know."

He does not seem to take his predicament seriously. Sebastian struggles to recognise the brother he knew; explosive and angry but never like this. Never defeated.

"You were a good student. I don't understand it. Do you like the way they jeer at you?"

Willy contemplates. He seems on the verge of forgetting the question. He examines his flask, turns it in his hands, allowing the liquid within to catch the light, tilting its surface. "I don't like it so bad."

Sebastian is flabbergasted. "Help me to understand, Brother."

Willy swigs before answering: "It's pure, this thing. It's in me and I let it out. Some people love that, some people hate it, most recognise it's in them too. You never wanted to taste blood? Sure you did. Sure you do! You're a carnivore, Seb, you like the taste of flesh. You might like it cooked, all that civilising of the flesh, but when you see me do what I do you see something older, right?"

Sebastian cannot imagine where this speech comes from. What is this? It is not healthy thought. "You think that's human, to behave like that?"

"It's more than human. It's all we humans is, Sebby, clip away the fine reasoning and a strip of tailorin'."

"But living in this hovel."

"I like it here, lil bro. I like the way we live. It's honest. True. We're a family, we give each other what we need, we don't judge. I can be the geek."

Sebastian looks around the caravan, takes in the objects: bottles, mainly, in all hues of glass. "That hawker, Willy. He's feeding you booze."

William does not even look at his brother to respond, his attention out the window. "You don't like booze? I even like that I need it. I like the savour of the need. I like the reward."

"He's got you trapped."

Now his attention is focused hard at his little brother. "No more trapped than back home and at least here it's true." He pauses, for thought or effect. "You know what's wrong with Ma and Pa?"

Sebastian is careful. "What you mean, Willy? True? I don't follow you."

Willy shakes his head slowly. "I don't know what's wrong with 'em, I only know I can't fix it. No one talked about it, did they? Sure, they was nice. Sure, they loved us. But they wasn't right."

Urgently. "Fix what, Willy? You can't just say this stuff."

"Pa was kind, Ma was kind, but they weren't all there. Pa preferred it away with the fairies."

Sebastian says simply: "Pa's dead."

William squares his shoulders. "Figures. Reason you're here." Takes another swig. "Guess he's happier now. Ma is sad. You know that, right? You see that?"

Sebastian stumbles. "Ma's sad because Pa's dead."

"Ain't that simple. She was sad afore. Sure she's sadder now."

--

A breeze enters the caravan, a freshness that subtracts from the mass of Willy. A young woman, compact and controlled in her movements and bright, a frosted spray of curled hair erupting behind her. Sharp eyes, aquamarines.

She performs a hesitation. "Willy, you never told me you was expecting no one."

Willy perceptibly warms even as he sees her, though maintains his disinterested tone. "This is my little brother, Bridget. Sebastian, meet Bridget, Bridget, meet Sebastian."

"It's a pleasure," says Sebastian, and leans out to shake her hand. Bridget smiles, and shrugs, and reaches back. In the grasping of hands, Sebastian feels the misplacement of digits, tries to adjust, fails. Embarrassed, pulls his hand away too rapidly. Bridget grins. "My special gift." She shows him her hand. Rotates it through one hundred and eighty degrees in front of his face. Thumb on the outside. She raises her left to display a counterpart to the first. Sebastian stares hard and long. The shift from the standard makes him doubt himself.

Bridget dances over to Willy and sits lightly across his lap.

"You never told about your brethren, Willy! Never knew." She strokes his face, using her thumbs to run the shape of his ears.

"What you been at, Bridget?" Willy doesn't seem to care.

"He's a upstanding young man, isn't he? Not like you, rapscallion." She musses Willy's hair.

"You been in the big tent, girl?"

She fidgets. "Aw, no takers for that nonsense this evening, Willy. This is a rodeo crowd. Been working tackle for the Jackson boys."

Sebastian looks direct at Willy. "Willy. Remember Japan? Remember Pa's climbing frame. It's about all I remember from Japan. All I properly remember."

Willy addresses himself to Sebastian. "Brother. I think our business is done. I don't have a message for Ma, nor for George."

He shifts Bridget on his lap. "I think you and I both know, if we're honest, Eric's not coming back."

"I used to love that game. We all did."

Willy looks direct at Sebastian. "I remember it. I can remember it for you. I remember how it played out. I remember I always ended up at one back corner, Eric at the other. How the moves always ended that way."

"Ma's in pain, Willy. Surely. I don't understand. She brought us up. Read to us."

"Pa's dead and it makes no odds whether I'm at his funeral or not."

"It's for her, Willy."

"I think it's for you, Seb. And I think you don't need me. I think I'm surplus to this." Willy is holding Bridget's hands in his own, turning them over. Admiring them. "You just so *dextrous*, girl. You handy."

--

The cards begin to arrive the following day, Howard's collapse having been so public. In the first days their friends in Washington society call with frequency.

Mary receives the Reverend Sterett, Howard's golfing partner. Sterett carries himself with the professional dignity of the pulpit. He eulogises Howard's company in respectful tones. Mary tires swiftly of the fine words and becomes grateful of the cover provided by the veil, her frowns and sighs distorted and concealed. Perhaps, she thinks, this is the true function of the veil: not to shield the widow's grief but to spare her guests her impatience.

Following discussion of the arrangements for the funeral, Sterett even confects to smuggle an inquiry after Howard's golf clubs into his questions around her sons' roles in proceedings.

Will the boys want them, he wonders? Under cover, Mary is able to reply sincerely. "Why, Reverend Sterett, I believe that Howard wished for Sebastian to have them. He has become quite the student of the game." The Reverend Sterett approves heartily of this wisdom and takes his leave swiftly.

Mary finds the jet reminiscent of lacquer-work of Japonerie. These surfaces. She moves around the surfaces. Howard's belongings. She sits within the walls.

She receives a card from a journalist from the *Post*. "Mrs Hinton, we at the *Post* share our deepest condolences." Mary sits down at her desk to reply, detailing Howard's American career, ignoring his many disappointments.

To be alone so suddenly. It is the absent surface of the man she notices now, the interior having so long ago absconded. She had been fond of the surface. The interior, when she glimpsed it, prompted an unsatisfying irritation.

The house is veiled as if it, too, were widowed. The knocker is tied up. The blinds are drawn. Does it chafe at its crepe? Alone, she stares into the jet and probes its reflective surface.

She hopes that Sebastian will arrive soon. In his last he told her that he had located William but that he was not reachable by mail. He had informed William of his father's death. The absence of further explanation communicates fulsomely. William was always such a wilful young man, occasionally wrong-headed in his stubbornness. Mary hopes he will not regret decisions he makes now. One lives with such regrets over the course of one's life, to whose form they mould themselves, responding to phases and shifts in tone.

She has received response also from George, who will make the week-long journey from Mexico, first by steamer and then by train. George and William will be a support. The idea of Eric cannot be approached directly.

SQUARE

☐

Some cards recall fresh memories. Ralph Whitehead describes their first meeting, at Montecito, which seems all too recent to Mary. He lists what they did that stay, describing Mary and Howard's union as "star-blessed". Mary surprises herself by feeling the kindness in this remark. She realises that what people wish to communicate to her is of greater significance than its truth.

William Swan Sonnenschein to Charles Howard Hinton

Dear Mr Hinton,   *25th Feb 1897*

I am in receipt of your letter of 22nd. I fear I am too much of an ordinary-minded individual to fully enter into your thoughts. I consider your speculations, so far as I have examined them, of much interest; but it appears to me that their application to every-day practice is fraught with much risk of error, not to speak of so mean a thing as danger. I should want a greater confidence in the sureness of my own mental strength before I ventured on so hazardous a line of action as such is and ever feel inclined to judge others by the standards of my own timidity: I can only wonder at others' confidence in themselves, & sometimes enjoy it.

I have sent your book to press today ("The New Era of Thought") on the following terms:

We to pay you £30 for the comp?

We to give you 12 copies of the book when out.

Please confirm these terms before the actual printing commences.

I was not aware that you had obtained a foreign appointment. What and where is it?

Yours truly,

Wm Swan Sonnenschein

14.

A small cape covered her head. An item of evening-wear, heavier than a shawl, reaching almost to her waist. A green velvet. A book of epigrams on the bedside table, maroon-bound in calf. A gold inlay.

Four grown sons. All out of the city at present. George out of the country. Eric God alone knows where. Willy, last he heard, heading on to some spit-ball place called Pocatello. Don worry about me lil bro I'm living the free life.

A rubber tube attached to a droplight. Brasswork, those heavy patterns, foxing on the metal. That room, that wallpaper: arabesques, paisleys; the old country. She loved that paper; had it shipped over. The lights unlit. The rubber tube extending beneath the cape. Swirling, proliferating.

She was an accomplished woman who wrote for the English periodicals. She was a poetess. She was a broken pair.

The door was forced open.

She was fully extended on the bed.

The neighbours summoned Dr L. L. Friedrich. That old quack. No use when he's had hours to warm up, next to dead if they had to raise him.

She had been an advocate of suicide, a staunch defender of it in the English periodicals. She had been despondent since her husband's death over a year ago. She'd seemed better. When they'd spoken, she'd seemed so much better. Better than him. He was to accompany her to Byrdcliffe, they'd spoken of it. She would have benefitted.

Illuminating gas.

Dr L. L. Friedrich pronounced her dead.

A book of gruesome epigrams concerning life and death. Swedenborg, probably, the kind of thing newspapermen think gruesome. She was always reading Swedenborg these days. She found it lightened her. Illuminated. She found it comforting to read Swedenborg.

He looked at the flowers, roses, orange-pink, the outer petals about to fall, their jar-water murky. He waited for the earthquake but it did not hit. He waited for the thunderclap but it did not come. He heard his neighbour push her sorry furniture into a new organisation within her rooms and he manipulated the tight muscle under his left shoulder blade that ached when he became tired and he walked through to his bedroom with the intention of lying down but it was too early to sleep as he'd only just raised himself and he knew he had to travel to Washington because none of the others would go or even know or read about it and the letters he would have to write. He walked back to the breakfast table and sat down to quell the vertigo and read a report of the tour of the author Mrs Varney but he did not comprehend the words merely sounded them. The timbre was wrong.

--

There was the death certificate. Preferring to defer the necessary tasks, Sebastian had the cab drop him before Friedrich's house, on the other side of East Capitol. He rang the bell and was welcomed inside with great seriousness by the Friedrichs' maid. She had him sit on a straight-backed Mission chair in the hallway. The doctor himself came quickly, apologising profusely in Austrian-accented English, shaking hands with excessive force and trailing the cologne of the previous days' drink. He led Sebastian into an office and with damp sympathy in his eyes described how little pain there was in death by asphyxiation through gas. Instructed him carefully in what he would now need to do, including taking the death certificate, which he would need to claim the body, to the city morgue. Recommended an undertaker, a true mensch, from Munchen Gladbach, so very honest. Sebastian, wincing internally, accepted with gratitude the documentation. Thanked the good doctor for his years of care and service. Thanked him for services he did not know the doctor had performed but thanked him nonetheless.

He made his way across the road and up to the doorway. Was admitted by Mrs Connelly who lived in 220 and apologised for the mess: they had broken down the door before taking his mother away, God rest her soul, though she did not believe in God, did she, and it was no longer her, not really. Nor would her soul be allowed to rest, given the circumstance, but she apologised for such thoughts. Still, she had been a good neighbour, she said, though prone to gloominess. Should have taken salts, had been recommended them a number of times, kept her own spirits up, swore by them. Sebastian thanked Mrs Connelly as her words pursued him up the stairs to the forced door and his mother's apartment. No one had touched anything, insisted Mrs Connelly, she'd seen to that, and Sebastian thanked her, his voice bouncing down the stairwell, for her vigilance.

Inside was minor disarray, the spectral residue of a panic. No gas smell, thank God, though a turned-over chair and a toppled vase in the vestibule. With little pause or fore-thought he stepped into her bedroom. Someone had made the bed, a small mercy whose benefit he felt in a swell, true kindness rendering him most vulnerable. The cloak mentioned in the newspaper had been folded and placed on the top of a chest. The book of epigrams was by her bedside. Scattered around the bed, papers: letters, documents. He picked one up. "Your loving father, James." From his grandfather, dead before he was born, to his father, dead one year. Nearest to the bed an official certificate, stamped. Names he did not recognise.

He ran an audit: cabinets and chest, a wardrobe, all would need emptying. He doubted there would be much that would be kept. He would need containers for the clothes. A photograph of Pa on the side.

He would make the decisions he needed to, on behalf of George, who had bestowed upon him that right. They had agreed that, after the funeral, they would go through whatever Sebastian had kept. Willy had said he wanted nothing and preferred not to receive any further letters, though Sebastian would write again, offering him the opportunity to reconsider, however forlorn his hope that it would be accepted. Willy's squaring of the shoulders more eloquent than his words.

In the sitting room, before the settee, the item of furniture that he knew would occupy his time. It had traversed a hemisphere, this inscrutable thing. It had sailed from Yokohama, made the journey by train to Princeton; stayed with his parents in Minnesota and Washington; and moved, after the old man had died, here to Ma's apartment. Six jet faces, gently bowed, divided, by a fine grid, into nine squares. The whole lacquered perfectly black. A truly remarkable piece of Japonerie. Craftsmanship of fine skill. His father had worked closely with the maker, a monk befriended at a temple, the family legend went, to create something according to his abstract designs. To Sebastian, the bamboo climbing frame was its skeleton, a cubic grid of three by three by three, fleshed out here in lacquered cedar wood; it was the small sets of cubes his father had sold through the adverts in the backs of his books. He had lost faith in those, towards the end; when Sebastian had brought a set down from the loft and asked him why he didn't use them any more the old man dipped his head and asserted that they might not be worth the great effort they required. He'd been evangelical about them in Japan: had recommended the process as a mental gymnastic to anyone and everyone; a way of training the mind fully to appreciate space. Moved through sequence in the correct way, it was claimed, using the exercises Pa himself had devised, why, it was possible, no, certain, that one could begin to perceive space in its over-ripe fullness. When Sebastian had brought him this old set he seemed merrily defeated; told stories of approving reports he'd received – one from a philosopher who lived in a place like Byrdcliffe in England – of those who had followed the system rigorously and gained great knowledge and peace from it. It had not led him to the expansion of mind he had hoped for, though, not in truth and on reflection, he chuckled. He remained rooted in this space despite the glimpses of the higher space he'd once experienced. Not rooted in this space any longer though, are you, Pa? thought Sebastian.

But this cube, this lacquer-work chest, this was something else. It reflected your vision with its sheen: you could see yourself in it, but could see yourself also beyond it; it was all surface, yet suggested such fathoms in its inky profundity. Never were superficies and regress so well comingled. So too was it a technical marvel. On each face, six of the panels could be opened by depressing the correct square surface to release a sprung catch. It took some familiarity with the chest to know which of the panels was so sprung. He knew the formula by heart though could not remember ever learning it.

There was a panel set in the top-most surface for accessing the central cube inaccessible from each of the lateral faces. This contained within its frame a geometric design: the entirety an octagon, a symmetrical lattice of lines within it describing the squares at each side, the cubes that might be projected from these; smaller squares in the overlapping corners, equilateral triangles contained within further overlaps; an octagon at the centre. Adjust one's perspective and one saw within the entirety – various three-dimensional projections, steps, tetrahedra; from a planar perspective, an arrangement of symmetrical geometric forms: hexagons, stars, rhombi. He knew that this was what his father called the tesseract.

The panel had been forced open to reveal the compartment beneath it, its contents removed somewhere.

Examining other drawers, he found deeds and correspondence. Letters from each of his brothers. Realised the logic – a face for each brother. And yet, he reasoned, if the topmost central cube is accessible from the centre of its face, what of the bottom-most?

He turned it over.

The base was unadorned cedarwood. The edges of a single, central square could be discerned. These he traced with his fingers. He pressed at this square and it unlatched as the other drawers.

Sebastian's breathing became irregular. The walls bowed as if throbbing.

He needed air.

He walked through to his mother's parlour. He approached the mahogany desk. He picked up the framed photograph.

He recalled earthquakes as learnt sensations: lurching, fearful, disturbances of equilibrium at the level of lived earth. A delirium tremens of the solid.

He recalled the climbing frame; a frame for so much of his Japanese memories. He was forever framing: X3, Y1, Z1.

He examined the photograph. He was his family. He was the boy.

Sebastian returned to the box to examine the uppermost compartment. It was empty. Peering at its base he discerned markings on the surface of the wood. He investigated with his fingertips. They were not carved but inked: gave nothing to the touch but grain of wood. He probed and pushed and felt some give. He pushed faster and a catch snicked; the base popped upwards, presenting an edge to be prised. He so prised, and the square rose up revealing a black lacquered underside; a black lacquered space within. Exploring the empty interior cube his hand slipped and his arm fell in. He felt his hand loosed from space. It seemed to go further than it should.

Reaching in he grabbed and pulled a leaf and the whole unfurled and unfolded.

A mille-feuille of notices and intimacies.

Contained by the lacquered space, a bundle of papers tied with a looped ribbon. He pulled these out. The lacquer box was evacuated, its interior made open to the world.

He untied the ribbon. A small daily book. His mother's handwriting.

Did he recall because there was a photograph?

Was the photograph what he recalled?

Nature, Letters Page, 26th March 1885
"Four-Dimensional Space"

POSSIBLY the question, What is the fourth dimension? may admit of an indefinite number of answers. I prefer, therefore, in proposing to consider Time as a fourth dimension of our existence, to speak of it as *a* fourth dimension rather than *the* fourth dimension. Since this fourth dimension cannot be introduced into space, as commonly understood, we require a new kind of space for its existence, which we may call time-space. There is then no difficulty in conceiving the analogues in this new kind of space, of the things in ordinary space which are known as lines, areas, and solids. A straight line, by moving in any direction not in its own length, generates an area; if this area moves in any direction not in its own plane it generates a solid; but if this solid moves in any direction, it still generates a solid, and nothing more. The reason of this is that we

have not supposed it to move in the fourth dimension. If the straight line moves in its own direction, it describes only a straight line; if the area moves in its own plane, it describes only an area; in each case, motion in the dimensions in which the thing exists, gives us only a thing of the same dimensions; and, in order to get a thing of higher dimensions, we must have motion in a new dimension. But, as the idea of motion is only applicable in space of three dimensions, we must replace it by another which is applicable in our fourth dimension of time. Such an idea is that of successive existence. We must, therefore, conceive that there is a new three-dimensional space for each successive instant of time; and, by picturing to ourselves the aggregate formed by the successive positions in time-space of a given solid during a given time, we shall get the idea of a four-dimensional solid, which may be called a sur-solid. It will assist us to get a clearer idea, if we consider a solid which is in a constant state of change, both of magnitude and position; and an example of a solid which satisfies this condition sufficiently well, is afforded by the body of each of us. Let any man picture to himself the aggregate of his own bodily forms from birth to the present time, and he will have a clear idea of a sur-solid in time-space.

S.

Cube

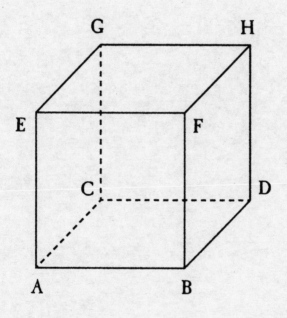

1888
Travels in Nippon
Mary Hinton, née Boole

I stroll after supper. While the maid clears away and Howard retires to his study to work on his MSs. I walk to the residences above the European settlement, away from the swamp and therefore the insects. There is a comfortable bench upon which I sit. It is quite safe: the Japanese stay indoors at this time and would in any case not wish to approach a gaijin woman. Many of the residences are concealed only by the paper screens that the Japanese favour. When first I realised that I became voyeur by the mere fact of casting my gaze at a residence I felt terrible pangs. As a scene of domestic intimacy played out in silhouette before my eyes, the shadows of the Japanese family therein cast upon the paper screens that were the only barrier between their home and the outside world, I tried at first to avert my gaze, a terrible conscience of eavesdropping weighing heavily upon me. Momentarily this eased, as the tenderness to which I was witness overwhelmed my awareness of intrusion.

A male figure: top-knot in the Japanese style. A female figure, the kimono giving a straight line. The male figure is kneeling. The female approaches and kneels before him. His hand reaches to her face. Her hand reaches to take his. She disrobes, the straight lines dissolving to the floor. The two figures move towards each other and become one in shadow: a unit defined by curves and angle of limb.

In awareness of the indiscretion, I returned the following night. The same two figures. On this occasion, though, the male figure moves with violence throughout the squared space. The female is in retreat, locating herself in corners. Her shadow blurs as she moves more deeply into the room, comes into focus as she approaches the screen. A sudden interjection – the extension of a line – and the shadows briefly intersect once more. The female figure falls, head bowed. The male stalks into the depths.

I could not contain this. On my return to the residence I shared the tale. Howard was delighted at my confession. You

are witnessing the phenomenal projection of the domestic nou-
menon, he declared. Do you not see, Mary? It is Plato's allegory.
The screens are the walls of the cave. I apologised for my ignorance of the allegory of which he spoke, so Howard explained,
expressing his delight that the nation of Japan supplied us with
such a superfluity of philosophical illustrations. But Howard, I
asked, what of the poor woman? Should we not intervene? His
frustration was clear but he agreed to speak on the matter with
his friend Bairstow the following day. Before returning to his MSs
he urged me to reflect upon the fullness of what had been taking
place behind the screen, and not simply the two-dimensional
projection to which I had been witness.

Howard has adopted a writer. An unusual gentleman by the name of Hearn. He has published ghost stories and exotic tales of his travels in Haiti. Howard enthuses over one of his, "Rabyah's Last Ride", which the man has presented to Howard as evidence of his literary prowess. Howard has invited him to live with us on this basis. I am to enjoy the company. He has many tales to tell. He was married to a mulatto woman in New Orleans. Howard delights in these. The tales are a higgle. Voudoun customs and French creole, working for the periodicals and tirades against tyrannical editors. His aunt is Irish and he grew up in the old country so we must be near family. Howard has given him a student – Clarke – and impressed upon young Clarke how fortunate he is to be studying with such an eminent author. Hearn rewrites Clarke's prose offerings so that not a word of the original remains. He declares himself satisfied with the finished work though it no longer bears any of the student's imprimatur. Hearn has fired off a missive to *Harper's* telling them of his dissatisfaction with the disrespectful way in which they treat his prose, altering his commas. He talks of rhythm as if he were a composer but professes to prefer the rhythms of primitive music – African and Spanish – to the northern European forms.

He has a somewhat untrustworthy disposition and looks very slope-shouldered. He is excited about living in Japan. He claims his name derives from the Greek island Lefka on which he was born. Lafcadio. His right pupil is not parallel to his left. It lags.

The shrine is made of many parts. There are glass vessels. There are blue pots with wooden fans to go in them. The glass vases may have green branches put in them if you like. The flat oil vessels have a cotton wick, not a pitch wick. The large base of incense you will see. You take a few together and set them smoking and then put them into one of the vases.

The cupboards in the shrine are for wooden tablets in memory of your ancestors.

There are one or two ribbed-fluted vases of wood. They do not belong to the shrine. You can put anything into them.

There is a large white vase and a small white vase. In one of these is a platinum crucible. I do not know which it is.

The room is not the room. It has shifted. I am askance to the room. It is not the room it was. It is improperly peopled. I am parallel to it. A pot slides. A book falls open, its pages flutter, its spine dropped. The words spill. The eyes of the children. One would expect trembling but there is not that. We have listed, we have yawned; we have not trembled. Water from the pot scatters across the tatami, droplets vibrato upon reeds. Something falls outside, a branch, a bird? And then the room becomes the room. A brief passage of time has been calved off, in a perpendicular room, so close to this one but abstracted, and has been sealed off to us again. The room has returned. It is peopled propitiously, water seeps once more. The eyes of the children no longer gape. They question: Mama, Mama, jishin?

I had not recognised it for what it was. Jishin, Mama, jishin. Papa, where is Papa? I lean to pick up the book. The opposite thereof is above the head, where nothing exists, but what causes man to be as it were mad, as is the case when juvenes are in yet thence, which is manifested by such traits as existed in the audacious spirit previously mentioned, who was in his adolescence, of such a nature, that no other was ever more insane. Where is Papa? I close the book and replace it in the shelf. Mama, is Papa safe from the jishin? Is he? He is. He is jishin. He is in the school. Should I be concerned? Has this shift been dreadful? Outside of this room has the world been made anew at an angle, its form tessellated into something fresh? Is there debris?

The stove is of iron. The mats are made from reeds. We shuffle on slippers. We do not speak. We gesture, we bow, we nod.

Eric fell from Howard's climbing structure. He was presented to me looking ghostly pale. He had been insensate for less than a two-minute. His brothers jabbered excitedly – it was an event. Eric could recall nothing of that morning. He wished to lie down. I did not wish him to sleep so I stood watch over him with a flannel. He thrice closed his eyes and thrice I coaxed him back to wakefulness.

Sebastian has been isolated. Howard observes him. Sebastian is the subject in a paternal experiment. Howard has become intense, his interest excited. What has caused this stimulation? It is a blessed pedagogical anomaly.

Felicity has been practising handwriting with the boys. Each was dictated a passage appropriate to his ability to copy out on washi. George had raced through some Thucydides in Jowett's translation; Eric had Prospero beseeching his charges to "be not afeared" (he would, as we know, prefer Mr Hearn's grotesquerie but Felicity knows my feelings on that matter). Felicity selected three sentences from Kingsley's *The Water Babies* for Sebastian and Sebastian pricked his ears for careful transliteration.

Upon inspecting the results of the exercise, Felicity discovered a marvel. Sebastian had recorded accurately the sentences read, with not a single error; not a single error excluding the orientation of his script. His writing was inverted, as if written by Mr Carroll's Alice. To demonstrate, Felicity held it to a glass for me and we read it together, as clear as day, in reflection.

How we delighted! The dear boy had produced something quite magical. Felicity claimed that such facility was scarce but not unknown; a governess of her acquaintance claimed also to have witnessed such looking-glass-writing produced by one of her charges. It was more common among left-handed children, she claimed, but would not impede the student's progress. Sebastian would surely revert in his own time.

On seeing the lines Howard immediately fell to deep thought. He muttered of cheirality. He began to expound upon Helmholtz's work on the horopter. Didn't I see? The boy's spatial apparatus was not yet accommodated to a space of three dimensions – here was evidence of perception loosed in four.

I dampened his enthusiasm with the suggestion that Sebastian was, perhaps without thinking, mimicking, imperfectly, the

Japanese mode of writing which he had no doubt witnessed in these past twelve months. Howard would not hear of it – it is lateral, Mary. The boy's mind was not yet conditioned, he insisted. It was a rare opportunity to observe higher spatial consciousness, raw and untutored.

Sebastian is seated before his father and asked to reproduce his visionary work. He cannot do it. His text is dutiful and correct, linear and standard. Howard is gentle, but I am keen to his frustration. He senses yet another higher spatial proof dissipating as steam from a surface, leaving not even a trace of moisture whence it was.

Ferrous and mercurial on the tongue. It has the appearance of quince jam, seamed through. The preparation of the fish is undertaken with great care so as to remove any filaments of sinew. It can separate at the seams. The iron flavour gives something of blood to it in the mouth. It neither tastes nor looks like fish.

Equal care is taken over the parcels of rice which are formed by hand into lozenges the size of an adult thumb. These are made to cohere through immersion in liquids. The finest rice is said to come from the Kochi Prefecture on the fourth island. The rice is graded by quality and sold in a distinct market. It defines its own economy. The word for meal is used as the colloquial term for rice: go-hang.

They serve it with the gratings of a fiery white root called wasabi. It is a species of radish. It turns to brown once it meets the air. The sauce they make from fermenting beans is served in its own bowl for dipping. This is a dark brown, inky in its depths, and powerfully saline. The colours should not be allowed to leak into each other on the plate.

Eric tells his brothers there are devils in the garden. They are native to the place. They eat the udders of cows. They are a type of vampire. How does he know about vampires? Mr Hearn told him. Mr Hearn told him about the devils. In the kingdom of the blind.

Sebastian is terrified, George distracted, William nonplussed. Eric enjoys the power his knowledge gives him. He plans a trap. He wants a devil of his own. Howard says of Hearn that he has fired the imagination. I tell Howard that I do not trust him. I cannot ever decide with which eye he observes me. I would have him leave.

CUBE

We enter through the low door-frame and into a six-mat reception area. Mr Yamamoto welcomes us with a low bow. We remove our shoes. He wears a dark-grey, worsted three-piece suit of an English style. A white cotton shirt with winged collars. A black bow-tie. Round, copper-rimmed spectacles. He ushers us to kneel around a table sunken into the floor in the receiving room.

Mr Yamamoto explains to Howard that he studied photography in Paris. That he once heard the great Daguerre lecture to two hundred at an école. That shashin represent the highest pinnacle of western technology that the Japanese seek to emulate. That he believes himself a humble moderniser. That his work is good for Meiji Japan. That his contribution is minor but no less significant for that. That we are his honoured guests. That western subjects are the most honoured because the shashin themselves will speak of great future collaborations between the modern west and Japan.

He speaks of time, frozen. Of the possibilities of successive instants lifted and isolated from their too-fluid catalogue. He speaks of the work of fixing and illuminating, of red light and blue, of yellow leaves and white blossom.

He speaks of the maximum amount of beauty and comfort with the minimum amount of trouble.

I inform Howard of my intention to retreat. I yearn for some peace before we leave this country. My reading in the religions of the Japanese encourages deeper engagement. I will go to a monastery. I have read of a place where they welcome Westerners. He may bring the boys if he chooses.

The monks also are in retreat. They are associated with the old rulers. There are those who would renew them. They have withdrawn to a mountainside temple from a larger accommodation on the plain. We make the journey and present our letters of introduction. They invite us to reside with them. In this way they will be seen to modernise. There is a small dwelling outside the temple grounds where we may stay.

The dwelling is rude but it will suffice. We sleep on futons. Life is simple. It pleases me. I am invited to meet with the women. The monks take wives since a new law was passed. We are free to explore. The boys can play in the woods. Howard is shown some blocks describing geometric problems.

The monk sits at his bench. He works with care. The ceramic bowl is broken. It is a beautiful bowl but it has shattered into parts.

The monk mixes powdered gold into a clear paste. The powder is ground from the metal.

The monk applies the golden paste to the edges of the cracks. He does this with the utmost care. He works patiently. The paste dries slowly so he can apply it without haste. He eases the two pieces of cracked ceramic together along the sharp join. He gently encourages them together. With a small blade he removes the excess paste. He returns it to a vessel.

The repaired bowl is placed upon a wooden rack to dry. It takes a day and a night. The cracks are highlighted in a seam of gold. The Japanese value this repaired bowl more highly than the perfect bowl.

I mime dropping a bowl. I mime inquiry. Does he recognise a question? I am sorry. Does sorrow appear? Does it mime? I trace the line of gold with my fingertip. It slides across the rough ceramic. I say the word "how". I pick up the two pieces of a broken bowl. I place them together and part them once more. I beseech with my eyes. He mutters a word ending "raremashta". Past. And passive? Intransitive? He stands. He takes a bowl from the shelf. He lets it slip between his fingers. I start at the sound it makes striking the floor of the cell. I am profoundly sorry. It lies cracked. It lies in three pieces. Raremashta. That was how it was broken. With deliberation. He kneels once more. I mime rogation. Can one mime such a thing? It is difficult but surely can be done. I mime shadows. I wish to speak in the noumenal. The man smooths the surface of the lacquer he has applied to a fractured cup. He glorifies the seal. I watch. I no longer mime. Can one cease to mime? He kneels.

Howard has befriended the monk Hizuita. Hizuita is the temple mathematician. Howard has discovered the art of paper folding. He sits with Hizuita and makes the folds, explaining in his patient way. "Point p1 can be made to coincide with point p2, like so. Point p1 can be made to occupy a position on line l1, like so. We can make a fold along a line that intersects both points p1 and p2, like so." The educator. Hizuita watches, and as he watches his hands work independently, creasing and uncreasing his own sheet. He produces a fox. The demonstrator. Howard chuckles to himself and continues to show Hizuita his geometric reasoning. The two pass sheets backwards and forwards, communicating through folds: lines and points replacing language. Serenity governs their actions, and the shushing of passed paper. Howard explains to himself as much as to his partner. Howard, again, in communion, his thought imprecisely expressed but made to travel nonetheless.

On tatami, at night, I see the shadow of the woman from Yokohama.

It is a sacred picture of scenes of the Buddhist paradise. It is called the Mandala.

The ground is brown silk – a rich golden brown but not having much individuality – capable of being the subject's colour but consenting to be only a foil. The "paint" is an embroidery made with human hair.

Most of the hair is black but hair of different shades is used for effect of light and shade and for glinting some of the scenes.

In the middle sits Amida Buddha – not Sakya Muni but perhaps a different incarnation of the same being.

Amida Buddha is the saviour of women and criminals and sudras.

Yumiko shows me a selection of characters, painted on a textured paper in sweeping strokes. I am to choose one to paint myself.

Yumiko pronounces each, carefully and slowly, and mimes.

"Chi. Chi." She kneels and pats the ground with an open palm. "Chi." She picks up a pebble. "Chi." Earth. Rock. Stone. She bends my arm and touches the biceps. "Chi." Strong.

She indicates the next symbol. "Mizu. Mizu." She makes flowing movements with her fingers. "Mizu." She indicates a stand of bamboo, and waves her arms. "Mizu."

"Hi. Hi." Yumiko's fingers are flames, flickering and crackling. "Hi." She touches her palm to her heart.

"Kaze." A sweeping arm, a breathing out. Wind. "Kaze." A motion away from her temple. Thought.

"Ku. Ku." She simply opens her arms, palms upwards. She looks towards the sky. "Sora." The sky. Less, and more than that.

I indicate the final symbol.

"Sugoi." She takes the paper depicting the final symbol and bows at me. She departs the room. I follow.

Howard and Hizuita fold together. Howard and Hizuita construct modules. Howard and Hizuita are making the Platonic solids, face superficies by face superficies.

Howard has received by return of letter from Alicia sketches of the cross-sections of the higher solids. Howard and Hizuita will fold these.

Howard and Hizuita have developed new forms. Howard has described geometric folds, Hizuita has combined them. They construct together solids beyond the Platonic. Howard rhapsodises. He describes intuition. He describes cross-sections. He describes a slice of the tesseract. He proffers a construction, a paper jewel, symmetrical and bewitching; an imagination of perfection; poetic in and of itself.

Howard has drawn plans for Hizuita. They will construct a box.

Yumiko carries under her arm a roll of paper. We enter an octagonal room on the ground floor of the pagoda. Yumiko unrolls the two sheets of paper and separates them. She places them on the floor and weighs each down. Yumiko goes to a chest and returns with some items: two small, white ceramic bowls and a jug; two brushes; a small item in a box; a black block. She arranges these on the floor next to the weighted sheets. She gives me a brush. It is some six inches long. Yumiko names it: fude.

The block has a recessed well at one end. Yumiko pours a little water from a small jug onto the smooth surface of this block. She takes a smaller oblong block from the box. She names this: sumi. She presses the end of the sumi in the water against the surface of the block and begins to rub. She continues this action for more than a minute whereupon she drags back some of the water from the trough onto the surface and continues to rub. She maintains this practice for some more minutes. It is restful to witness the action.

Yumiko places the block on the floor. She tips the ink into the white ceramic bowls. She indicates one to me, with a small bow. She takes her fude and dips it into the ink. She makes a sweeping, horizontal mark upon one sheet of the paper. The line takes a swooping form, mimicking the fude that made it. It is deeply black and pure against the white of the paper. Yumiko is pleased. She indicates for me to do the same. She takes my hand with the fude and demonstrates the action. A fluid motion in the wrist. I dip the fude in the ink and make the mark. It is clumsier than Yumiko's. Yumiko nods.

Yumiko dips her fude again. She makes another line, at the left of her first, a large apostrophe almost abutting it. She indicates for me to do the same. We continue in this fashion. Two more horizontal lines, then four vertical, like a gate. Beneath these, four more: one apostrophe and three made in quick succession, dipping with the fude like a crane dipping into water, to make three angled in the opposing direction.

Yumiko bows. She indicates my sheet and says: sugoi.

Howard's boots, crumpled and collapsed. Wardrobe boots. Encrustations of mud imprisoning wrinkled, sagging leather. Could they even accommodate him any longer? Could they be made, once more, supple enough to wear?

I realise that Yumiko is the first person in whose company I have felt any comfort since England. Felicity, sweet-natured though she is, does not inspire in me a sense of trust. What would she make of my truer thought? That Howard's progeny is all but corrupted. That there is a woman on the surface of the earth – a woman who knows not her own name – who has caused such pain to me that I find all of humanity distorted by her image. That to think of Maud so appals me that I must build anew an idea of people. That I must force my determination towards freedom internal so as not to be consumed from without. That I can no longer read Tennyson.

Yumiko simply sees my actions and responds to those. Hers is a companionship offered freely and equally. Though I know not what I bring to this company, I sense that we learn from each other.

Yumiko has laid out the sheets, the blocks, the sumi, the bowls and the fude. Beside these sits a puzzle box.

I grind the ink. I dip my fude first. Yumiko watches intently. I take the fude from the outside of the sheet and make a fluid, continuous spiral. Yumiko follows my lead. We make two spirals, flowing inwards.

I take my sheet and I fold it in half. I fold it in half again. Yumiko mirrors my actions. I continue this series of folds until my sheet will fold no further. I give the folded sheet to Yumiko. Yumiko takes both sheets and places them in the puzzle box. She slides sections of surface so that it is once more closed. The spiral sheets are removed.

Ceanothus bloom
Coral blossom crowns jade leave
Bark-form'd thorns beneath

空

Tesseract

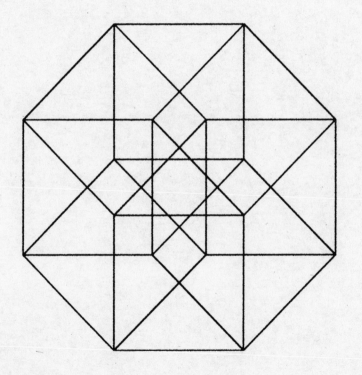

Compositor's note

There are, nested in the archive of the Californian writer Gelett Burgess, a small number of papers relating to the obscure British author Charles Howard Hinton.[1] On his sudden death in 1907, Hinton's family had appointed Burgess literary executor, presumably with the idea that Burgess would survey Hinton's correspondence and works in progress, oversee the publication of any outstanding pieces and promote the Englishman's intellectual estate. As is the way with such collections, Hinton's papers had remained in Burgess's possession until his own death in 1951, at which point both authors' literary remains were gifted to the library at Berkeley.

Hinton's papers hold a special interest for contemporary researchers into the occult, of whom I am one. Three years before his death, he had published a collection of essays, *The Fourth Dimension*. These detailed the culmination of his many esoteric lines of thought relating to the idea that space exceeds the mundane three dimensions of length, breadth and width. Most of the essays are, truth be told, extremely challenging reading, but the fold-out colour plate at the front of the book provides a very useful visual guide to the system of cubes Hinton had developed to assist his readers in following him into the fourth dimension of space. It is easy enough to find images of this illustration online. According to the account books of his publisher Swan Sonnenschein *The Fourth Dimension* was

---

1 Burgess was, among other things, the originating mind of the neologism "blurb". For an example of this form, see the back cover of the current volume.

not a commercial success but to his loyal readers it offered a summary account of the author's life's work and an invaluable aid to his method.[2]

A novel, *An Episode of Flatland*, was published in 1907, some mere months before Hinton's sudden demise. This novel brought his writing career full circle by giving tribute to the text that had lent it early impetus, Edward Abbott's 1884 novel *Flatland*. *Flatland* was narrated by A Square, a two-dimensional character who becomes a heretic in his own home for attempting to convince his fellow Flatlanders of the sacrilegious existence of spheres and cubes. Its popularity had briefly made the idea of the fourth dimension quite the mode in the mid-1880s. Committed theorists such as Hinton were given a springboard, as were more enterprising minds, who jumped on the fad with gusto, publishing ghost stories and parlour games of higher dimensional illusion.

In Hinton's addendum to Abbott's novel, the inhabitants of another two-dimensional world undergo an immense spiritual and intellectual blossoming through their contact with three-dimensional models. They experience an awesome inner awakening and great connection to their countrymen. It is difficult not to read this final fiction as a form of imaginative wish fulfilment on the part of its author, whose own system of models had not been taken up with quite the same level of enthusiasm despite his hopes for it. It seems like the last dice-roll of a writer who sensed his imminent obscurity; not so much a heretic as an afterthought.

---

2 These are held in archive at Reading University which also houses the archive of Samuel Beckett, within which is contained a conker belonging to the writer. *The Fourth Dimension* appears to have sold 243 copies. All copies are first editions. My own, purchased at the Oxfam bookshop next to the British Museum, cost me only £40 in 2009.

The publications of these books, with their sense of summary and completion, therefore begs a question: if Hinton had been clearing out his cupboard in the years preceding his death, what remained in the archive passed on to Burgess?[3]

The items are fragmentary. There is the draft of a form of memoir called *The Travels of an Idea*, narrating Hinton's life in Japan and America but written as if from a "higher" perspective. This is an interesting, if flawed, piece of narrative: episodic, omniscient, occasionally urgent, it attempts to describe the author's life through its defining philosophical position.

There are prose poems that read like notes towards a distinct mode of narrative, a reaching for a new voice. These alternate between the first-persons singular and plural and the third-person before settling on the impersonal intermediate voice "one" as preferred mode of address, occasionally doing away with pronouns altogether. It would not quite be correct to think

---

3   In truth, this question is begged of few. Hinton scholars are a rare breed. The stalking of fringe historical figures across the sparse scholarly highlands is not encouraged in the contemporary academy, where collaboration, meetings and synergies are favoured over selfish hours in crusty archives. We are required to justify our existences before panels of our peers by confecting shared interests. For those of us who decline to justify our existences to ourselves, attempting to do so for others seems a doubly redundant operation. I was warned off this material, not because it was thought dangerous – would that one of my colleagues had been capable of that insight – but because it was deemed injurious to a fledgling career. There will be no one to speak to about it, they said. No one will be interested. Certainly, I faced more than my fair share of the politely baffled and barely awake on the conference circuit. I tried sexing up my presentations to forestall the glassy-eyed stares, introducing visual props to demonstrate the shift from two dimensions to three and therefore, by analogy, from three dimensions to four. I used animated PowerPoint slides. I recreated a set of Hinton's cubes and compared these to Froebel's gifts, to show the lineage of the idea of using physical objects to learn extended space. There were hands-on, 3d printed cross-sectional models of the tesseract to pass around. I sold myself as a researcher into material cultures, as an investigator of historic senses of affect. More often than not someone would ask a question about relativity theory that I was unqualified to answer.

of these as Modernist, though they share with Modernist poems certain formal characteristics.

There are philosophical apercus, odd and stilted but tonally familiar to Hinton obsessives. "Being is being for others." "Behind the noumenal there is yet another realm. This we shall call the psychemenal." "The higher life is real and accessible to all." Many of these are scribbled on the flipsides of other documents: geometric sketches, patent applications and suchlike. The handwriting is only partially decipherable and one must make educated guesses to fill in the gaps in sentences. It is demanding work.[4]

There is a technical notebook containing speculations about the material form of books, speculations that are more akin to Hinton's writing on practical experiments in spatial consciousness. These consider the book itself as a form of spatial technology, discussing the "diptych of the page", the "spatial form of the volume" and its "higher potential". He considers in such passages the form of the book at every level, moving from macro- to micro; binding, page, print and material. Take, for example, the below passage:

"And yet, looking at the same printed papers, being curious, and looking deeper and deeper into them with a microscope, I have seen that in splodgy ink stroke and dull fibrous texture,

---

4   Many readers will surely have experienced the phenomenon of type appearing to move on the page. When we are tired, or inebriated, letters themselves can seem to shift or deliquesce; even to dance. We try again and again to fix them with our eyes but the more closely we focus, the more slippery the words become. Dyslexics who become disorientated by words may be trying – pre-consciously – to solve abstract, printed, two-dimensional symbols by working with them in three-dimensional space. Perhaps this is what was happening. Perhaps the words wished themselves to be treated in higher dimensions. Perhaps the Dalì-esque melting of sentences was also that. Perhaps.

each part was definite, exact, absolutely so far and no farther, punctiliously correct; and deeper and deeper lying a wealth of form, a rich variety and amplitude of shapes, that in a moment leapt higher than my wildest dreams could conceive."

Most intriguing, though baffling, are a set of paper squares, imprinted and divided by horizontal, vertical and diagonal creases. These bear the inscriptions of multiple curvilinear arrows indicating directions of fold. Yet many of these folds are impossible to recreate, seeming to indicate directions in which the paper simply cannot be persuaded to move. These have to be marked down as curiosities and nothing more, and indeed are catalogued by the archivists as "miscellaneous objects".[5] The notes on the obverse of one of these declares an epiphany – not unusual for Hinton – that extends a particular speculation from his earliest work.

In the essay "What is the Fourth Dimension?", Hinton had described how access to a higher-dimensioned space might provide the observer with privileged insight into spaces shut off from those in the lower-dimensioned space. Realising that this was quite a difficult concept to grasp, Hinton provided an illustration: as a three-dimensional being – a mundane human, for example – might examine the interior of a two-dimensional square inaccessible to a being confined to the plane of that square, so a four-dimensional being might, from its higher perspective, examine the contents of a closed cube. On the scrap in the Burgess archive, Hinton extends this line of thought towards closed "volumes" of all forms, including books, secret notes, collections of correspondence: all text would be open to the inquiring higher mind.

---

5 An author of my acquaintance, a specialist in the so-called New Weird, when I told him of these squares, began rhapsodising about impossible folds and new developments in origami that enabled the application of the practice to solids. I need not stress the absurdity of such speculations.

The documents assembled below are all contained within one section of the archive. They detail, in the form of correspondence and clippings, the events of a few years in the life of Charles Howard Hinton as witnessed from the perspective of outside observers. It is not clear how they came to be in Hinton's, or Burgess's, possession.

I have read across the source materials before selecting, editing and collaging the text that has been compiled here. I present these documents as found, re-contextualised and shaped for narrative. While I hope that the reader will encounter the events as they unfolded in the period – or at least, as they were noted for personal record, exchanged between correspondents or published more broadly – I realise that it may be useful for a reader to meet in advance some of the characters who correspond here.

First is Henry Havelock Ellis, who would become famous as a ground-breaking researcher into sexuality and sexual behaviour. Educated in Croydon, Ellis lived for five years in rural Australia where he worked as a teacher. Making the most of his long periods of solitude, Ellis read extensively, becoming particularly interested in the philosophical writings of James Hinton, Charles Howard's father. On his return to England in 1876, Ellis made contact with the Hinton family by letter. James Hinton being only recently deceased, Ellis became friends with his widow Margaret, through whom he was introduced to a number of James's closest acquaintances, including Margaret's sister, Caroline Haddon, and her son, Howard. The Hinton family assisted the funding of Ellis's studies in medicine. Ellis's journals, written around the time he moved back to London, are a rich resource of intimate detail on Ellis's intellectual hero.

Second is Olive Schreiner. The daughter of South African missionaries who rebelled against her parents' Christianity, Schreiner travelled through the Cape working as a governess before sailing for England in 1881 to pursue her dreams of studying medicine. Too ill with asthma to study, she committed herself to writing and became the literary success of the season in 1883 with her novel *The Story of an African Farm*. Ellis reviewed the book approvingly and the two met. Their love affair, never consummated, nevertheless resulted in a voluminous correspondence. Through Ellis, Schreiner met and became friends with Mrs Hinton and knew Howard as Ellis's friend. Letters from the correspondence that refer to Charles Howard Hinton are sampled here.

In 1884 Schreiner was invited to attend the first meeting of the Men and Women's Club, founded by Karl Pearson. Pearson, who would go on to become a leading Professor in statistics at University College London, holding a chair in eugenics, was a tyro intellectual in the early 1880s. He founded the club to discuss frankly one of the great questions of the age: the relations between the sexes. Schreiner became emotionally involved with Pearson and this pair also corresponded a great deal. As with her correspondence with Ellis, Schreiner would sometimes write to Pearson a number of times in the same day.

If Schreiner's strong attachment to Pearson was erotic – and there is debate over this subject – it was not reciprocated in kind. Pearson married Maria Sharpe, the Secretary of the Men and Women's Club and the younger sister of Elizabeth Cobb, a society figure and wife of the Liberal MP Henry Cobb.

When Olive Schreiner suggested to the members of the Men and Women's Club the discussion of James Hinton's work, which rehearsed a number of highly unconventional ideas around sexual relations, including the advocation of freer forms of family organisation, a highly charged correspondence between a number of members of the club brought to light further details and rumours concerning James Hinton's approaches to a number of women. The letters included here written by Emma Brooke, a campaigner for women's rights who wrote one of the first New Women novels, 1894's *Superfluous Woman*, are exemplary in this regard.

A formal invitation to speak to the Society extended to Caroline Haddon was rescinded. Hinton's posthumous reputation and social standing infected his philosophical thought, no matter how his supporters – Ellis and Caroline Haddon in particular – argued for the significance of his work. Olive Schreiner, who had been interested in James Hinton's work, was repelled from it by the disclosure of allegations, but she remained friends with the family members she knew, including the mysterious Mrs Weldon, who she had hinted was Howard's mistress.

When Charles Howard Hinton was subsequently arrested for bigamy in 1886, to the members of the Men and Women's Club it seemed confirmation of the terrible risks associated with the Hintonian school of thought. Correspondence between members was once again filled with gossip about the Hinton family – Elizabeth Cobb's acid letters are sampled here – and Ralph Thicknesse was despatched to court to report on Hinton's trial.

Olive Schreiner alone stood by her friend Mrs Weldon, Hinton's bigamous bride, now revealed as Maud Florence.

Many of these letters survive because Karl Pearson and Maria Sharpe maintained an almost full set of records relating to the Men and Women's Club and correspondence between its members. The record is *almost* full because Pearson did not keep records of his own letters: such of these as survive must be located from alternate sources and I have not sought them out. I have little time for eugenicists.

I describe my role in this affair as that of a compositor. In letterpress printing, the compositor sets the metal blocks of type in a composing stick. So have I selected letters and set them here. I ask you, dear reader, to make of them what you will. Contemporary scholarship has been all but mute on the subject: it is an obscure footnote.[6] My sense is that it has greater significance than that.

---

6   Which must make these obscure footnotes to the power of two. There has been some interest from scholars of the occult, for good reason. I am wary of including the following story and do so only with its subject's permission and on condition of anonymity. One of our most eminent literary scholars, who has worked her entire career on myth and fable, on hearing of my interest in *A Life* once told me of a very peculiar experience. As she waited at a networked printer in the copy room of her university department, the machine began to spew out sheets of paper. This was not unusual, as remote printing was possible, but it seemed to her to be occurring with greater urgency than was typical. One particular sheet containing an illustration of an extrapolated cube caught her eye and she examined the pages churning from the mechanism. She had some awareness of Hinton, through Borges, so was further intrigued to notice that he appeared to be the author of the work issuing from the machine. Assuming it to have been printed by a colleague, she left it on the printer and endeavoured to identify its source, eager to discuss the work. No one could be found who had any idea of the document. When she returned to the print room it was no longer there. She searched for the title online, thinking to buy a copy for her son, a sculptor with an interest in higher geometry, only to find it unavailable. She is certain that the printed work was entitled *A Life in Many Dimensions*.

1880
The Private Journal of Henry Havelock Ellis
Jan 6th 1880

*Went to dine at 6 o'clock with Mrs Hinton, Miss C. Haddon,
& Howard Hinton, the first time of seeing them.*

*They did not quite seem to care for the "Life and Letters";
Miss H said his spiritual biography had yet to be written. Miss
Hopkins only knew him 2 years before his death. Miss H said
if they put all they knew about him it wld. not be believed. The
Life only contains what was credible.*

*Was fond, specially in his earlier days, of poetry, but never
wrote on literature. He gave up his profession chiefly to have
time for reading. Shelley he loved greatly and above all. Also
loved Mrs Browning; especially that sonnet:-*

With stammering lips and insufficient sound,
I strive and struggle to deliver right
That music of my nature, day and night,
With dream and thought and feeling, interwound,
And only answering all the senses round
With octaves of a mystic depth and height,
Which step out grandly to the infinite
From the dark edges of the sensual ground!

*And really, that does seem to describe Hinton with wonder-
ful precision.*

*His love of music and his intense delight in the way in
which music is constructed was wonderful. Miss H had often
seen him gloating over music scores. Had sat beside him at a
Monday Pop. concert when he had buried his face in his hands
+ afterwards looked as if he had passed through some great*

spiritual crisis. Loved Mozart: would say after listening to some piece of his how "Mozart had as little to do with that as I have; it is music itself": but he recognised the superiority of Beethoven.

His love of pictures was remarkable as it did not develop till relatively late in life. Above all adored Turner but also greatly liked Constable; they had not heard him say much of Gainsborough. Before some pictures he said he felt inclined to kneel down. He sent some of his pictures – among them delicate pieces – to – I think it was – public houses, and wished them at times to be explained to the people. After his death his pictures were sold.

Mrs H said he was wanting in practical wisdom. He lived, as it were, in the future. Also, that he was extremely eccentric, would do the most inappropriate things. "Oh, he was such a troublesome man, Mr Ellis; it was so hard to get him to have his hair cut + have his photograph taken. And he never could be got to a dinner party."

When a boy – or at all events when young – he was walking with the future Mrs H + her brother and it was pouring with rain and he was holding an umbrella over the former and holding a discussion with the latter about the radii of a circle. They differed apparently on the subject, and, at last, Hinton, in order to convince his companion, put down the umbrella leaving his future wife standing in the rain, said "Look here, John" and proceeded to describe a part circle on the pavement to demonstrate his argument.

He had a high opinion of teaching; considered it superior to his own profession and brought up his eldest son as a teacher. He considered it monstrous that children were taught nothing of morals and of their duties as citizens.

Used to spend every Friday evening with Stopford Buerk;

Mrs H could generally tell by Buerk's most recent sermon what had been the subject of their discussion. Rev Mark Wilks was his most entire disciple; the Rev Tipple of Norwood was his friend but not so greatly influenced by his ideas.

Saw a fine photograph of Hinton; superior to that reproduced in the Life, though taken at the same time; with the same intense thoughtfulness but with more wealth of compassion, a rare mingling of breadth and delicacy of compassion.

Saw also photo of his second son Willie who died about 3 years after his father. One of the loveliest faces I ever saw; rich sweet mouth and dreamy eyes, and hair falling on his shoulders, not in ringlets, but with occasional tendency to ringlet.

Hinton used to develop and philosophise on the most trivial and insignificant remarks made in his presence. Everything, said Miss H, was like Hinton's apple to him. Mrs H said that at last she got afraid of saying anything in his presence.

Went March 1st 1880 to Elizabeth House, High Barnet, to stay with the Hintons for three days. Have not, this time, heard very much further about Hinton although had an enjoyable stay. Took the index to "art"; suggested a volume on art and feminine called, say – "Thoughts on feminist art", agreed to collaborate with Howard in making such a vol and perhaps accruing a share of profits. He only got £20 profit on "Art of Thinking".

My most important discovery is in regard to H's social views. Mrs H said in latter part of life he thought intensely about social evils, specially of the wrongs of woman. She almost dreaded the arrival of the newspapers every morning they affected him so deeply and he had found the remedy. This remedy makes it inadvisable to show his MSs to people except to a small circle of intimate admirers. It is easy to imagine the nature of the solution he proposed; and from some of the MSs

*Mrs H has lent me I see it distinctly as expressed in this princi-
ple: put others first. Pleasure then rests on self-sacrifice.*

Nov 6th 1880

*Went to Mrs Nettleship, Harwood Square. Saw Mrs H and
Miss Haddon.*

*Miss H remarked that H used to say it was painting that
broke down his morals.*

*Mrs H said that not long before he died, when as she said
his mind was enfeebled as well as his body, he seemed to go
back on the now familiar conceptions, asked her once to pray
with him + prayed for forgiveness etc. in the old orthodox
style.*

*In regard to H's beliefs on sexual subjects Howard told me
at Uppingham that he once asked his father's advice concerning a friend of his. Howard thought he ought to form
a connection for the sake of his health. Hinton said: "The
remedy is worse than the disease." He disliked making woman
a saviour for man. He thought more of making man to save
woman in this respect. He seems not to have fully believed
his own directions, as Miss Haddon says a number of women
always clung to him.*

1881
Meeting of Mr Hinton's friends at Mrs Bury's, Friday April 1st 1881

Mackay told me that at supper once Hinton was talking to Mrs Chambers about the condition of the poor. He flourished the carving knife and exclaimed with deep emotion: "We want blood, Mrs Chambers, we want blood!"

Mrs H said that he said once to her: "People will say when I am dead that I was such a good man. Will you always say that I was not. You know I am not." "You are a darling," she replied.

1882
June 27th 1882

*Mrs Hinton says that they (JH and herself) at one time thought
of "marrying a girl". I do not think they had decided who
the girl would be. Mrs H seems quite to have entered into his
beliefs. He was uncertain whether his social views ought to
be speculative or practical first. He said sometimes the one
enlivens the other.*

1883
June 21st 1883 at Miss Jones's

*She read part of her paper on Hinton and herself (a sort of
"Confessions of a beautiful soul").*

*She said he was considered by many (and seemed at first)
"serpentine" and insincere. She once wrote an intimate
account of her own feelings etc. at his request. Said he profited
by it and he showed it to someone else. She did not like that +
got it back + burnt it. She means to write it again.*

Aug 1st 1883

*In regard to Hinton's spontaneousness, Miss Jones tells me he
once went barefoot + dressed as a beggar down Fleet St., in
order, I think, to understand a beggar's feelings.*

*Also, that he once got drunk in order to find out whether
he would attack his wife. The results, I believe, were not
remarkable.*

1884
Olive Schreiner to Havelock Ellis

St. Leonards-on-Sea, 25th February, 1884.

My dear Sir, on my return from a visit to London I found your letter which my publisher had forwarded here. Had I received it sooner I should earlier have written to tell you of the pleasure your expression of sympathy with the little book An African Farm *gave me. Thank you for having written.*

Olive Schreiner

1885
Havelock Ellis to Olive Schreiner

Sunday evening, Feb 11th 1885

I'll tell Mrs Weldon that you will probably be coming to Brighton in a few days, shall I? Instead of mentioning the exact day. It's best for you to go just when you feel inclined. Brighton is an immense place. You'd better take the bus to the sea front where it stretches along both ways. To get to Bedford Sq where Mrs Weldon lives (no. 32) you turn to the right.

Olive Schreiner to Havelock Ellis

Friday 3rd April 1885

You know I can't help wishing that [Howard] Hinton would go down to Brighton & find Mrs W--- with someone else. I wish it; then he would learn the value of sincerity. We can trust each other so, you & I that's so sweet. What you told me about feeling sad when I said was happy so so good of you. You can always say anything to me.

    Olive

Havelock Ellis to Olive Schreiner

Sunday morning, April 12th 1885

I am going to Brighton on Tuesday morning, shall probably stay at 32 Bedford Sq. that night; on Wednesday morning I want to come to Hastings. Shall I just come & walk up to your room? If you don't want me to come, or have anything to say about it, write at once. – You needn't write to me in Brighton unless there's something special to say. Olive, I wish you & I could spend a little while somewhere quite free & alone, so that we could rest together perfectly.

I shall be with Howard Hinton at Brighton. He came to me yesterday – plunged straight at once into a favourite question of his – "Space-relations" – walking eagerly up & down. But I knew he had something more definite than that to talk about & by & by he plunged into it with a good deal of confusion and hesitation. Olive, why is it people want to trust me so much & tell me things they don't tell anyone else. It is sweet when you love anyone a great deal but not else.

Olive Schreiner to Havelock Ellis

Weds 17th June 1885
41 Upper Baker Street, Marylebone, London
Mrs Weldon gave the love to [Howard] Hinton that you want, & now she talks of revenge. But it is natural you should want that kind of love. Even with the bitterness & hatred & lifelong separation that comes after it.

The Private Journal of Henry Havelock Ellis
Sept 17th 1885

Mrs Farcourt Barnes told Olive that [James] Hinton said to her more than once "If I had had a mistress this would never have occurred." According to her, Mrs Boole really was his mistress. (A striking resemblance between Mrs Howard Hinton + Daisy, but perhaps only accidental.) Daisy, aged about 14, Mrs Barnes says, she has seen running about naked in the room where Hinton and his son were. She says that C. H., as you could tell from her face when she sat on his knee – was the woman who more than any other felt intense favour for Hinton. Mrs Barnes admired him as a man of genius, doesn't wish anything she said to be used against him, but considers that he had "every vicious instinct". (She is a woman of the world who has evidently had lovers.) Hinton used to make love to her. She endured it, she says, but considered him a very repulsive sort of creature.

Caroline Haddon to Karl Pearson

December 11th 1885
Dover
Dear Mr Pearson,

*I am flattered by your wishing me to write a paper on
"Hinton's Treatment of the Sexual Relations", although I
must for the present decline. I could not in any case prepare so
important and difficult a paper in such a short time.*

*I should have to make a careful study of a great deal of MSs
and unpublished printed matter to make sure that I did not
misrepresent his views.*

*You see I never read a word on that subject for seven years
after his death: it was all too painfully associated with his
suffering and his death. Not until I was in the Black Forest three
years ago had I ever read his woman papers. I felt then that at all
hazards they must someday be given to the world. But I do not
see any way to doing anything at present. Another reason for
declining a paper just now is that my book on Hinton's Ethics
The Larger Life is just about to appear. I have had all the second
set of proofs and I hope that it will be out before the date you
mention. I should rather people judged of his ethical philosophies
in themselves without having the judgement prejudiced by one
particular application of them. I should be glad to be a listener
at the club meetings for a little while and gradually get to know
the members by joining in the discussion before I venture upon a
paper. When I do so it will not be with the idea of making prose-
lytes to my "Master's" opinions or should I by the fact of stating
them imply my non-adhesion. The fact is I feel more and more
how ignorant I am and how much practical knowledge I should
need before I am competent to give an opinion. I rarely feel that I
have opinions when I hear what goes thoroughly against them.*

Of one thing I am sure that our only hope is in liberty. I suspect that it is in that idea and in its advocacy of openness that the Hintonians of the club see hope.

I hope to see you on Sunday as Miss Schreiner has invited me as her guest. I remain, dear Mr Pearson,

Yours sincerely,

Carrie Haddon

Caroline Haddon to Karl Pearson

December 14th 1885

Mr K Pearson

Your letter is naturally very painful to me though I am grateful to you for speaking plainly out to me what it would have been easier and pleasanter for you to have kept to yourself or to have uttered only to others. It would distress me far more if I could thoroughly take in but it seems to me still after all your plain words so incredible that anyone who knew James Hinton could use the word shame in relation to him that I must believe it is all a misunderstanding that will be dispelled by further knowledge. I can have wish but that you should know all. That you should read every word he ever wrote and if that were possible that you should understand.

I fear nothing but the lie that is half the truth and ever the worst of lies. Not that I defend, or ever did defend, all that he said and did. No doubt he made grievous mistakes and no one has suffered through them half what my beloved sister Mrs Hinton did.

Yours sincerely,

Caroline Haddon

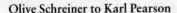

Olive Schreiner to Karl Pearson

December 21st 1885

I send you Mrs Walter's letter. I have been thinking about Hinton. We, I, must not be too bitter against him. I am sure that he was mad. He was open in what he did. Mrs Barnes has thrown a great deal of light on his character to me. She says that he often told her that if when he was forty he had "quietly taken a mistress as other men do, nothing of all this would have happened". He used to sit Miss Haddon naked on his knees, & play with her: his theory was that a man's wish for contact with a woman's body was right, & must be gratified.

His theory & his practice worked it out of physical contact between women & men. My loathing for Hinton grows so strong that it is painful to mention him, but I want to be just to him. I think the depth of degradation to which he sinks woman makes it harder for me than it would otherwise be.

Mrs E. M. Walters to Olive Schreiner

December 17th 1885
Dear Miss Schreiner,

Nothing could induce me to take up the repulsive task of trying to recollect what I have heard of Hinton but the conviction that you must have a good reason for asking it. And the only good reason can be that the evil he did lives after him and you want to stop it.

The little I know is not worth much, as none of the worst facts came within my personal knowledge.

Before I was married, a great friend of Hinton's – a married man – said to me "You really must know Hinton" in such a way as to make me think it wd be an immense benefit. Then I heard Hinton wanted to know me. An accident took me to his house: I accompanied an American lady to consult him professionally about her child. For half an hour I watched his face and form. I had to leave before he had finished his operation as I had promised to meet Mr Walters somewhere (it was a week before we were married). Hinton seemed very disappointed – he followed me into the entrance hall and begged me in whining tones to stay, saying he had hoped to talk with me after the Americans were gone. He took my hand and leant over it, not quite kissing it. That was all I ever saw of him, but the impression was sickening.

Creeping, insinuating, lascivious – anything but bold and honest he seemed to me. Then I was often hearing of him wherever I went. One rather known worker amongst prostitutes wrote me that she was baptised for the lead – meaning Hinton. She used to sit for hours with him by the sea, and she assured me his heart was nearly broken for the sufferings of women!! She still believes in him.

Then one friend of mine, a widow, enlightened me a little. She had met Hinton in society: he had attached himself to her and gained her interest on philanthropic subjects. He travelled 60 miles several times to see her and wrote to her constantly. Suddenly she awoke to his real meaning. He may have pretended he was ministering to her needs – she had no such needs and indignantly repelled him. It was some few years after that she told me of this – her face scarlet at the recollection – saying that his letters were too shameful to repeat. She said she had heard he suffered great remorse on his death bed for what he had done.

One acquaintance of mine used to have her hand kissed and worshipped by him when she went to him as a patient. "What a lovely hand!" with a fond face at it.

*I often heard of this kind of "service" to "other's needs",
and of his spiritual-wife theories, but I never knew anyone
whom he had gone farther with than seduction of the mind.*

*One of the present dangers of his influence is in the teaching
Caroline Haddon may give the girls in her charge. An old pupil
of hers at Kettering, hearing of "The Future of Marriage" said
to me Caroline H cannot possibly help giving out to the girls in
her school all that she is a believer – not openly, perhaps, but
insidiously and purely.*

*How any woman, especially a wife and sister-in-law can
believe in such a wretch, passes my understanding.*

*You know I am not squeamish – you know I am not fond
of any social proprieties – I always rebelled against the word
"duty" and I can advise love often when society would
condemn it – but Hinton excites the intensest loathing in my
mind. Far better be a bold and boastful seducer than a squeak
spinning webs of fine moral reasoning to catch his victims.*

*You know he was the son of a dissident minister – that
explains much—*

*Thank you for your card. I cannot, alas! leave home – my
husband is laid up for weeks, anyhow.*

*Tell me what you do and hear and come and see me if you
will.*

Yours affect.

E. M. Walters

Olive Schreiner to Karl Pearson

December 17th 1885

*There is something very pathetic to me in the fact that as
Hinton was in his dying state he cried out that it was all a*

mistake all wrong, wrong, wrong. That everything he had
written in the last seven years was to be burnt & thrown away.
Poor old brother soul, rather than crush it, let us find out some
better & nobler mode of relationship than he or the past have
dreamed of. I say this not preaching to you but to myself.

    OS.

One must be very careful of what one says because of Miss
Haddon & her school. We must not crush other human lives. It
is the men Hintonians that I feel so bitter against.

1886
The Private Journal of Henry Havelock Ellis
Feb 2nd 1886

Dined with Donkin and Karl Pearson at Saville Club. Donkin said it was said during his life by some medical man who knew [James] Hinton that he had flummata of brain. He died of cerebral tumour; no hardship. Its syphilitic character seems to me very doubtful.

Olive Schreiner to Havelock Ellis

September 24th 1886
Dear Havelock
  *After Monday afternoon my address will be 35 Acacia
Road, St John's Wood. I am going to board with Mrs Hinton
till I can find quarters.*
  Olive

Olive Schreiner to Havelock Ellis

October 11th 1886
Dear Havelock
  *I had two trying visitors today (trying because one wishes to
help but hasn't the means).*
  *The other woman this afternoon is one whose son has
seduced a woman & had two children by her; now his wife
has found it out. Both she & the other woman are in such a
wretched mental condition that one does not know which to
pity the most.*
  *This is one of the most painful cases I have seen. I will tell
you about it some day. The poor old mother was walking up
and down my bedroom crying and wringing her hands long
after it was time for me to start, so I must with my head full of
many things to the club.*

The Diary of Edward Thring, Headmaster of Uppingham School

Wed October 13th 1886

A strange and piteous thing this afternoon. Hinton came in with his wife and his sister (I understand) to say he had committed bigamy and that they had persuaded him to give himself up to justice. It is fearful and these things make the world rock about one, so marvellous is the breakdown from conventional morality, and consequently the noise where there is ruin. The good and evil are so much more positive than in quieter times. There seems much that is noble in this unhappy business but I know not how.

He goes tomorrow, never to return. I must do what I can of course. I have at once written to put off my journey to Hambledon for Monday. I am wanted here. After such a tragedy the daily things seem trivial.

Alas for poor Hinton and his unhappy ladies.

The Times, Friday October 15th 1886

CHARLES HOWARD HINTON, aged 32, of 35 Acacia Road, St John's-wood, described as of no occupation, was charged on his own confession with having committed bigamy by intermarrying with Maud Florence, his first wife being then and now alive. Prisoner went to the Bow-street Police Station and made a statement to the acting inspector to the effect that he was a schoolmaster and, on April 21, 1880, he married Mary Ellen Boole, at Marylebone Church. He married another woman, whose name he did not remember, in or about January, 1883, at the Registry office in Bow-street. It was stated that a marriage had taken place before the registrar as described by the prisoner, but at present the second wife had not been found. The first wife attended and said she did not wish to prosecute, and prisoner had only given himself up as a matter of conscience as they did not wish to have a secret in the house. Prisoner was remanded for further evidence.

Olive Schreiner to Havelock Ellis

October 15th 1886

My Havelock, Howard Hinton as you see is in prison; it is all lies, lies, lies. None of them speak the truth. In the end Howard speaks it as much as anyone.

I am going down to Bow St now to be with Mrs Weldon as she has no one else with her. She too is false but she is all alone. I think you might come & see Howard some time in prison.

Yours

Olive

Spent all yesterday afternoon with Mrs W- in the court.

Olive Schreiner to Havelock Ellis

October 15th 1886

Imploring letter from Mrs Weldon. I must go to the Old Baley to be with her Come to me there. If I'm not back I'll be back as soon as I can.

H. Ellis Esq

To be given to Mr Ellis if he calls.

Olive Schreiner to Havelock Ellis

October 16th 1886

Couldn't come to my boy.

Terrible day at the Old Baley.

Come tomorrow if you can You know my brain has given way. It isn't Mrs Weldon or Karl, it's just the slow sure change that's been going on since that night at Eastbourne.

It's so dreadful to be so young & watch your own brain dying I was quite mad last night.
   Olive

THE DAILY CHRONICLE,
SATURDAY, OCTOBER 16th 1886
POLICE INTELLIGENCE
BOW STREET

THE STRANGE BIGAMY CASE – Charles Howard Hinton, aged 32, giving an address at Acacia-road, St John's Wood, which was charged on remand, on his own confession, which was given yesterday, with having committed bigamy by marrying Maud Florence, his first wife being then and now alive. The first wife stated that she did not wish to prosecute, but that her husband had given himself up as a matter of conscience to them both, as they did not wish to have a secret in the house. Maud Weldon, formerly Maud Florence, living at St Albans, said that she was married to the defendant on Jun. 19, 1883, at Bow-street Registry Office. When she married him she knew he had been married before and that his other wife was then alive. She lived with him about a week after they were married in Argyll-square,

Kings-cross. He went back to live with his former wife, and witness went away. Since that time, until very lately, they had been intimate. She had twins eight months after she was married. It was to give a colour of legitimacy to any children that might be born that she married and not in any way to injure the prisoner's wife. She first proposed that they should marry. Sir James Ingham: You knew he was married to another woman and thought there was no harm to joining the other woman in partnership? Witness said she did not think she was doing wrong. The witness, on being asked to sign her name on the deposition, said "What is my name?" – Adelaide Nettleship, of Melbury-terrace, Marylebone, said that the defendant was her brother. She was present at the first marriage. He had three children of the first marriage now alive. About three years ago the defendant told her he had married another woman. The registrar of marriages for the Strand District produced the register of the second marriage, and Sir James Ingham committed the accused for trial.

Olive Schreiner to Karl Pearson

October 16th 1886
Dear K. P.

Your letter was very refreshing to me when I came back from four hours in Bow Street Court. I cannot live among human creatures & not live in them & for them if they are suffering. I can feel them & their very own abstract intellectual life bubbles up clear & free at once. Ought I to? That is the question I ask of myself.

As I write Mrs Nettleship has come in to ask me to get Mrs Weldon to come & take a room near this till the trial, so that I can look after her. They are afraid she may run away or kill herself & then Howard will they think kill himself: He really loves this woman he doesn't care a straw for his wife as compared to her – but you don't want to hear about my individuals!!

It is horrid of you not to like that poem – it's nearly as wicked of you as not to like my little stories. I've got a number I'd like to show you, but I'm ashamed to.

You don't know how terrible it was in the court yesterday. That poor woman would have been there utterly alone if I had not been there with her: all the others were together; she seemed such an outcast. The case will be tried on the 25th.

Olive Schreiner to Havelock Ellis

October 18th 1886

This trial affair is so terrible; they are all so false. What a terrible deadly thing that Hinton theory is, like a upas tree blighting all it comes in contact with because it is false to human nature.

*I saw John Falk on Friday. I am going to get Mrs Weldon to
stay here till the trial & I am going to sit with her at it.*

*Do you know I can't help hating Mrs Howard Hinton. She
is the only one I can't feel sorry for. Poor Howard looked so
beautiful when he went into the prisoner's dock. They say he
will likely only get a few days - & then*

I can't think about anything else.

Olive

Olive Schreiner to Karl Pearson

October 18th 1886

*The Hinton affair gets worse & worse. They are now
trying to prove that the children are not his but another man's.
Perhaps they are right. Life seems to have been to me like a
grim face with a smile of despair on it since I came to town.*

*If in this letter I have passed the bounds of what our friend-
ship allows, please put me back by a letter however short a one.*

Yours faithfully

Olive S.

Emma Brooke to Karl Pearson

October 19th 1886
Dear Mr Pearson,

*I have no doubt that you know of the enclosed strange
case. I had no idea of it – Miss Wedgwood having given me
quite a different account of Mr H. H. who was, you may
remember, her friend. One cannot but be sorry for these
people. Is there not something very feeble-minded about the*

whole proceeding – as though they had got into an unwhole-some excitement and lost the ordinary power of reasoning about morals and reading between the lines, one knows that the whole matter was organised on the Hintonian principle: straining after transcendental right whilst doing very commonplace wrong always ends flatly I suppose.

But will not this give the desired publicity to the Hintonian dogma to stop the secret teaching? Nothing could come as such a satire on the deadening emotions as this short and sordid account.

I think he must have intended to get out of his false position. And if so, does not that merit respect? But I am sorry for the innocent victims. The two sets of children and his mother.

I am not speaking about this to anyone but you – I do not wish to. They have quite enough to suffer.

Yours very sincerely,

Emma F. Brooke

Olive Schreiner to Havelock Ellis

Friday October 30th 1886

I have just returned from the city (11pm) where I have been to see Mrs Weldon who is lying alone & ill in a miserable little public house near the Old Baley.

Hintonianism falls like a blight on every thing it touches, because it is false to the profoundest laws of human nature, & because its first principle is not remorseless truth.

I have had my Friday afternoon this was the most painful one I ever had. It's so glorious that I shan't have any more philistines for a week.

Yours

O. S.

Report of Ralph Thicknesse to the members of the Men and Women's Club

At the Central Criminal Court on Wednesday 27th of October 1886 Charles Howard Hinton schoolmaster was put upon his trial on the charge of bigamy with Maude Florence. The case came on at the end of the day, the last case before the Recorder.

Maclure for the prosecution mentioned the case and stated that the prisoner was arrested on his own confession and pleaded guilty.

Sir Thomas Chambers said that he had read the deposition and that it was a most painful case and one in which it was not advisable that the facts should be made public.

Mr Bexley for the defence made a statement on behalf of the prisoner expressing his regret for what had happened.

Sir Thomas Chambers in giving sentence alluded to the fact that the prisoner went through the process of marriage with Maude Florence at her request she being fully aware that his wife Mrs Hinton was then alive. He sentenced the prisoner to three days imprisonment. The prisoner who had been detained since Monday 25th was thereupon released.

N. B. Maclure was a school or college friend of the prisoner at Balliol or Cheltenham.

Elizabeth Cobb to Karl Pearson

November 7th 1886

*I was so glad I had your letter of nearly a fortnight ago
& so glad you spoke to me of this wretched case of Howard
Hinton's, it had come upon me with a sudden shock of how I
was unable to see anyone with whom to speak of it, & I wondered much what others might be thinking. I wished to write
to you, till perhaps knowing a little more of the circumstances
I knew better what I really thought I could tell you. You will
know the end now? How there was practically no trial, no
investigation or report. Prof Jowett and Mr Thring wrote letters in high terms of the character of C. H. Hinton. & George
Lewis, whose wife is Ms Nettleship's friend "managed it well"
to have no exposure or sentence. One hardly feels as if it was
fair, it seems as if it would have been better if James Hinton's
name had come in, & people who think about him, had understood more. And yet one can hardly wish that more cruel pain
would have fallen on those who perhaps are innocent. It would
have been hard if Mrs Hinton whom Olive Schreiner describes
as looking like a woman who has been killed, has died and had
come to life again, & Miss Haddon said it was a good description – should have suffered the worst exposure thro' her son.
When I saw it in print in the paper I thought how strange it was
that the fear Miss Jones, was it not, expressed they had after
J. H.'s death, some terrible retribution should overtake them,
should be realised in the son. And it seemed a lesson, how
people cannot go on a wrong, false track alone. They must
always take others with them. But at least in the matter of any
wide exposure, the relatives seem spared just now. As however
to where the suffering will end one cannot see. I realised a
little how it was coming home to them when I had to see Mrs*

Nettleship on business last week. She wrote to me she did not think I could know of the trouble they were in, & perhaps ...

I hardly know how but she [OS] has taken the guardianship of this unhappy Mrs Weldon on herself. She had been to see her, thro' Mr Ellis who as a doctor attended her, some time ago before she even knew she (Mrs W) had anything to do with H. H. A policeman had come to Blandford Sq. also, to find Mrs W. But I do not know how much you know of the circumstances, & they are not to the point except that the details of pain realised gauge the depth of the wrong-doing, at least they do to me.

OS is wondering if she can help Mrs W away to work at the Cape; is seeing her constantly. I hardly understand why she should so have the weight of it, except that she is such a generous little thing, that indeed she is. But she kept saying in real perplexity, "I wish I could be sure she was perfectly true, then I could help her better." I cannot but wonder she should doubt this. Surely it is impossible for the poor unhappy thing to be quite true, she has been wholly false. She deceived H. Hinton's wife in her own house & later let her see the children not knowing whose they were. It is the "necessity" there has been for "telling lies all round", as Olive says they have done, that shows the miserableness of it all. Anyone who learns such complete deceit may have flashes of truthful life, but it is not to be counted on, surely. Olive describes her as speaking of this hateful Hinton doctrine, & saying why don't they burn all their books, & bury everything relating to him. And then the curious part is that Mrs Hinton, and I understand Mrs Haddon also, deny that this case has anything to do with the father's doctrines. To every outsider the connection seems too obvious. Of course, it is not as preached, there was to be a sacrifice on the wife's part, who was to ask for the thing to *be done, and here the wife was deceived, but it only seems as if the general confusion of ideas took a little different form. This dreadful Hintonianism, O. S. says, with harmful influence on every life it touches ... I feel a gratitude to Miss Brookes that thro' her opening the subject to you, you showed it to me also. It would have been a great shock to me had it come upon me unprepared. As you say, it shows me Miss Haddon's doubleness, she never ought to have seemed to speak with me so openly as she did, leaving so much unsaid. I asked her straight out if Hinton ever carried his theories into practice, & she said no, but had he lived he would have done. She must have known then of the son. I quite feel what you say & pity for him. And it is very sad in more ways than one, that he has sacrificed what seemed to be a really good and useful public career. What a tangled world we live in ...*

Elizabeth Cobb to Karl Pearson

November 8th 1886

I remember her answer quite well. "Oh! Yes, many people knew, he (H. H.) was always telling them about it."

My intimate connection with the case, my wish to be clear in my own mind about it, of course all comes from my former friendship for Miss Haddon, my still great admiration for her many admirable qualities, all mixed with pain and bewilderment as it is, for I cannot understand her. It is impossible to reconcile what you have said with what she writes to me – & it is impossible for me to believe she is telling a deliberate falsehood. "Poor Howard was never for a moment misled into thinking he had been acting according to his father's theories, & it is one of his bitterest thoughts now that he may have been the means of deferring the time when his father's ethical doctrine should be accepted." & again "he cannot believe that any readers of his father would make the mistake of in any way associating his errors with his father's teaching."

All the family are shattered & all have to join together to support this man & wife & all the children, in their utter material ruin. He is trying to get mathematical pupils and hopes to be able to be an independent tutor but one fears that given the degraded state of his reputation they will perforce struggle.

Olive Schreiner to Karl Pearson

November 8th 1886
Monday night 1.30 am
Dear Mr Pearson

When Mrs Cobb called the Friday before last she said that you had not been writing to her on the Hinton trial.

I did not make any remark. She then said, you had told her about Howard Hinton a year ago, & she asked me whether I was the person who told you.

I made no answer to this question either, but simply looked at her, because I could not feel her right to ask it me. Now I have thought the matter over, & feel that if you think that you ought to tell Mrs Cobb what I may have told to you, you may freely do so. If you have still any of my letters & would like to you can send them her.

Please, feel with regard to anything I tell you or write to you that you may do with it exactly as you would with information you had gained for yourself; if you used it in a way I did

*not approve of I should think it an error of judgment; I should
never question your purity of purpose.*

Yours

Olive Schreiner

*Please send this note with yours to Mrs Cobb if you write to
her on the matter.*

*2.40 a.m. I moved away from you very rudely tonight. Do
you never feel that you can't bear any more, that you'll break if
anything more happens?*

*Please tell Mr Parker I will try to write a paper note for the
next meeting on the marriage (freedom in forming).*

Your face was so white tonight, it was so white.

Olive Schreiner to Robert Parker

November 26th 1886

9 Blandford Sq

Dear Mr Parker

*I take the liberty of sending you the enclosed. Do you know
of any people who might be likely to care to attend the lectures? I believe that H Hinton is quite genuine on the purely
intellectual side. He has nothing to live on. I am very anxious
he should get some subscribers.*

*I fear it is not likely you will know of any one, but could
think of no one but you to whom I could write.*

Excuse my troubling you.

Yours Sincerely

Olive Schreiner

MR HINTON M.A.,
(*Late Exhibitioner of Balliol College, Oxford*)
**IS PREPARED TO GIVE INSTRUCTION
ON FOUR-DIMENSIONAL SPACE**

MR HINTON holds that it is possible to obtain a mental conception of shapes and figures in four dimensions similar to the conception which everyone has of objects in three-dimensional space.

The instruction is not specially mathematical, and requires no previous knowledge of mathematics; it is directed towards developing in the student the power of conceiving shapes in four dimensional space – a power more akin to that which the sculptor or mechanician has of conceiving complicated space figures, than to the analysis of a mathematician.

For more of the bearings and applications of this study see "Scientific Romances" (SWAN SONNENSCHEIN & CO.)

2, Melbury Terrace,
Harewood Square, NW

CUBE

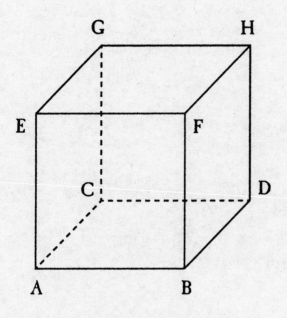

They fit like coiled spirals.

He had started – as he did – on the matter of space, stuttering through some abstraction and her response had been to observe him flatly and to ask a series of simple questions. Why must space be so? Why only four dimensions? Why not five? He was well used to polite boredom and occasionally to baffled concentration, but never before had his orations provoked such serious engagement in such company. He sensed that the inquiry contained some more complex emotion. He fixed her gaze and imagined he discerned beneath a splinter of mischief. The curiosity of that reciprocal gaze had led to their promenading together in a garden at Cheltenham.

He had blathered again as they had walked amongst knipho-fia, away from company, and she had allowed her fingertips to brush against his. He felt such tension in himself, wishing it to be purposeful, but could not be certain how to understand this idle and passing touch, so subtle was it.

When they had parted and he had bent to kiss her goodbye, expecting her cheek to be proffered, she had instead pushed her lips to his and his astonishment at the brash warmth of that eager cohesion where he had expected smooth, powdered surface was what again and again triggered his imagination and yearning. Had any of the other guests witnessed that kiss it would have been an unthinkable scandal. Instead, it became insurmountable for him, a rucked carpet for his mind, repeatedly tripping him as he gazed from the window of the cab that carried Mary and him to the station. He could not stride beyond that kiss. It had replayed in his mind's eye as a blossoming and sharpening of colour, fresh tinctures novel to his perception, bright scarlets and oranges.

His actions since had been single-minded in achieving a repetition of that experience. He had written to her requesting to meet. Her reply had been by return of post, received within hours. They had met at the front of King's Cross. Upon seeing her it was as if he were meeting an old acquaintance for the first time and he felt discombobulated: she appeared urbane and confident. He had suggested a stroll to view the impressive lobby of the Grand Midland Hotel. Her hand had grasped his firmly, her fingers interlocking into his in a fashion so decidedly intimate that he had approached the reception desk as if in a waking dream and inquired as to the availability of a room for one week for Mr and Mrs Weldon.

That room now, opulent. An iron bedstead. Too warm, coals only recently allowed to die in the grate while outside the sun had broken through the cloud sending streaks of sunlight onto the muddied road before the grand station.

She had listened to him at that garden party. Had teased him. She wished to have him respond to her.

She exited the bathroom, naked. He made to jabber but was caught. She was unapologetic in her nudity. She accommodated the warmth of the room. She took his hand and pulled him to the iron bedstead. She lay back and raised one knee, pliant.

He rushed, clumsily, to remove his clothes. Her seriousness erupted into giggles. "Howard. My Howard. Be calm, darling man. We have hours."

They had taken days. They had shuddered into each other. He had thought of the Kilkenny cats, twisted together by their tails. There was no outside of the room and such interiority. He had felt the air. She had examined his body, stroking his legs, inspecting as a physician might a newborn. He had reciprocated. There had been honesty in that exchange. They had learnt each other, parsed each other by touch. He had become more human in that.

He had become embodied, in her body. He had assumed angles, for perspectives. Seen the mound of her pubis as viewed from the level, its tender, proud rake forwards from her flatted stomach. She had put her cheek on his thigh next to his prick. When they had coupled a tergo, in his spasm he had metamorphosed from beast to burden, from rutting to holding her, binding her breast with his arms, pressing his chest into her spine. They had taken a postponement from the exterior. As the days and nights became indistinct, so too did their sense of their own bodies. He had recognised the resemblance between them, the echoes of form. She had sensed the edges of herself dissolving into fluid rhythms. "You" sublimating "I" condensing.

Muto, mutas, mutat – mutatis mutandis. Become, becoming, repeating, becoming. Let this point be a. "I" extend the point to a second point, b, make a line, A.

"You" extend lines from points a and b to points c and d to make two lines perpendicular to, and of the same length as, line A. Let these be lines B and C. You complete the square by extending a line from point c to point d to make line D.

She was the correct height for his height. His chin might rest upon her crown.

Self-elements had been obliterated. Left and right lost their meaning. Up and down were persistent. Self-elements had been dissolved. Absolved. Resolved. One imagines oneself within. There was no left or right, there was only rotation within one's self.

O
b
j
e
c
t

A

intersects with object B

Subject A intersects with Subject B.

Mu. – mutatis mutandis

Point.

Goosebumps on her flesh in the cooled room, he had sent for more coals. They became. Come into the garden, Maud, a lyric of Tennyson. For a breeze of morning moves, and the planet of love is on high. Surmounting sense of self. O young lord-lover, what sighs are those, For one that will never be thine, But mine, but mine. And the soul of the rose went into my blood.

She heated a copper tub over the grate and bathed his feet in warm water as he sat naked. By the end of the stay, so comfortable there unclothed with her as he had never before been unclothed with anyone, despite the theories of those he had best loved. Here was the living of it. Here in a room. She made to dry his feet

with her hair and he would not have it but made her sit, washed
her feet, her legs and fell to her once again, wishing, kissing her
blooming lips.

--

A lost week. Subsequently, letters, chanced and hidden. Days
and nights in Brighton over months and then years. The shock
of the realisation that their elopement had been fruitful, their
communion complete and yielding new flesh. The inevitability of
succession. The registry office, the dream of the Weldon couple
inscribed in ink, strangers press-ganged as witnesses. Visits. Ellis
attending the birth as midwife in Maud's rooms in Brighton.
Sworn to secrecy. Twin boys. Charles and James. Secrecy becoming unmanageable, Howard spoke to his aunt; knew Ellis had
shared the news with Olive.

For a period, the sense of a new way of living. Maud and
the babies came to Blandford Square as he thought to allow
his beloveds to meet, though not at that stage to disclose all.
Maud was discreet and Mary enjoyed her direct mode of
conversation. He began to wonder if the distinct cells of his
life might not be combined? His intimates, Aunt Carrie, Ellis,
seemed not to have judged him harshly: had taken the side of
humanity. Might the parallel lines be made to meet? Must they
be extended to infinity? Then, one afternoon in her house at
Brighton, Maud proposed that the boys be Christened and an
argument ensued. Its sudden bitterness a shock to Howard's
vision. Imperceptibly at first a fault-line formed. The marriage for Howard had been a mere practicality, the textual
disguise for the one thing he had so hoped and to which he
had sacrificed, well, risked, all; nothing less than the purest
communion of two subjects, absolute selflessness, achieved in

ecstatic physical union, but this charade, no longer, not in the eyes of the God his father so needed at his deathbed.

Then, one morning in Uppingham, a letter arrived, pleading, distraught, confused, singing of abandonment. He secreted it. The next day, in an effort to muster a response, found it gone from its niche. The inevitability of events now far exceeding his agency as the groove in the aether through which his life passed was felt to run over him this one, singular way and he confessed, asking for forgiveness into perpetuity from Mary, now pregnant herself, their fourth son, his sixth heir, also inevitable.

Square

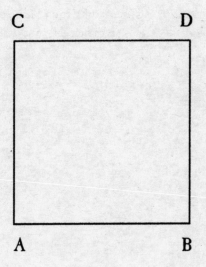

He has split the men into teams. He insists upon shifts of no more than eight hours – the companies delude themselves if they think they have productive work from the men beyond this period though there are many who expect the labour they would from livestock. This is demonstrably counterproductive and he has written charts to demonstrate it to the board. He has read of initiatives in Scotland and Yorkshire in which the men are offered extra-curricular education. He has established a small classroom. He tests them on writing and reading in Spanish. Each man must be literate.

He offers voluntary lessons in English. The men file to the door. He welcomes them in, naming each as he enters and therefore recognising any newcomers. There are several newcomers each week. He has always been blessed with a finely detailed memory and this small matter of speaking to the men by their given names allows them, he feels, to converse as equals for the duration of the class regardless of their roles within the mine. He is working to tutor them in a practical use of the language, building up a stock of everyday terms; giving them, indeed, the terms for the objects and practices they encounter in their working day so that they might, should the need arise, find work in an English-speaking mine; that they might become professional in the business of mining. It is, besides, a considerable pleasure to hear a man who has laboured under the earth for eight hours, borne picks and dragged carts, attempt to form words alien to his tongue. The men enjoy the lightness of it, and trade words. They like to call him jee-orj.

In similar intention he trains his gang leaders in the basics of engineering. This is a practical concern for him, also, enabling him to realise his plans for the mine more effectively. The virtue of this arrangement has shown itself on many occasions. Men who understand the need for a new channel and how it might be achieved are better able to assist in its construction and to make the decisions required should any small obstacle arise. Should the same men have nothing but plans and instructions they will require him to advise on every nail to be struck.

He has mapped the shafts of the three prospects and has this chart pinned to the wall of his office, a rough shed of sturdy construction. A fan system of his own invention – driven by the flow of a small outlet stream – circulates air and takes the worst out of the starchy heat; any shade is welcome during the hours at which the sun is highest. He lights a small stove as soon as the sun falls behind the ridge and by the time it has set, and the desert chill has taken hold, this throbs heat.

He envisages more expansive automation throughout the operation. A system of picking tables like interlocking gears, sifting at staged diameters and dropping slack and nut into appropriate hoppers. A belt-driven shaking table. He pictures it much like a bicycle: there are gears, chains, wheels, interlocking and shifting, accelerating and decelerating as the need arises. He believes it might be possible. His sketches have been prepared for presentation to the board. Given the profitability of the claim, he is confident that the case can be made for greater investment in efficiency of extraction.

--

Two days away from the mine he arrives at a plateau on which lies a small settlement he has visited before. Some days five miles is distance enough. Mephitic climate and terrain, one vertiginous barranca steepling out of the next, the chills of the shades curtaining into rough, furnace-winds in the open; the splintered teeth of the earth bathed in its acrid breath.

Ted was a lifeline in this wilderness. Ted was the finest saddle mule he had ever encountered, a quietly determined creature, sure of foot and well-balanced. So good, in fact, that a mine surveyor in Aguilla had offered 2,000 pesos for him – at thirty times the value of a cow still not an offer that George could ever contemplate. The money would be useless without the luck and timing also that had allowed him to find Ted. Despite this, the animal can walk no more than five miles a day in this terrain and while the pack mules might have endured a mile further, Ted is the decision-maker.

He approaches the hut with caution. The Indian couple he'd befriended on his last trip are not expecting him on this occasion. He does not wish to startle them. They had two children. One had been malarial and George had administered to the child 25 milligrams of quinine sulphate from his personal supplies. The family will doubtless be grateful for that, though in this country there are no guarantees. There is no guarantee, indeed, that they remain in the hut; have not been usurped by bandits seeking a temporary hideout. Makeshift fencing for corralling goats and a washing area seem to indicate continuous habitation. He calls out when still twenty feet away. The father comes to the door of the hut. George removes his hat and waves. The father beckons him. George dismounts and approaches. They shake hands.

George returns to his mules, forages in Ada's saddle bags and removes two packages. One contains medicine – quinine and iodine. He knows these supplies to be of the greatest value to these people, three days' travel from the nearest pharmaceutical supplier. The other contains salt and cheese. He returns and gifts them to the father with a small bow. The father nods his thanks and directs George to the rear of the hut where there is corn and water in a trough for his mules. George thanks the father. He ties Ted, Lenina and Ada to a post, fills their nosebags with corn and begins the process of brushing and checking each as they eat.

He uses his fingers to feel the fur behind the withers, below the tail, where the cruppers catch; behind the forelegs where the cingle chafes. An untreated cut and the animals will be lame within three days. He bathes a graze on Lenina's foreleg but does not judge it to be of any danger to the animal. In the lowlands each morning the mules have to be checked for the bites of vampire bats which can turn into a suppurating ulcer. In the desert, the risk of coral snake bites is greater. Here, on higher ground, ticks and sores are the enemy.

Foot by foot he checks their shoes. He shoes them himself every six weeks, not trusting the local blacksmith not to cut corners or to shoe them imperfectly without first shaving the feet equally. An unsure mule can mean disaster. He carries extra shoes and nails, extra saddle-pads and halters. Satisfied that the mules are in good shape, he removes his cot from his saddlebags. Given the risk of rain he knows he will have to sleep in the hut. He will be afforded seven feet by thirty inches of space, just sufficient for his cot.

Inside the hut the mother welcomes him and one child – the one he has treated – smiles to him through a mouth full of tortilla and cheese. He will not ask.

On the first occasion he slept in such a dwelling he had followed his hosts and went barefoot. The following day he experienced a boring pain and the curious sensation of a pleasurable but frustrating itch around several of his toes. The next day the pain increased and the itching worsened. White haloes of skin surrounded small black nodules. The pain became particularly acute at night and on return to his hosts they identified nigua infection. Several of these parasitic ticks, sand-dwellers, had secured domicile within his foot. Desquamation of the skin followed. They emitted trails of faeces and a watery secretion. His hosts treated the infected area with the juice of a kind of apricot and advised that he return to his home. He had to cut short the trip and attend to his feet lest he himself become lame. Under the wrong conditions, ulcers and suppuration might occur. Since that time, he has never gone barefoot in rude dwellings regardless of whether or not they have sand floors.

Here, in the highlands, the floor is mud.

--

He sets out into virgin territory with the rising sun cresting the forested ridges. He has never before travelled North East from this location. His hosts had described to him a trail that leads up the valley and into a heavily wooded region of mountains. While farmers are increasingly felling to extend their territory, this valley remains unspoilt. George is hopeful of discovering a range of specimens.

Before striking out, he has unpacked his drying furnace and set it upon his cot in preparation for his return. Having lost two trips to mould, he has learnt very early in his collecting career that moist samples are his greatest risk. Leaving samples to dry in the sunlight for an entire day does not ensure complete desiccation. In previous years he has cached furnaces along his route but on the current expedition he is trialling his new prototype – a telescopic furnace of his own design. He does not require it in the field for the day so readies it for use on his return. The samples must be bright and crisp when packed. This furnace will dry them perfectly within twenty-four hours and can contain some two hundred samples at a time. He has transferred from Ada's bags to Ted's some one hundred corrugated cardboard folders.

He rides for two hours into the woods enjoying the steady swing of the mule's march. Finding himself in a clearing he scans the ground. Much of the flora is familiar to him but he recognises slightly altered environmental conditions to anywhere he has yet collected. He has come to realise how little the locale need be distinct for the possibility of as yet unrecorded species.

--

Rounding an abutment in the face of the cliff he finds his way blocked by two men no more than ten feet before him, their faces concealed by bandanas in the manner of the hill-country bandits. The foremost of the pair points a rifle at him. The path is too narrow and the mule too slow for a retreat. With a weary familiarity he raises his arms and slowly dismounts. He carries no firearm about his person and never has: guns are more valuable than gold in these hill-towns and invite violence rather than deter it. He prefers to reason. A lone traveller with openly carried weapons is an enticement to violence, an advertisement of wealth and a statement of suspicion. The rifleman indicates that he should hand over his saddlebags.

Maintaining his passive stance, he addresses the highwaymen. "No tengo dinero."

If they are surprised at his Spanish they give little indication. The rifleman leans into the stock of his gun. "Danos tus maletas."

"Solo tengo plantas," states George. He knows not to plead. He moves slowly towards the tarpaulin bag closest to him, sensing the increased nervousness of his captors, and slowly and gently opens the buckle, raising the flap. He presents the bag towards them, showing them his samples. "Solo plantas."

The rifleman instructs his partner: "Verifica el otro."

The second man moves towards Ted's left flank and begins

rummaging in the tarp bag. In awareness of the need for calm at this juncture, George quells the irritation he feels at the disruption to his samples. As the first man questions his distracted friend – "que ves?" – George reflects on how the turn of events in which he finds himself would have unfolded in the adventure stories he read and loved as a young man. He would swiftly reach beneath the right-hand saddlebag. The rifleman would catch his movement too late. He would swing his rifle back towards George but not before George had loosed a single round from the revolver concealed beneath Ted's right-hand saddlebag. In those stories, the rifleman would fall. His partner would scrabble on the opposing side of Ted. George would step away from his mule, towards the downed rifleman and pick up the weapon. The scrabbling partner would sprint towards the abutment back in the direction of George's ascent and George would watch him go.

The stories would omit what George had witnessed on three separate occasions: the unpleasant materiality of the wounding. Say the bullet entered the man's throat through the bandana and beneath the chin. The rifle swing would carry the man's fall backwards, awed distress lighting his eyes. A wet wheezing sound would be broadcast from the man's throat as his blood-dampened bandana flapped in the breath emitted through the wound beneath.

George would approach the victim slowly and carefully. He had heard tell of men killed as they attempted to administer aid to men they had shot. In theory, he would murmur the viaticum, the only noble act left available to one in such a distressed situation, and he runs through it in his head now: "Padre, tu hijo, Jesucristo, es nuestro camino, nuestra verdad y nuestra vida. Mira con compasión a tu siervo quien ha confiado en tus promesas. Has refrescado a él con el cuerpo y la sangre de tu hijo: que él ingrese a tu reino en paz pedimos esto por Cristo nuestro Señor."

The frothing would, eventually, subside, leaving a bloody foam cresting the bandana. He would attempt to tip the rifleman from the side of the path but would find his body too heavy to shift. This would be a struggle. He would sweat and heave and it would require contact with a bloodied and warm corpse, copper and sweat in his nostrils. He would watch the puppet-like tumble down the steep side of the barranca with relief. He would nervously check the path and hope that the partner was not lurking around the corner, his courage recovered. George would stow the rifle among his saddlebags, hoping that it would not make him a more obvious target for future attacks, and remount Ted.

In either version, he would say to his mule: "Not far now, old friend."

--

George, grounded, with his arms raised, says to the rifleman: "Tengo un arma." The rifleman tenses at the word but is confused. It was not uttered as a threat. George continues: "Vale más que las plantas. Puedes tenerlo."

"Donde esta?"

"Debajo de esa alforja." George indicates the saddlebag with his chin. The rifleman instructs his friend who, with no discussion, makes his way around Ted. He finds the revolver strapped beneath the saddlebag and brandishes it towards his friend. There is a moment of doubt. For George, some apprehension. He has calculated that the relief at finding the weapon will make the pair grateful towards him. He knows certain of these mountain people. They are impetuous and poor, and are driven to criminal acts through hunger, but they are not bloodthirsty or vicious. There is, however, no generalisation that cannot be overturned in an instant.

The partner inspects the handgun. It is a decent enough piece, a snub-nosed GAF .38, though no treasure. The men seem pleased. They have overcome their confusion. George understands that he must now confirm the exchange in which his life is valued equivalent to a weapon. "Es todo lo que tengo de cualquier valor. Es tuyo." The rifleman nods. He lowers his gun. He moves to one side of the path.

"Puedes continuar en el camino."

As George takes Ted's reins and leads on his mule train, he reflects on the many versions of the story that conclude differently. He reflects also on the relative difference in value between a firearm and a previously undocumented plant. He reflects upon the equivalence between an undocumented plant and his own life. He anticipates the packaging and postage to Kew of his latest samples, a bullet in his back banished from all possibility in his own mind as he marches Ted up the hill towards the mesa and the scent of fresh pasture. Given his poor eyesight, the GAF has been modified for use with hollow rounds which give an improved spread if a shorter range. He manufactures this ammunition himself so he knows the technical skill required to make the firearm useable. He can reassure himself that he will not have been the source of further violence.

--

He fords the Balsas river, the tarp bags hitched up as high as possible the best to protect the specimens, just south of Los Placeres del Oro. He rides wearily on to home and the herbarium.

En route he delivers his packages to the post office. Duplicate parcels, each containing thirty-nine new samples. One is addressed for Dr Isaac Ochoterena at the Instituto de Biologia, Universidad de Mexico, and fulfils his legal obligations to deposit a sample of each new varietal discovery locally. Initially, Dr Ochoterena returned his samples: did not know what to do with them so did not want them. At his urging, Ochoterena has developed a catalogue at the University. The duplicate set are for Smailes at Kew. Maria, the post mistress, beckons to him. She hands him a letter stamped from Minnesota. A letter from Sebastian. He has not heard from his brother for some months and returns home with interest. What news from North America?

His cataloguing completed, the mules fed, watered and safely stabled, George settles at his writing desk. Father's funeral always at such moments at the forefront of his mind. Kind words from the assembled. Gelett Burgess grasping him by the hand, proclaiming his father's soul of a poet. Offering to help in any way he could. When George consulted with Sebastian, they decided to request that Burgess execute the literary estate, not knowing how to do it themselves. Burgess was overwhelmed with pride though had achieved little practically despite some mutterings about assembling a posthumous biography from notes.

Students of Father from Minnesota and from Princeton, who'd read of his death in the dailies. Wanted to say how Father had changed their lives with his instruction. Ralph and Jane Whitehead representing the bohemians. One only remembered those who were there, not those who weren't. He could hardly remember Mother there.

He remembered Singer. He remembered a feeling of deep gratitude that this young man who had met his father only once, on a train, had attended the funeral to express his condolences and fond memories of that single conversation. Singer had read of the sad loss in the *Post*; tipped his head to the side in sympathy, responding with "Ah!" to every remark. Asked after George. Expressed fascination in mining and indicated that he would like to correspond, if George might do him the honour. Touched,

George had exchanged addresses. Over the years their correspondence had mutated. George now knew full well that when he deposited samples with Singer's proxy at the Smithsonian, alongside notes on his collecting, detailing, at Singer's request, encounters of all forms with people of all descriptions, these were for intelligence purposes beyond the entomological.

He alone of the brothers knew why their mother and father were intimately estranged. He alone had any memory of Britain. Those memories were slight though iridescent. He had no one with whom to rehearse them. They had been corroded and reformed, rusted and polished, within his own memory and no other.

He saw his father framed in the hallway following a period of absence, his own infantile joy overwhelmed by the sense of seriousness and the whispering of adult conversation. Mother was surrounded by babies. He remembered the smell of the books he pretended to read. Father went again and Mother showed him paintings of Japanese ladies. Eventually the mail brought a summons and they set off for Portsmouth to follow.

He separates the flap of the envelope with a letter knife and withdraws its contents.

Winnetka, November 24th 1923

My dear brother,

Thank you for your last. I read of your account of your continuing exploration of the highlands of the Sierra Madre del Sur with great interest. You are a cowboy of the old school, sat upon a mule.

I am always heartened to hear of your collecting passion. The collecting instinct is inherited from Father, is it not? I am minded of his strange objects and trinkets from Japan, his netsuke and paper constructions, his odd-coloured blocks inscribed with kanji.

I have been thinking much of Mother and Father recently. It is more than fifteen years since she died, sixteen since Father led the way. For many years after I could not think of them happily. I realise that is no longer the case. It was a difficult time, was it not? We are not a long-lived family. And yet, everything changes.

I find in my mind I return again and again to one particular memory. The time Eric fell from Father's bamboo climbing frame in the garden at Yokohama. That climbing frame has always been my strongest memory. I find I can remember nothing of Eric's fall beyond it happening. Cannot remember seeing it but can picture him on the structure.

I, too, have followed some family traditions. Like you and Father, I have applied for a patent and it has been granted. I attach drawings of my patented climbing structure. They are too flat, but they describe it well enough. The first of its kind will be installed in the playground of the Winnetka School this spring. I trust that many generations of children will be able to experience the pleasure of being commanded to X3, Y2, Z1, or even, simply, to horse around.

I realise that you are more than content down there. I wonder if you mightn't think of coming up here one of these years? It would be a pleasure to introduce my long-lost brother to Carmelita and Jean, Joan and William to their uncle. But then again, I don't think I will ever make it down to you so perhaps we are best served by an honesty of corresponding exchange.

George, take care down there. Love to you and yours.

Sebastian

Oct. 23, 1923.

S. HINTON

1,471,465

CLIMBING STRUCTURE

Filed July 22, 1920   2 Sheets—Sheet 1

Inventor:

Sebastian Hinton

By:-

Ottis, Poole + Hinton Attys:

276

Oct. 23, 1923.   1,471,465

S. HINTON

CLIMBING STRUCTURE

Filed July 22, 1920   2 Sheets-Sheet 2

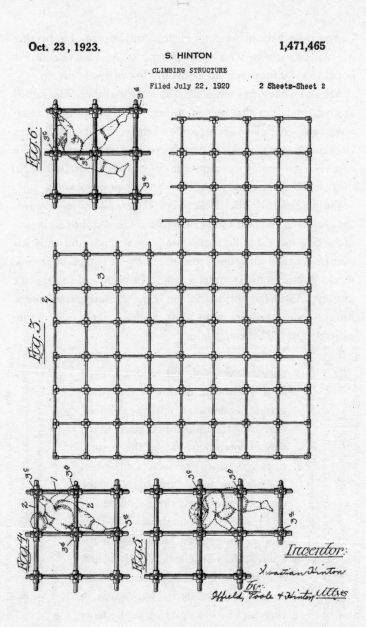

Inventor:
Sebastian Hinton
By:
Offield, Toole & Hinton, Attys

George eases back in his chair. He folds up the plans. His brother has made something worthwhile, he thinks. An achievement. He hopes to see it in playgrounds, the shadow of a wild dream.

Sebastian has always wanted to do work for others. He trained as an attorney for that reason, to help those who wished assistance through the law. Sensible. He is selfless in that way, ponders George. A practical kind of selflessness. One that does not entirely – impossibly – imagine the self away but tries, instead, to make it substantive and to describe and adapt its location.

He pushes back the wickerwork chair and moves towards the shelves at the rear of his herbarium. Here, in boxes, he has archived papers. He finds the family box. Odds and ends left over from the winding up of the estates: one or two photographs, letters to him from his father salvaged from the old chest, some jottings considered surplus to the literary estate passed on to Burgess; one or two poems of Mother's that had not made it into collection or the little magazines.

He fishes out the letter, on fine paper now foxed and yellowed. Even at this distance in time it feels dangerous, its desperate energy explosive, exceeding the limits of the page. In the way of correspondence of this period, lines written to the side of the page, the bottom, filling any space on the sheet. He has long since worked out its significance, though when he stole it from his father's hidey-hole in the study he had little idea what it meant, a hopeless, heartbroken spiral, running both forwards and backwards, in time and in space, its vortical energy

Please come to me spare me from myself. Please do not harden yourself I see you harden as it progresses I see you remove I sense your transcendence I know that you protect yourself in this way I know that the love such as we felt for each other cannot simply ebb cannot dissipate cannot cease to be

It is too much to bear I lose heart I lose soul in these rooms I wash you from me as I once washed your feet do you recall it was tender but there is no tenderness now I can spare none beyond that for the boys. Howard what will I call the boys? I do not know my own name anymore simultaneously centrifugal and centripetal. Howard, my Howard. His father referred to as a Lord, a master, essence, divine. Such language. Talk of flesh. Biblical. Signed by his ever-loving Maud.

George returns to the desk and reads it one final time, twisting the page, before effecting its overdue disposal.

Line

_____

A   B

The devil of heredity. The environment has shaped her sons, forged of them wilder boys than any she had known in England, but lineage cannot be altered. She has allowed only the slightest trace of their father into their universe and regrets even that.

Her nerves had never quite recovered from the journey, arduous enough without the prolonged anxiety of caring for perpetually mobile infant boys. She had worried about their safety at the gang-rails, clutching them to her skirts while picturing doll-like hands sliding beneath waves. At the docks at Madeira as they scampered amongst sailors, clambering over ropes coiled like serpents, ready to strike them down with whip-like force, she willed herself to withhold. In the cabin as they slept atop an immensity of breathless, churning ice she had suffered from terrible dreams in which she was forever judged. She had requested a name from God himself and none had been given. He had found her wanting.

Her letter of introduction from Miss Schreiner had led her at point of disembarkation to the man Edmond, a rough man, standing beside his trap. A farmer in the lands back from the Cape he was quite simply more beastly than she might have imagined. They had barely two bags between them and these he threw into his cart as the sun pricked her skin with its needlework of splintered light. As they trundled over pocked tracks, Edmond told her how he hoped for companionship, being unwilling to converse with the blacks in his ownership, and she heard threat in his words. She retreated into her room in the farmhouse with the boys and there came more shame-filled dreams from whose shadows her daylight thoughts could not emerge.

For the first months she had clenched her boys too tightly and sobbed as they squirmed to escape her grasp. Once escaped, they explored the place, too small to fear its savagery as she did. The serpents were here. Edmond showed her one after he had separated its head from its body with a spade; black, with red, yellow and white bands.

The boys grew into the place, their feral explorations natural to them. They did not distinguish between white and black; they played games with the enslaved children, learning from them the wild places and things. Edmond tutored them in tool-use. They became increasingly distant from her. She remained in her first-floor room and lived for her letters from friends in Brighton, which would arrive once a month as the postal service allowed, or every second month should she wish for a response to her own. Nuggets of news as inconsequential and dazzling as gemstones.

She had months alone with her thoughts. Her memories of her previous life were interrupted. She had no recollection of entire days around the trial. Her life was an intimate journal from which entire pages had been torn free and discarded. She had allowed him to open her. Together, they had read her, marking and annotating her in anticipation of return. What he had opened to her was not legible: blank pages and arcane symbols. It had not been an exchange. Over the years before the discovery of their secret readings, they had returned to certain passages of her. Having been discarded, she would never again open herself in such a way.

She wished she had not allowed the boys the cubes. She had, at first, thought it important that they possessed them: a memento of a man to whom she had once surrendered, whose expansive thought had so enchanted her soul that she had wished to incorporate its source. She had seen no harm in it. The boys had played with them quite normally in their early years, but approaching adulthood, Jamie's interest had become something else, no longer mundane.

She had begun to recognise in Jamie more and more of his father. He was easily distracted, prone to spiralling imaginations, liable to explain his thoughts in terms inaccessible to others. Charlie found him tiresome, Edmond incomprehensible. He had such eyes. He made angles of everything. He projected. It was Howard.

She had once been enamoured of this speculative geometry. In Howard's zealous performance it was possible to glimpse a truth beyond the mundane. His conviction was a sweet madness, transmissible through the force of his will and razor-like gaze. Imagine the experience of the square for the planar being and one could project the experience of the tesseract for the higher mind. Just as one could raise a triangle from its plane into space, turn it around and return it inverted, so could a fourth-dimensional being invert solid objects. Just as a solid occupies multiple planes at the same time, so must a hyper-solid occupy multiple spaces. Just as it is possible to see inside a two-dimensional object, so were we all transparent to higher beings. He believed all child minds, preconditioned, to be higher-dimensional consciousnesses. There was love in all of this, though what it became – what extrapolation led to – was no longer love.

--

The drawstring bag was handmade from velvet, a fine fabric whose softness was nowhere else found in the farmhouse. His mother's skin he remembered as equally soft but since she had become disinclined to allow him to touch her, the bag of cubes had become his consolation.

Jamie was compelled to manipulate them. He had made wonderful discoveries with them. He would stack them to produce regular patterns so that, for example, a blue diamond was apparent to him in a purple face created by twenty-five cubes stacked together. He found it satisfying then to stack a layer of cubes behind these so that the diamond shrank to contain the central purple cube. In the next rank the centre cube alone would be blue, while a fresh diamond would have begun forming at the perimeter in, say, white. He found these arrangements pleasing and could continue with them for hours on end. He began to apprehend the forms he produced within the blocks as shadows of the truer versions.

The changes had commenced shortly after his mother had withdrawn. Jamie was playing with the cubes, shuffling them through sequences, when he sensed that the cubes wished to be inside him. He opened himself to the wish and felt himself above his own body, looking down on himself. It had happened so slowly that he had experienced it simply as a spatial expansion of his perception. He had experienced something similar when dreaming but this was different in degree; he was fully conscious when it happened and he was able to manoeuvre his perspective at will.

When he returned to his own body, he felt invigorated and rushed to Charlie to tell him. Charlie was in the back, whittling some branch, admiring the blade he had sharpened that morning. He could scarcely feign interest in his brother's wild rantings. Jamie retreated.

Over the course of several months Jamie gradually extended his range and found himself able to pass perceptibly – though still in his mind, he was quite sure – through solid boundaries such as walls and ceilings. He was able to manoeuvre himself around the entire farm and to enter into barns and out-houses. He glimpsed his mother as she shuttled herself around the house to avoid Edmond; could see her in plan, as from above. He gradually extended the range and speed with which he could perform this mental egress.

The ability was intoxicating and he could barely wait to go to bed at night so that he could indulge it freely. He spied on the girls in their huts. Sometimes during the daytime, he slipped into it without wishing to, finding himself drifting off at inopportune moments, visiting other places that had captured his interest; a watering hole; a kraal. The cubes were no longer required as catalyst, their lessons incorporated into the organ of thought, his expanded proprioception now entirely autonomous.

He experienced genuine wonders. Time expanded for him. Instants would become hollowed out, eternities unfolding within them, astonishingly vast terrains of time. He could discern the topography, the crevasses and chasms within his own consciousness. He felt as if he were standing at the edge of an ocean of himself. He feared what might happen should he plunge in. Hours became years while he was in this state.

Having gained sufficient familiarity with the process that he could relax into it, he began to become more open, allowing himself gradually to flow into the ocean. There was at first a disorientating sense of dissolution: a terrifying loss of self within this profundity. By degrees, a diver discerning submerged forms in murky waters, he began to sense the edges of other structures within these fugues, structures that he thought of as structures of being. He began to explore the edges of these, their sides and surfaces.

Following one particularly intense trance he had returned to his bedroom to discover a most startling phenomenon. Before him on the floor lay a small but intricately folded paper structure. He had no recollection of having been engaged in any physical activity while psychically abroad but here it was. He was certain no one else had left it. He redoubled his explorations, mapping the contours of the various structures he encountered on his voyages. He ceased eating.

He had decided that the forms he could discern within his trance must be available to ingress. He simply needed to discover the correct method to enter one. They were arranged in some kind of network, with connections between them. He thought of it as something like a root system, or perhaps branches of a tree, and that each form was something like a leaf or hub. He did not know why but he felt an incredible sense of connection with these structures. As he had approached each, he felt something extraordinary, an emotional surplus, an excess of intimacy. Series of images had presented themselves to his mind. Images produced by others.

--

When James failed to come down for breakfast, Maud asked Charlie where his brother was and he as much as laughed at her. She was struck with a realisation: that there was always a carelessness to their fraternity. Alert to deep connections, mysterious to outsiders, she had often wondered how one might manage should the other no longer be there. Here was indication from one side: Charlie would simply square his shoulders.

As she climbed the stairs to James's room, a terrible, irrational panic pounced into Maud's mind: what if he *had* disappeared? He was frequently as good as absent, particularly since he had become enchanted by Howard's cubes. What if he had simply slipped out of space? Howard had told such tales. She rounded the frame to his room consciously quelling this panic by naming it, calling it unfounded fear, and feeling the oil of her reason sit atop the surface of the unreason beneath. The moment she saw him sitting at his desk, marvelling at a sequence of cubic paper sculptures, a lightness washed all away.

Maud reached her hand towards one of these constructions

before suddenly thinking she ought to ask for permission. She looked her son in the eyes and, feeling herself cast off-balance by the intensity of his gaze, asked, "May I?" as much to be able to avert her gaze as to be allowed to inspect the object.

"Of course, Mama," came his reply.

The structure was pleasing, a jewel constructed from paper in two tones. She shivered at the thought that the geometric gift was inherent, yet it was so, clearly. James had never received instruction.

"This is wonderful, Jamie. How have you learnt to do this?"

The boy shrugged. He turned to her again. "I do not so much make them as find them, Mama."

"Well, then," she said, "they are well found." She ran her hand through his hair and he looked at her beseechingly.

"Please stay, Mama."

Why did he ask this? He could not know her thoughts. Did she reveal herself in other ways? On occasion, since he had commenced his study of the cubes, she had been struck by these strange intimations.

"Your mother has no desire to leave," she lied, and planted a kiss on his forehead. "Come now, you must remember to eat."

Back in the kitchen, they sat at the table, Maud and her two sons. She settled herself. Jamie and Charlie talked, of discoveries on the farm, and she listened, becalmed after her secret turmoil. She knew that Jamie would not mention his cubes; knew that Charlie was not interested. Their talk bubbled. Their plates cleared, they moved into the yard, and Maud followed. They took up a game with a ball, bouncing it backwards and forwards, each attempting to outfox the other with spins imparted by wrist and fingers.

She observed them, twin lines, drawn from the same point but diverging. Just so, she thought. They should have their own lives. She sensed that they might do so here, in this old world. She accepted this.

If the lines should conduct her boys to a distinct plane, well, then all was well. The fact of their origin could not be erased. She was it. She was the originating point, her ink smudged, perhaps, but no, not erased.

Point

● A

Hinton, for me, is the key figure. The whirlwind, energising principle. He puts it all up in the air. But he's crazy, he's out of himself. He erodes his boundaries; he spills. And it's up to others to interpret his work, to take it on and carry it through.

[...]

We give ourselves up, let go, stalk up on ourselves unawares. We walk into our own outlines; we are there before. Howard is become his own father.

Iain Sinclair, *White Chappell, Scarlet Tracings* (1987)

ACKNOWLEDGEMENTS

Hinton contains many historical documents and the compositional strategy surrounding these is almost as outlined in the 'Compositor's Note' that opens the 'Tesseract' section. I have been assisted over the years in tracking these down by archivists at the special collections of UCL, Reading University, Bristol University, the University of Cork, UCLA and the British Library. I have also benefitted greatly from the Olive Schreiner Letters Online, an admirable piece of digital scholarship: https://www.oliveschreiner.org/. I would particularly like to thank Gerry Kennedy, a Boole descendant, the source of some of the most astonishing documents and details here.

Warm thanks to Iain Sinclair for permitting me to quote from *White Chappell*, *Scarlet Tracings*, the book in which I first encountered Howard and James Hinton.

All possible care has been taken to trace the rights holders and secure permission for the texts quoted in this book. If there are any omissions, credits can be added in future editions following a request in writing to the publisher.